I. A.

"Fired?" she chokes. "B-b
Either women are getting
crankier. Lately, not one cam
than *why*, and at least a dozen others found ....
similar predicament as Ann.

I'm an asshole. Nice to meet you.

"What did you expect?" I cross my arms. "A promotion? You failed probation." I reserve the patronising tone of my voice exclusively for women I fuck and my best friend and business partner, Nick, if pissing him off is on the agenda.

It often is.

Whoever invented the probation period deserves a Nobel Prize. I've been hiring, fucking, and firing women on repeat for two years, causing no problems for our HR department as long as my victims aren't employed longer than three months. None lasted half the time thus far, so I'm safe.

Advertising the job and interviewing new candidates every few weeks caused unnecessary staff downtime, though. Nick, lost his patience once or twice.

Maybe more, but who's counting?

He threatened to stop my extracurricular activities if I kept dumping the workload on his assistant, Anthony, whenever I fired mine. To keep my hobby and maintain my business partner's good mood, I organised an open day, gathering twenty CVs to minimise staff downtime. To secure the position, a potential candidate must possess four qualities: tall, skinny, blue-eyed, and blonde. Slutty is a bonus but not a necessity. They all fall at my feet eventually, whether it takes a week or three.

Panty Peeler. Nice to meet you.

Nick considers my attraction to that specific type of woman a mental problem. He even suggested I should see a specialist because I, apparently, have issues.

Yes, yes, I do.

Not in that department, though.

There's no concrete reason behind my hair colour preference when it comes to women I fuck. I simply like blondes. I like their blue eyes, long, light hair, and even longer legs. Five-foot-eight is a minimum, and heels are a must.

Ann grips her waist on both sides like an outraged high school teacher ready to scold my wicked behaviour. "You're firing me because I had sex with you?"

I had sex with you doesn't paint the picture all that well. *You fucked me* describes the five minutes Ann spent holding her legs wide open much more accurately.

"Yes." What else can I say? Lying would be thoughtful, but I don't have much thoughtfulness, and whatever I have, I don't hand out to just anyone.

Her eyes widen, and lips part, but words pile up on the tip of her tongue. With an exasperated huff, she exits the office, slamming the door—a theatrical outlet for the frustration triggered by losing her job and not reaching an orgasm when her big boobs were pressed against the wall ten minutes ago.

Not one assistant I ever had held back longer than a month before giving me the green light. I could fuck them more than once since they hand themselves over on a silver platter, a bow tied around their waists, but once is enough. Round two with my assistant, or any other woman, never ends well. I learned the lesson hard when Nick and I started the company...

Grace was perfect. My kind of perfect: tall, skinny blonde with eyes like sapphires. She was a model we hired for a promotional clip. Half an hour after introductions, she dragged me to my office, took her panties off, and spread her legs on my desk. Ten minutes later, she left like a good girl should.

We repeated the little ritual for a week. I was careless back then, and Grace sucked dick like a vacuum cleaner. All was well until she invited me to a party. She was *so* excited because her friends were *dying* to meet her boyfriend. A week of quickies somehow made her think I was looking for a relationship. A

Editor: Dave Holwill
Cover Design: Net Hook Line Designs

I. A. DICE

One

Nice to meet you

THOMAS

I glance over my shoulder, finding my assistant, or rather, ex-assistant—Ann—sitting on a round sofa in my office, adjusting her clothes. She pulls her blue skirt down, then slightly up once she realises she's covered too much silky-smooth skin. She irons the creases marking her blouse, getting it back to its previous state, and stilettoes across the room with a seductive sway of her hips.

"Is there anything else I can do for you, *sir*?" She licks her lips, looking me up and down in a slow, shameless once-over.

One. Please... just *one* woman who won't expect round two, three, or a ring. One who won't fish for declarations, proclamations, whispered confessions, or my number. One who'll let herself out, not looking back, like a good girl should.

Am I asking for too much?

Shit.

"Yes," I say, my attention on the paperwork littering my desk. "Pack your things. You're fired."

few minutes on my desk doesn't scream, *I care about you,* but Grace saw the world through rose-coloured glasses.

From then on, I adhered to the sacred, golden rule: once is enough. And that *once* doesn't last longer than fifteen minutes because I don't do warmups, kissing, or foreplay.

I also don't give a fuck if they come.

Sue me.

They usually do, but I lose no sleep if they don't.

I'm a dick. Nice to... see what I mean?

I take out a pile of CVs from the bottom drawer, open the first one, and call the girl. Marie Hill promises to show up at nine am sharp on Monday morning. Little does she know the job is hers if she hadn't gained weight or dyed her hair dark.

Twenty minutes later, Nick enters my office holding two white paper cups of coffee and sporting a cloudy expression that has me bracing for another monologue titled *Drawbacks of fucking and firing your assistants.* The bitter, heavenly aroma prickles my nose before he closes the door louder than necessary—an enraged display of his disapproval for my utter disregard of workplace ethics.

He sits across from me, pushing a takeaway latte my way while drumming "We Will Rock You" on the armrest.

I raise my hand, stopping him before he gets going. "Spare me the whining, Nick. I know. You disapprove. We talked about this already."

He shoots me his signature annoyed look: eyebrows drawn together, lips pursed, eyes narrowed. "Yes, we did. Like ten times, but you ignore everything I say, Thomas. You want to keep changing your assistants every fortnight? Fine, have it your way, but quit fucking them at the office. Anthony's uncomfortable when they scream bloody murder here."

Nick doesn't care about his assistant's feelings. He just enjoys giving me shit for no reason, like with his fiancée, Amelia. Every so often, he tells me to stay the fuck away from her even

though he knows that for exactly three different reasons, I'll never touch her.

Boundaries—dicks and assholes have them too.

Reason-slash-boundary number one: Amelia—although I prefer to call her Mel—is Nick's fiancée. Girlfriends, fiancées, and wives are off-limits, just as sisters, mothers, and the rest of the family. Maybe apart from cousins. Those are a grey area.

Number two: Mel is five-foot-five, a redhead, and curvier than I usually go for. It's not a bad thing, just not *my* thing. Even if she weren't engaged to my best friend, AKA business partner, AKA the massive pain in my ass, I don't find her attractive.

And three: even if she weren't his, bleached her hair blonde, grew three inches and lost fifteen pounds, I still wouldn't touch her because I like her. We have a cool, platonic relationship going on. Once a girl slips into the drawer in my brain labelled *friend zone*, there's no coming out.

Amelia's fun, which is a rarity these days. She's also easygoing, although that's not a rule. Sometimes she's an even bigger pain than Nick, but it makes me appreciate her more. Not many girls stand up to me. Not many guys either.

Come to think of it... none, actually.

Nick doesn't count.

"Next time, I'll wait until Anthony leaves." I raise the cup to my lips, hiding a grin. "What time are we leaving?"

His face brightens at the mention of our afternoon plan—a trip to the airport to pick up his little sister, Nadia. He hasn't shut up about her since she told him two weeks ago that she's coming home for good.

Nick went bat-shit crazy with happiness.

Literally.

Fine, not literally, but close enough.

I understand that brothers love their sisters but what Nick has going on is a borderline psychotic obsession. He worships the ground below Nadia's feet. The guy would happily lie down in a puddle, letting her use him as a bridge. It never ceases to amaze me how much he cares about her, but I'm yet to find out why he sounds like a fanatic whenever her name leaves his lips.

"Any time now. She lands in an hour, but you know how bad the traffic gets around Heathrow. Especially on a Friday."

"Fine by me." I push the paperwork aside. Nick walks out the door before I slip into my jacket. "We're done for the day," I tell Caroline as we pass the reception desk in the foyer. "Marie Hill will be here on Monday for an interview."

Caroline too is a blonde supermodel. I've never touched her, though. Not that I didn't want to.

I can't.

She's married to our brightest accountant. Good, honest accountants are harder to find than slutty blondes, so Caroline remains the only blonde girl who ever worked at C&G Records, whom I didn't fuck.

Before taking the wheel, I light a cigarette, hanging my jacket at the back of the car. Looks like I won't need it today. The temperature reached thirty degrees Celsius three days ago, and according to the weather forecast, it won't cool down for weeks. *The United Kingdom hasn't seen temperatures like this for seventy years!* the newspapers claim... every year, really.

In the passenger seat, Nick fiddles with the radio, looking for his favourite station. "Is the boot empty? Nadia will have a lot of luggage."

Of course. As he mentioned just fifty-eight times since Monday, Nadia lived in New York for two years, so coming home means she packed all her belongings and will therefore fly back with several suitcases. Honestly, I wouldn't have figured it out if he hadn't told me.

"Yes. It's empty as always. We can stash a few bags on the back seat if it won't all fit in the boot."

An ear-to-ear grin threatens to split his face wide open when I pull out of the car park, taking every shortcut I know.

As much as I enjoy Nick's company, I don't want to hear, yet again, how excited he is that his little sister is coming back.

The emphasis he puts on *little* has me convinced Nadia's three inches tall.

Nick pushes his shades up his long, slim nose and finishes his coffee, discarding the paper cup by hiding it in the door pocket. Cheeky so and so.

Despite talking about Nadia twenty-four-seven, he didn't once ask me to keep my hands off her. I can't help but wonder if he realised I have some decency or if he forgot about the warning me in all his excitement.

She's not blonde, but neither is Mel. I expected a lecture, especially since Nadia's one of the most important women in his life. Correction: undeniably the most important woman in his life. I last twenty minutes before curiosity wins the battle with common sense.

"No *Stay away from my sister* speech? You're slacking, Nick."

He chuckles, glancing at me from above his red Lennon shades. "There's no way she'd trade Adrian for you."

Ah, that's right. Nadia has a boyfriend. Nick mentioned him, but I chose to forget.

To be honest, I pay little attention when he babbles about his sister. I recall vague information he's spewed all week, like the fact she studies art, but not much more than that. Instead of listening, I busied my brain with more important matters like what's the worst thing you can put in a recycling bin?

Where the fuck is Greenland?

Why do people use cutlery to eat a burger?

Hear me out. How can you trust someone who doesn't trust themselves with a fucking sandwich?

We speed across the city, reaching the airport ten minutes ahead of Nadia's scheduled landing. Nick exits the car, beaming like a lunatic as he leaves me behind to wait. I shove *Die Hard* into the DVD slot for the seventh time this month and wait as instructed.

The boot opens forty minutes later. I look into the side mirror, curious about the *little sis*. Dark-haired, she stands by a trolley filled with suitcases stacked higher than Nick's head. He lacks the muscle to load them into the boot, so I step out, rolling up my sleeves.

The first thing that hits me is Nadia's height. She's not the three inches I expected, but I don't think I ever saw a shorter girl. Or maybe I did, but five-eight is a minimum to grab my attention. Nadia won't hit that even if she jumps.

"My Range Rover is getting valeted. Mel left a can of Pepsi on the dashboard in full sun," Nick says. "You've no idea how much mess one small can makes when it explodes."

"Then whose car is this?" she asks, her voice pleasant, melodic, but not too high.

"Mine." I watch her spin around. "Thomas Calix."

Surely, she knows who I am, but we've never officially met.

I take her hand, kissing the back softly, discovering a gentleman in me to please Nick. He was born with old-fashioned manners. I'm not as polite, but I figure it won't kill me to make an effort once. Despite being as far from my type as possible, I'd have to be blind to miss how attractive Nadia is.

I like blondes, but that doesn't mean I consider other girls ugly. Nadia's immediately shelved under *gorgeous* in my head, and few girls hit that rank. In fact, only one other girl deserves the *gorgeous* tag—Maya. Maya, who'll turn three in a few weeks.

Nadia and I check each other out in the parking lot, mildly curious. She's pursing her lips, scrutinising me like I'm a sample under a microscope, and for the first few seconds, our eyes don't lock. I watch her face, small nose, full lips the colour of peaches, and dark-brown hair complementing her olive skin. Her eyes linger on my chest longer than appropriate.

Longer than my eyes lingered on her boobs.

That's... unexpected. Just as the sense of intimidation wash-

ing over me instead of expected pride.

She tilts her head back to look at my face—that's how short she is. She'd need a fucking ladder to get eye-level with me. Another two seconds pass before our eyes lock. Once that happens, my heart stops beating.

Earth stops spinning.

Birds stop singing.

The wind stops blowing...

I could go on, but you get the point.

Some kind of a prodigal shift happens out of fucking nowhere. Centipedes with icy feet stomp up my spine, and I'm uncomfortable in my own skin looking into Nadia's eyes.

They're a window to her scarred, broken, tormented soul. I've no idea how I know this, but every cell in my brain pulses with knowledge as if I have a first-row seat to her thoughts.

I don't. I simply recognise what hides in those dull, lifeless eyes because mine are the same. Almost dead.

She seems at ease, sporting a cute, adorable smile but hurt and pain hide underneath the mask. Nothing save for her brown irises betrays she's hurting. And hurting greatly.

I wait, hoping she'll say something, that she'll react somehow because the cat sure got my fucking tongue right now. Instead of opening her mouth, she sizes me up again, her pupils blown when she peers up with a tiny frown.

"You must be Nick's sister," I say, my mind void of better ideas for a casual opener.

Our stare-down lasted fifteen seconds, but with my heart skipping a dozen beats, it feels as if an entire goddamn century just casually passed me by.

"Nadia." She offers me another dazzling, fake smile.

Her proximity is both soothing and disturbing. I want to avert my gaze and keep staring at the same time.

There are more things I want to do with her—or to her...

I want to taste her lips, touch her skin, rip her clothes off, and fuck her right here in the parking lot to check if I can breathe a bit of life into her with a good orgasm.

I want to bend her over the hood, grab a fistful of her hair, and have her screaming my name.

I want her... I don't know why, though.

We just fucking met. Two minutes ago! She's not blonde, tall, or slutty, but desire erupts under my skin as highly inappropriate images fill my mind.

And then, *boom*! A small piece of information that eluded me thus far leaps out to knock out my front teeth... she's Nick's sister. His off-fucking-limits little sister. I can't have her.

Considering I always get what I want, not being allowed is frustrating, to say the least.

Within seconds, Nadia changed from a girl I had no interest in into forbidden fruit. That means trouble. *Big* trouble.

Fine, not that big: five-feet-two, give or take.

Nick struggles with the first bag, so I step up, busying my hands because all they want is to touch Nadia. Frustration finds a way out of my system when I lift the heavy bags. It'd prove more helpful if I could hurl one across the car park.

Once everything is loaded, I slam the boot closed, pumping my fists to rid the tension. Nadia's safely tucked in the back when I take the wheel, and Nick's messing up my radio station list again. I should tie his hands behind his back before letting him in my car next time.

"What's the plan? Or should I just ask who's coming?" Nadia's voice penetrates my armoured walls.

"We'll have fun tonight, sis. I promise."

Nick planned the evening in detail. First, a house party, then a night out because Nadia loves dancing. Half an hour ago, I looked forward to spending quality time with friends.

Now?

Not so much.

Considering what I want from Nadia, being in the same

room with her might be a bad idea. She brought me to my knees within thirty seconds. What the hell will she do to me when she has an hour or two? The evening ahead just turned into a game of survival, and I fucking suck at games.

I squeeze the wheel harder as I join the rush-hour traffic. My eyes dart into the rear-view mirror, watching Nadia. Those full lips of hers will haunt me in my sleep.

"Nothing changed here," she says.

Nick turns in his seat, barking out a laugh. "You were gone two years, not two centuries."

Two years too long. I would've met her two years ago if she hadn't left for New York. Not that I have a single idea how we'd spend two years since I'm not allowed to touch her. Even thinking about her the way I am is a no-no.

Nadia ignores Nick's remark. "How's my flat?"

"About that. You'll stay with me for a few days. The painters weren't available last week, but they're starting tomorrow. They should be done by the weekend, so you'll move then."

I ignore Nadia's presence, tuning her out, but it's like ignoring my own fucking hand. God, this must be what dogs feel when staring at a chocolate bar. They can look and smell it but can't eat it. I'm in the same position with Nadia. I'm not allowed to have her. No wonder dogs give in when no one's looking. The frustration inside me already drives me nuts.

"You've got three hours for a nap before everyone comes over, sis."

"I'd like to see Dad first." She looks into the rear-view mirror, locking eyes with me. "Would it be a problem for you to drop me off there, Thomas? I'll get a taxi back."

Instead of forming a coherent reply, I'm sidetracked by how my name sounds on her lips. The *s* is a touch longer than when anyone else says it.

"Can't it wait until tomorrow?" Nick asks. "I'll take you over there tomorrow morning."

"I've not seen him in two years, Nick." She huffs out a heavy sigh. "It's okay. I'll just order a taxi."

I search for her eyes in the mirror. Since leaving the airport, I spent more time watching her than the road. Not the wisest idea. "I didn't say I won't take you, Nadia. Do you want to go straight there or Nick's house first?"

"Straight there if you don't mind."

I flick the indicator on, parking by a tall, brass gate ten minutes later, and turn around to look at her.

Fucking perfect lips.

Fucking beautiful, big, sad eyes.

"Thirteen Lakeside View?" she asks.

Nick nods, taking his wallet out to give her cash for a taxi— a taxi she won't take because I'll come back to get her. As inappropriate and idiotic as it is, I need a few minutes alone with her, even if it means blue balls for life.

I won't tell Nick in case he gets the wrong idea, though. Not that he shouldn't. The things I want from his sister are precisely the things he failed to warn me about.

Two

So thoughtful

NADIA

I place a bouquet of lilies I bought by the cemetery gate on the headstone and sit in front of Dad's grave. Two years have passed since I was here, looking at the letters carved in marble.

Arthur Grimwald
A loving father, a caring friend.

For a while, I stare at the letter I wrote, then inhale a deep, soothing breath and open my mouth, reading quietly.

Daddy,
I'm back for good. I know I still have another year before graduation, but I can't stay in New York any longer. So many things have happened during the last two years… I don't know where to begin.
I guess I should start by telling you about Adrian. We've been dating for over a year. He was perfect, loving, and helped me see past grief. I've never met anyone as passionate about life. He stalked me for a whole

month, asking me out any chance he got. I grew tired of telling him no, and after that first date, we were inseparable.

You should've seen Adrian and Nick together. They were best friends after half an hour. Nick adored him, but five months ago, everything changed. I'm not sure if I should tell you this. It's hard, Daddy. It's still fresh, and I'm not even sure I've made the right choice.

I pause, skimming the following pages. I don't know if I have enough courage to tell Dad why Adrian is no longer a part of my life. This isn't a conversation I should ever have with him, but I guess this isn't exactly a conversation... it's easier to tell someone who can't answer. Someone who can't judge.

I flip back to where I stopped and start whispering the words, hoping that telling the story will help me move on.

Four pages later, I start the last one, feeling lighter but still just a shadow of the girl I was three years ago. Happiness has been hissing out of my life since my eighteenth birthday. When I met Adrian, I thought he could make me happy again, that I'd find peace thanks to him, but it was just an eerie calm before the storm. Now I'm stuck—reliving the worst times again, looking for a way out of the cold, dark maze.

I've had enough, Daddy. I booked a flight, called Nick, and here I am, wondering if I did the right thing. Adrian would never leave me like that. He was there when I was breaking apart. He picked up my pieces and put them back together so I could keep living.

I should've done more to help him, but I don't know what else I could've done. Thanks to Mum, I find it hard to trust people. Adrian knew that. Months went by before I started trusting him, and when he failed me, there was no way I could trust him again.

I wish you could be here to tell me where I made a mistake. Although, if you were here, I'd never tell you about this. Just like I won't tell Nick. He wouldn't understand. Knowing the truth would hurt him too much.

On the bright side, now that I'm back, I can help Mel more with the

wedding. Maybe running errands for my future sister-in-law will take my mind off things. I wish you could enjoy the wedding with us. It'll be fantastic. I love you, Daddy. I miss you so much.

Tears stain my face when I tuck the letter into the back pocket of my jeans. Talking to Dad is difficult, but it's all I have left. I like thinking he can hear me, even if he can't answer. With one last look at the grave, I walk away, my head hanging low. I should call a taxi, but I don't pull my phone out until I walk through the brass gate.

"Nadia."

I peer up from the screen, finding Thomas waving me over, halfway out of his BMW parked across the narrow footpath. Dark shades hide his striking cinnamon eyes. I take a few wary steps toward him when he gets back inside, leaning over the passenger seat to open the door for me.

"You didn't have to come back. I would've called a taxi," I say, getting in.

He slides his shades off, eyes scanning my face and growing heavy with what looks like genuine concern. "I had no other plans, and Nick asked if I could bring you home."

"Did you wait long?"

He shifts the gear, pulling out onto the road. "Why were you crying?" He steals a sideways glance my way as if trying to catch me lying.

Not many people would ask that, knowing where I spent the last hour. "It was a difficult conversation."

"Conversation? Your dad's not here. You can't call it a conversation, Nadia. It's a monologue."

My lips curl upwards at his ignorance. I enjoy brutal honesty. We're alike that way—I don't care for vagueness either. At least I never did... now, honesty is harder to muster.

"That's why I talk to him, not anyone else. Because he can't answer. He can't pretend to understand what's happening when he sure wouldn't."

"How do you know?"

"How could he if even I don't understand it?" My guard's down, my mind at ease. Words escape my mouth before I can stop them. The few short minutes I've spent with Thomas so far are enough to pique my interest. Even though I rarely have trouble reading people, I can't riddle him out. He doesn't come across as approachable, yet he's easy to talk to.

"That makes no sense," he says, stopping at the traffic lights. "How can you not understand what you tell him about?"

"I've been asking myself the same question for months."

He turns back toward the road. There's something incredibly intimate about how he rests his elbow on the armrest, leaning toward the middle and consequently toward me. His woodsy cologne fills the space, wrapping me in a strange, masculine blanket, and muscles in my abdomen contract when he grazes his thumb across his bottom lip, deep in thought.

"Maybe you should talk to Nick? Maybe an actual conversation will help?"

I shake my head, focusing on the view out the window. "I know my brother. I can screen-write that conversation for you. I know what he'd say and how my words would impact him. You'll understand what I mean later when he asks about Adrian." I gather my hair into a low bun. "Dad knows everything because he's not here. He can't judge me. I can just get things off my chest."

We turn onto a woodland road, and within a hundred yards, we arrive at our destination. Nick's house resembles a pretty screensaver—a medium-sized, traditional British cottage surrounded by tall trees and a dark artificial lake. Although *lake* is an exaggeration, it's more of a glorified pond. Nick always wanted to build a house by a lake, but there aren't many around London. He couldn't relocate, so he dug out a small lake and built the house beside it.

I smile at how much has changed during the past two years.

When I left, Nick was renting a one-bedroom flat and driving an old, battered Ford Fiesta. He told me about the record label idea soon after our father died. That's also when he mentioned Thomas for the first time, but we never met before today. I spent my days at a psychiatrist's office back then and moved across the ocean before the record label kicked off.

Now, Nick owns a beautiful house, is about to get married, and makes millions thanks to C&G Records.

"Thank you," I tell Thomas, my hand lingering on the door handle. "Will I see you tonight?"

He drapes his arm over my seat, his gaze jumping from my lips to my eyes. "You will."

Nick chooses that moment to exit the house, beaming like a child in a toy shop. I only manage a nod before leaving the car, my legs weak. Thomas raises his hand, acknowledging my brother, then holds my gaze as he backs out of the driveway, disappearing behind the trees.

"So? What do you think? Not bad, huh?" Nick approaches with an ever-growing smile.

"Not bad? It's amazing."

"Wait till you see your room. It's overlooking the lake." He winks, taking my hand to drag me inside and show off the warm, cosy décor as if he were the one who chose the colour scheme, not his wife-to-be.

Dark wood and copper-coloured carpets create an illusion of the indoors being an extension of the outdoors. I collapse on the corner sofa in the spacious living room, sinking into fluffy pillows. An eight-hour flight and a five-hour time difference are creeping up on me. I haven't slept much lately, plagued by nightmares that not even an elephant dose of sleeping pills drowns out. Now that I'm home, my energy evaporates like air escaping an inflatable mattress. Hopefully, I'll sleep better here, a safe distance away from Adrian.

Thomas's striking cinnamon eyes flash before mine... I can't help it. He's a sight to behold with dark, messy hair, barely-there stubble, and what I'm sure is a flawless body he hid under a white shirt.

"What time is Mel due back?" I ask, changing the course of my thoughts.

"Shortly after six. How about you get some sleep? I doubt she'll resist waking you up when she comes back."

He's not wrong.

Three hours later, I walk out of the bathroom after a long, hot shower, dressed in a beige skater skirt and a white long-sleeve top. Mel tackles me into a bear-hug as soon as I step into the bedroom, her cheeks pink, eyes glowing.

"Oh my God! I can't believe you're finally here!"

I laugh, wrapping my arms around her tightly, rocking us left and right. "Me neither." I pull away when her bright red hair tickles my face. "How did the fitting go?"

"Okay, I guess. We're on schedule, but there's still so much to do! We only have two weeks left before I start work." Her voice climbs an octave when panic kicks in—she's famous for the ultrasonic tone whenever she's stressed.

"Don't worry." I squeeze her hand. "We'll get everything done on time. I promise. If not within the next two weeks, I'll deal with whatever's outstanding once you start working."

She sits on the bed, picking her nails. "I know. I can't believe it's happening. I mean, would you have guessed I'd marry your brother when we were in high school?"

"Not a chance. You didn't like him back then," I chuckle, remembering Mel always bickered with Nick when we were teenagers. "I'm glad it's you, Mel. You're perfect together."

It took a while before I got used to the thought of my best friend dating my brother. I freaked out when Nick first told me about them. I was afraid my relationship with Amelia would fall apart if things didn't work out between them.

I couldn't imagine they'd last a month, but the longer they

were together, the harder I rooted for them. It wasn't until Nick proposed two years ago that I got my peace. I needed tangible proof, like with everything else in my life.

Now I can't imagine a better fit for either of them. Amelia's caring, resolute, and bossy, which helps her tame Nick's impulsiveness. He managed to get her hyperactivity under control.

Slightly, but that's enough.

"Who's coming tonight?"

"Thomas is already here. He freaked me out arriving before everyone. He's always late. Ethan should be here in an hour. He was over the moon when Nick told him you're coming back. Scorpio is coming with Jane, too."

"Ethan?"

"Ethan Marks!" she exclaims, eyes wide, lips falling apart. "Oh my God, Nadia! How can you not remember the guy?!"

"I remember. I just didn't think he'd still be around. Nick never liked him very much."

"They worked things out, and they're good now. Oh, and Alex might join us later." A curtain of red hair covers her freckled face when she busies her hands, redoing her ponytail. "She's in love with Thomas. It's fun to watch when she's all puss-in-boots cute eyes while he just doesn't give a shit."

"Not his type?"

"Neither are you, Missy."

"What?" I spin around, two wrinkles creasing my forehead.

"You're blushing, babe. I get it. He's hot, alright, but he's not the guy for you. He doesn't do monogamy, and you're in a committed relationship."

"About that relationship... I've got something to tell you about Adrian."

Mel's lips curve into a Cheshire-cat grin. She glances at my hand, searching for an engagement ring. "If it's what I think—"

"Don't get ahead of yourself."

She ignores me, smiling like a maniac. Figures. She always

dreamt of a double wedding, so I'm sure she already imagines how to make that happen.

I finish my makeup, and we move downstairs, where Nick and Thomas wait in the living room, the latter casually sprawled in the grey wing chair by the panoramic window.

My step falters.

My mouth turns dry.

Instead of a suit, he wears black jeans and a *white* t-shirt. And hanging over the armrest? A *beige* jacket.

Talk about coincidence.

A diametrical change in his style added a few points to his good looks. He peers up from his phone, those striking eyes roving me up and down. Despite standing at least ten feet away, I notice how his chest broadens when he inhales, his eyes taking me in inch by inch.

"Sleep well, sis?" Nick pats the space beside him.

I hesitate, knowing damn well that if I sit there, he'll be touching me a lot. Nick's a very physical being.

I used to be too. I enjoyed nuzzling my head in the crook of his neck while we watched a movie. Not anymore, though.

"Not bad." I sit further away than I normally would've. "Although it's weird without all the noise outside the window."

"Missing New York already?" Thomas cuts in.

"I bet it's not New York or the noise you're missing," Mel chirps, bouncing in the doorway with another broad smile. "Go on! Spill it!" She looks at Nick. "Nadia wants to tell us something about her and Adrian."

Nick's reaction matches Mel's one hundred percent—he smiles softly and checks my hand for an engagement ring.

So much for calm news breaking.

Here they are, expecting an engagement announcement while all I have is bad news.

Nick winks at Thomas, drinks his whiskey, and looks back at me, failing to contain his excitement. "So? How's my future

brother-in-law? When is he coming?"

Nick met Adrian last Christmas and accepted him as a part of the family less than a day later. Nothing surprising there. Adrian makes a great first impression. He's a guy any brother wants for his sister—kind, caring, affectionate.

I glance up briefly, looking for strength in the blue ceiling. "He's not coming."

"What?" The smile on Nick's face morphs into a frown. Disappointment rings in his voice like a church bell. "He won't fly over for the wedding? Why?"

"I told you not to get ahead of yourself," I tell Amelia, my stomach churning with dread. "We're not engaged." I pause, letting that bit sink in. "We broke up."

Amelia clasps one hand over her mouth, unnecessarily theatrical as per usual. "You *broke up?*" she mouths, plopping down by my brother.

Thomas chuckles softly, drawing my attention, amusement written all over his face as if he wants to say *I see what you meant.*

"You dumped him?" Nick snaps. "When? Why?"

He's not helping my mental well-being with the higher-than-normal tone and disappointment casting an ugly shadow across his face. I glance at Thomas again, looking for help, even though he can't. He's not trying either, but the intensity of his gaze burns my cheeks.

"Who said I broke up with him?"

"Oh, please!" Nick throws his hands in the air, slapping his own thighs before he jumps to his feet. "He's over his fucking head in love with you! Why did you dump him?"

The accusation ringing in his voice drives me up the wall. All the ugly truths threaten to spew from my lips unfiltered, each one begging me to scream at the top of my lungs what Adrian did, but it won't help the situation. It'll make things worse.

I swallow the lump lodged at the back of my throat, grounding myself with the first technique that springs to mind:

I grab a cushion, touching the soft fabric. Velvet, I think. Orange, smooth. Small. Light. White stitching. A geometrical pattern of a wolf on both sides.

That's better. My breathing stabilises, and I meet Nick's eyes, controlling my emotions. "Adrian changed. He's not the same person you met last year." Nothing's left of the passionate guy I fell for. He's just a shell of the man he once was. A shell filled with anger, drowning in his addiction.

"What does that mean?" Nick asks, squeezing the crystal glass he holds so hard his knuckles pale.

"Oh, for crying out loud!" I fume, shaking inside. "Let it go, okay? I know you liked him, but we're over. End of story."

For the past month, I replayed my relationship with Adrian a thousand times. There's nothing I want more than to leave it behind. Forget and never think about him again. Everything reminds me of Adrian back in New York. In London, nothing can trigger unwanted memories, and if Nick stops talking about him, with a bit of luck and sheer belief in the little strength I have left, I might move on.

God knows I want to start a new chapter and pretend the nightmare never happened. So far, no luck. Adrian lurks at the back of my mind despite my best efforts. I still have feelings for him, as ridiculous and plain reckless as it is. I still miss him, and it scares me beyond reason.

I'm fast approaching desperation point trying to rid my heart of him. There's not much I won't do at this point if it means regaining peace. I'm tired of tears... I want to draw a line separating the past from the present.

Nick remains silent, eyeing me with a frown. He drains the last of his drink and leaves the room without another word. I assume he needs a few minutes to wrap his head around the unexpected news, and I almost regret yelling. All he wants is for me to be happy. In his eyes, Adrian deserves a chance to make that happen. Hell, in his eyes, Adrian *makes* me happy.

Unfortunately, not anymore.

"I can't believe you kept this quiet this long!" Amelia clips, then takes my hand, huffing a sigh while glancing her thumb over my knuckles. "How are you holding up, babe? You need a girl's night out?"

"I'm fine, Mel." I pull my hand out of her grasp, not comfortable with being touched. Even by my best friend. "Really. I'm okay. It's for the best. You better think of some cute guy who'll be my date to your wedding."

"I'll take you," Thomas says, seemingly casual, but the heat behind his gaze makes me tingle all over.

"You're not cute, Thomas," Mel says, "but thanks for being so thoughtful." She never knew when to shut up. I'm dateless. Thomas is handsome, ergo—good enough.

"Can you dance?"

"No, he can't."

Thomas curls his lips into a one-sided smirk. "Wear comfortable shoes."

Nick returns with shot glasses and a bottle of tequila, still annoyed. He can hide his lousy mood behind a mask, but the softness of his features does nothing to hide the anger gleaming in his eyes.

With a stern face, Mel wraps her arm around his neck and pecks his lips, scratching the back of his head with long nails. "Guess who just offered to be Nadia's date to our wedding?"

Nick glances between his best friend and me. "It might not be a bad idea. You're my best man; Nadia's the maid of honour... you won't entertain dates, and you'll focus all efforts on ensuring everything runs smoothly."

It sounds like he's convincing himself that Thomas and I attending together is okay, but I know he dreads not seeing Adrian at my side in seven weeks.

Three

Missing posters

THOMAS

The more time passed without Nadia around, the better I got at rational thinking. Whatever spell she cast on me outside the airport evaporated once I parked my car in my garage after I dropped her off at Nick's.

I stood in front of the mirror in my bathroom for ten minutes, staring at my reflection. Nothing about my appearance changed since the morning, but I felt different. All because of a gorgeous baby doll with eyes the colour of dark chocolate and the size of walnuts.

A doll I can't have, despite wanting her like I never wanted anyone before. I can't have her because she's Nick's off-fucking-limits sister; she's a brunette, and after twenty minutes with her alone, I *like* her.

All the reasons not to touch her are checked off... too bad it doesn't mean shit. I still want her. I fucking crave her.

My brain didn't take a holiday. It disappeared. Giant *Missing* posters hang all over London while I search for it. I shake my

head, amused at how much I've been thinking about Nadia. It's not like I ever gave a second thought to Ann, Grace, or any other blonde, but Nadia occupies my mind non-stop.

At the end of the day, I just want to fuck her. Nothing more and nothing less. As much as I want that, I can divert my needs to some nameless blonde when we hit the club later.

Problem solved.

My foolproof plan—fucking the first good-looking blonde I'll lay my eyes on, works perfectly well right until it doesn't...

I follow Nadia outside a few minutes after Nick finished interrogating her about Adrian and even fewer minutes after I offered to be her date for Nick's wedding.

How very fucking thoughtful of you, Thomas.

Taking girls out is hardly my style. Fifteen minutes is all I need. Inviting them out means spending more time with them, which means complications, like the inability to drag two or three girls to the toilet during one party.

Whatever.

I can abstain from acting like a world-class jerk for one evening if it means Nadia won't be accompanied to the wedding by an even bigger jerk. By the look of Mel, I know exactly *which* jerk she'd lined up for Nadia if I hadn't offered. No way I'll let him take care of her. I wouldn't let him take care of a fucking fruit fly. I should've thought the idea through a bit, though. While the stunned disbelief was nothing short of what I expected from Mel, the same look on Nadia gave me the creeps.

She knows.

She knows what kind of a man I am.

Mel must've filled her in by now, and for the first time in my life, I'm ashamed of my lifestyle.

Nadia sits on a fallen bough Nick failed to get rid of. The sun heads west, and the first rays of orange paint the grey sky, creating a spectacular view over the calm lake. It wouldn't be half as spectacular without her in the picture.

"You look gorgeous, baby doll," I say, lighting her cigarette with my Zippo.

Gorgeous is a fucking understatement. I don't think there's a word good enough to describe how stunning Nadia is. How she keeps her hair draped over one shoulder, falling down her chest, her petite posture, and how she holds a cigarette between those full lips is hypnotic. Even so, I can't put my finger on why I'm so hooked on this girl. She's pretty, but it's not her looks that pull me in like an invisible rope.

The fine hairs on my neck rise when she licks her lips. The sight induces a fit of shivers sliding down my spine and a head rush that makes standing tricky. I sit beside her, which might not be the best choice. Her perfume has an equally powerful brainwashing effect.

"*Baby doll?* Is that supposed to be rude or flattering?"

I inhale a drag and exhale the smoke, trying to focus on something other than her proximity. Something other than the spark passing between us, but I can't while my heart beats its way out of my chest with a fucking sledgehammer. "Not rude," I mutter, eyeing her lips. "Tell me what you're thinking about right now."

The air around us becomes too thick to inhale once the atmosphere shifts, no longer casual but roaring with lust.

"I think you're too close," she sighs softly, redirecting the blood flow in my body toward the inseam of my jeans.

Instead of moving away, she inches closer. I think she wants me to kiss her as much as I want to do it, and that's all the green light I need to flush my friendship and partnership with Nick down a drain.

All for *one* kiss.

How can I not think about making love to her when she sighs like that?

What the fuck?! You want to fuck *her, Thomas.*

God, I'm doomed. Is my brain never coming back?

Everything else disappears when her nose almost brushes mine, less than an inch parting our lips. I'm about to move in, seal the deal and steal a kiss when she jumps back as if I fucking clocked her. I don't know what the hell is happening until a familiar, suddenly very loathed voice fills the air, coming from the open patio doors.

"Nadia!" Ethan exclaims, charging right at her.

My first thought is to nail his face before he gets near her. A deep breath later, I rein in the sudden possessive shit wreaking havoc in my head and stop short of knocking out my friend.

Nadia eyes Ethan, a hint of dread tainting her pretty face. If I wasn't so focused on her, I would've missed how she glances around as if looking for the fastest way out. Before she makes a move, and before any other brilliant idea pops into my head, Ethan helps—read: *forces*—Nadia up, pulling her into his arms.

She goes perfectly still as if frozen. I can't see her face, but her body language speaks volumes, clearly saying that Ethan's greeting is the last thing she wants. She awkwardly pats his back with a trembling hand, wriggling out of his embrace after two seconds. He covers up an edgy, abashed look with an eager smile.

"Amelia told me you'd be here," Nadia says, stepping back.

Ethan drapes his arm over her shoulders, pure joy sparkling in his clear blue eyes. "I wouldn't miss it for the world, cutie."

I swear she flinched hearing that shitty endearment. Once again, she frees herself out of the blatant invasion of her personal space. The fear and pain I saw in her eyes earlier are much more prominent now.

I don't like what I just witnessed.

I don't like her reaction to Ethan or that I don't understand the last of this.

I offer Nadia my Zippo when she sits beside me, putting another cigarette between her lips. Our fingers touch accidentally, and I watch, dumbstruck, as she stops trembling. What's more, she calms right down.

What the hell is going on?

"You good, mate?" Ethan smiles wide, showing off the perfect, too-white teeth he had done last month. If he had a tail, he'd be wagging it all over the place.

Pussy.

My jaw locks along with my fists. It's not like I stopped wondering whether to knock him out. The urge to break his nose comes stronger now that I witness Nadia's anxiety. Has he upset her in the past? Hurt her somehow?

Fuck, maybe they were dating, and the jerk broke her heart...

A surge of protectiveness jabs at my mind. I don't know what I'd be protecting her from, but I can't shake the feeling. The burning need appears out of nowhere, knocking me off my damn feet. Nailing Ethan would definitely help me cool off. If not for him, I would've kissed her by now.

Then again, Nick would nail *my* face if I did, so call it even.

What I got out of this situation is worth the wait. I can't deny myself her perfect lips when I know she wants me to taste her. Or maybe I'm just justifying my weakness.

I glance at the oblivious Ethan. "I'm good. You?"

"All the better after seeing this fine lady. How long has it been? It sure feels like a century!"

Kiss-ass.

Nadia heads back inside a moment later with Ethan at her side. I stay, needing a minute or two to get my act together. I've been a bouncing ball since she arrived. When I touch the ground, i.e., when Nadia's nowhere near, I'm okay with her off-limits status. Once I bounce up, my reason dies a tragic death. Considering that a bouncing ball spends way more time in the air than on the ground, I'm fucked.

Everyone's at the table engrossed in a casual conversation when I get back inside a few minutes later. Ethan's gaze is fixed on Nadia, a visible softness in his baby blues, but she doesn't notice his hearts and kisses attitude, busy talking art with Nick.

Scorpio arrives with his girl, Jane, an hour later. Like Ethan, he hugs Nadia, stamping a kiss on her cheek. And like with Ethan, Nadia's suddenly absolutely still. Only this time, I see her eyes.

I was right.

She's fucking *scared.*

She endures the few short seconds of Scorpio's unwanted closeness, mindless-animal panic etched in her eyes. I'd bet good money she's screaming inside. I glance at Nick, his unfazed expression throwing me off track. No one seems alarmed by her behaviour, and that's the only reason I stay in my seat instead of shoving Scorpio away.

Maybe I misread her emotions.

Maybe it's not fear but distaste.

Maybe she's just not a hugger.

I squeeze my neck, frustration growing by the minute. Instead of trying to kill the obsession, I push forward, deeper into the madness. Deeper into the unknown.

"Taxi will be here in an hour. We better get a move on."

"We're going out?" Nadia asks, sitting beside me again.

It might be wishful thinking, but I swear she's closer than she was moments ago.

"We booked the VIP booth at Vertigo," Ethan says, but if you'd rather stay here—"

"No. I just need to change my shoes." She sprints out of the room, followed by Ethan's and my gaze.

He's smiling; I'm frowning, and Nadia looks relieved to catch a break. I mentally thank Nick for his lack of common sense because he picked a house project that didn't include a downstairs toilet. I get up without needing an explanation, then climb the stairs, following in Nadia's footsteps.

The door at the far end stands open, and Nadia sits on the floor, her back against the bed, a bag on her lap. She rummages through it, pulling out prescription meds—*seven* different kinds, then she swallows five tablets, eyes closed. My stomach swings up to my throat when she wipes her eyes with the back of her hand, drying off tears I hadn't noticed from afar. That's too fucking much for me... I can't deal with that shit.

Instead of doing something, *anything to* help her, I hide in the bathroom like a coward, so she won't catch me lurking out there. My heart races faster than my thoughts when I rest my forehead against the cool tiles, fists clenched at my sides.

Well done, asshole.

A long time ago, Nick told me Nadia saw a psychiatrist after their father died. He mentioned medication, but I can't remember what kind. I should've paid more attention to his Nadia ramblings. I could do with knowing what pills she took back then. Maybe it's the same thing she's on now. Maybe I'd understand her behaviour better if I knew what she's popping.

Shit, why is she even still taking pills? Their father died almost three years ago.

Nadia's heels click on the wooden stairs jolting me out of my chaotic mind. I exit the bathroom, gawking at the closed door to her bedroom. I have no right to snoop. None whatsoever, but damn if checking the labels on those orange prescription bottles isn't all I can think about.

Nope. Not happening.

I turn around, heading back downstairs.

Nick stares at Nadia's arm, inspecting a small gun tattooed on the inside of her wrist. "When did you get it?"

"Last month."

She outstretches her fingers, imitates a gun, and pulls the imaginary trigger. A *genuine* smile lights her face rendering me speechless. Lord, she's so fucking beautiful when she smiles like that, eyes sparkling and all.

A moment later, with Ethan by her side, she leaves for a smoke. Not that the jerk smokes...

Nick rubs his face with both hands once the door closes behind them. "It's like I don't even know her anymore. First

Adrian, now the tattoo. What else is she hiding?"

Looks like more than he can imagine. The trouble is that he doesn't notice her problems, and I have no right to ask.

"You're such a girl, Nick. Grow a pair, will you?" Mel huffs like a pissed-off Chihuahua. "She broke up with Adrian. So what? It's not the end of the world. You thought she'd marry the guy? She's twenty-one!"

"He'd never leave her. *She* dumped him."

"You don't know what happened. Why do you only blame her? I mean, when we met him, Adrian was perfect, but Nadia must've had a good reason to leave him."

"What reason, Mel? He's a fucking saint for dragging her out of mourning in the first place. I like Adrian. I owe him big time. They were good together!" He snatches a shot glass from the table and throws the disgusting tequila at the back of his throat. "I wish she'd tell us what the hell went wrong."

"She will. Give her some time."

I'm only half involved in the conversation. The other half of my concentration goes into keeping my ass seated while Ethan is outside *alone* with Nadia. I can't see them, so my imagination runs wild. I rake my hand through my hair and urge Scorpio to drink a shot with me before I shove my hand in the front pocket of my jeans, pulling out cigarettes.

I'm ridiculous. Nadia and Ethan were friends long before I met them. They're just talking. Well, if they're just talking, there's no reason not to join them, right?

Right.

Ethan stands with his back pressed against the wall, intense gaze on Nadia as if she's a genie, about to grant his three wishes. Her breathing hitches when I sit beside her. Containing a triumphant smile proves almost impossible, but Ethan helps me out when he opens his mouth.

"We could go to Pesto; it's a great Italian restaurant."

Whoa. Did he just ask her out? How did that happen? He's

afraid to chat a girl up when we go out...

"How about we go play pool?"

She could've slapped me, and I wouldn't know the difference. Less than two hours ago, she sat in the same spot, ready to kiss me. Now she's planning a date with Ethan.

I should've nailed him when I had the chance.

A vein throbs on my neck when he retreats inside, unharmed and winning. "Ethan? Really?" The accusing tone of my voice rings a whole level too desperate.

Nadia pulls her eyebrows together. "I don't follow."

"Why are you going out with him?"

"He asked me."

I grip the bough with both hands. "That clears things up."

"It's nice that you care, but I already have a big brother, Thomas. Unless Ethan's a rapist, a drug addict, or a murderer, you can let Nick do the worrying."

Big brother? When have I acted like an overprotective brother? I'm further than far from being her big brother, small brother, or any other fucking brother.

She toys with a lock of dark hair, drawing her lip between white teeth and pulling slowly. A rush of heat pools in my chest. That date is just a ploy. She won't go out with Ethan. She wants me, but she wants to play a little.

And I'm all game.

"You're right. It's none of my business. Just don't leave me hanging. You're my date for the wedding."

"Of course, I am."

The atmosphere relaxes once we leave the house in one big taxi. Nick's good mood reappears, which can only mean one thing—a conversation game. He's obsessed with those.

He looks around, scanning the confined space. "I spy with my little eyes something beginning with *G*."

Amelia bounces in her seat. "Garden! Ginger!" Her eyes come across me. "Grumpy face!"

"A *gun*," Ethan says, smiling at Nadia. "My turn. I spy with my little eyes something beginning with *C*."

I have the urge to roll my eyes. He's overdoing it. "Cutie. I spy with my little eyes something beginning with *J*."

That one is obvious, isn't it?

Apparently not.

At least not to six people sharing the taxi with me. No one guessed, but their turns lasted the rest of the journey. Twenty minutes later, Nick, Scorpio, and I head for the bar, leaving the jerk to escort Nadia to the table since she's apparently incapable of walking twenty metres without assistance.

Scorpio sneers under his nose, watching Ethan's piss-poor attempts at wooing. "That didn't take long. Were they a thing before Nadia left?"

Nick looks over his shoulder, a sad smile on his lips. "No. He's had a crush on her ever since I can remember. He asked her out once, but she was sixteen and not interested in boys. He had a long-term girlfriend later, and when they broke up, our dad was already dead, and Nadia was a mess." He turns back to face the bar. "If he's trying to make up for lost time, he'll be thoroughly disappointed. Nadia will be back with Adrian soon."

"She seemed certain they're over," I say.

"I don't think such a term exists when it comes to them. You've not seen them together. Adrian's *the* guy. Nadia's everything to him. He's so in love with her, he makes me look like an amateur."

Surely that's not possible. Nick loves Amelia like a beaten-up stray dog loves a new owner who offers a cosy bed and an occasional pat on the head. He loves her more than his work and life combined. Not more than Nadia, but still a-fucking-lot. How can Adrian love Nadia more?

"What can I get you?" A tall, skinny, blonde barmaid stops before me even though Scorpio's the one impatiently tapping his knuckles on the bar, waiting to be served.

"A bottle of tequila."

"And an Appletini," Nick orders Mel's favourite drink. Scorpio elbows my ribs as if it's my fucking fault he attracts less female attention than I do. "Two of those."

"Should I order another? Does Nadia drink that?"

Truth be told, if I had a say, I'd cut her off. She swallowed *five* pills less than an hour ago. Flushing them down with alcohol might not be the brightest idea.

Nick pulls a face. "Not a chance. She chose tequila, so she needs to stick with tequila. She can't mix. It never ends well."

Noted—no mixing.

Ethan approaches when the barmaid finishes up with our order. He raises his chin in greeting because we haven't seen each other for three whole minutes, then moves his gaze to the blonde with big boobs.

Is she a sign? A tall, blue-eyed sign telling me to leave my best friend's sister alone and fuck her somewhere at the back of the building? Maybe that's not such a bad idea. Nadia has issues, and God knows I have enough of my own.

"Two Coronas, one with two limes," Ethan orders.

There was a time when I liked this guy. Deep down, I still do, but damn it, he sets my teeth on edge. He's an annoying discomfort like gum stuck to a shoe or pigeon crap on a brand-new Armani suit. All because he's after the girl I want. It wouldn't be an issue with any other girl, but in this case, Ethan can have Nadia. I can't.

Nick frowns, hinting who the two-limes Corona is for. Pissed off again, I snatch the tray from the countertop, making my way to the table. Nick can cover the bill this time.

I give Nadia a shot. "Drink up."

"Ethan's getting me a Corona."

He'll choke on it later.

I outstretch my arm over the back of her chair, leaning closer. The sweet and spicy perfume she wears targets my nose,

driving me wild. Everything about her drives me wild. I want to hide my face in the crook of her neck, graze my nose along her smooth skin and inhale her like a fucking creep. "I'd rather you didn't mix."

She purses her lips, eyes drilling a hole in me like a pneumatic hammer used at roadworks. I think she's getting ready to snap at me. Her eyes narrow, but she downs the shot, holding my gaze.

"Thank you." I take the empty glass from her, setting it back on the tray bottom up.

Mel watches me from the other side of the table. I know her well enough to interpret her facial expressions, eyebrow movements, and the wrinkles marking her forehead: vertical equal confusion or annoyance; horizontal equal surprise; one eyebrow raised is for disbelief, and if coupled with a pout, it's a wise idea to run for cover.

Right now, she's perfectly balanced between confusion, disbelief, and shit... she pouts, holding my gaze. I should probably check if I'm not at the bar.

I scan the dance floor for a perfect blonde who'll take my mind off the perfect brunette. The barmaid is plausible, but I know there are prettier girls around here tonight. Nothing changed since this morning—Nadia's still off-limits.

I also still crave her; fuck knows why, so it's time to take drastic measures. Before I zero in on potential prey, Alexandra joins the party making my skin crawl.

"There you all are. I've been looking *everywhere*." She hovers her lips close enough to my ear that she's breathing down my neck. "Good evening, handsome."

Creeped out must be a spot-on definition of my facial expression right about now. I don't acknowledge her presence when she sits opposite, hanging her bag over the back of her chair. I don't have to look at her to know she's watching me with what she considers cute eyes. In reality, she's a drugged-up

Chucky doll. The sting of her gaze burns holes in my lips, cheeks, and retinas.

"There you go, cutie." Ethan sets a Corona on the table.

Good boy.

Nadia smiles, reaching for the beer. Her smile slips when I snatch the bottle first, bring it to my lips and take a large swig, proving a point. "Got something you'd like to say?"

"There are many things I'd like to say right now." She extends her hand, cheeks heating. "My beer, please."

"Don't mix, *please.*"

Her determination lasts three seconds before she drops her hand, forfeits the beer, and gets up, smoothing out her skirt. With one last look my way, she takes Amelia and Jane to the dancefloor.

Shit. I can't watch her from where I sit.

With two shots, I move to an empty seat beside Scorpio.

"You alright?" he asks quietly, motioning at my clenched fist under the table, caused by the jerk turning in his chair, his eyes searching for Nadia. "What is it?"

"Nothing. I'm good."

"You can't lie for shit, mate. Why her? And don't pretend you don't know who I'm talking about. You've not taken your eyes off her all evening."

I should've known he'd be the one to notice and figure out the reason behind my uncharacteristic behaviour. We've been friends for years. He knew me before Nick did and before my life turned into a pile of regret and a guilty conscience. I shake my head to indicate I have no idea why, of all people, it's *her.*

"Whatever the reason, you better forget about it." He motions at Nick with his chin. "He'll have your balls in a blender if you touch his precious little sister."

Yeah, that's probable. We partied together enough times after Nick argued with Mel, so I know he's capable of some crazy shit. Nick, Scorpio, Ethan, and I hit the clubs whenever they fight so he can get wasted. The problem is that Nick is

unpredictable, fucking uncontrollable once past a certain level of alcohol in his blood. He was cuffed and locked up a few times for the night, leaving me to lie to Mel and pick up his sorry ass from the police station the following day.

So yeah, the blender thing will happen if I touch Nadia. And as I don't think I can back down, it might be a good idea to wave bye-bye to my balls. I'll miss them one day, but the brain in my pants doesn't care.

Four

The right push

NADIA

Sean Paul's "Get Busy" resonates through the club when Jane, Amelia, and I find enough space on the dance floor for the three of us. Jane moves like a professional stripper, every move sexy, seductive, and way too out there, but she keeps safe, shoving guys away whenever they come close. She glances at the table every so often, where Scorpio keeps a watchful eye on her.

Amelia's moves are less provoking and don't attract as much attention, but it doesn't stop my brother from making sure she's okay. Their protectiveness reminds me of the times I spent with Adrian. He was just like them. Maybe even *more.*

I sit on Adrian's lap, tucked against his chest, my legs sprawled on the couch, a Corona in hand. I watch the partygoers while he talks to his best friend, Ty. The music blares throughout the house, shaking the windows while frat guys play beer pong, and ultraviolet lights bounce around the crowded room. People dance wherever they can, and my friend, Jasmine, has been waving me over for ten minutes now.

It's been four weeks since I started dating Adrian, and this is the first party we came to together. He's known around campus. Anyone who's anyone heard the rumours about the up-and-coming boxer.

He stamps a kiss to the nape of my neck, letting his lips linger in the spot, then slides them higher, nipping my earlobe. Despite the loud music, I hear him inhale a deep breath. "Go," he mutters, tucking my hair away. "Have fun, Puppet."

I shake my head, eyeing the crowd of drunk guys groping every girl out there. "I'll pass. They aren't dancing. Guys just want to get laid, and girls try not to get groped."

Ty chuckles, leaning closer. "No one will touch you, Nadia. They know that if they cross you, they cross Adrian, and no one here will risk a one-on-one with him."

Adrian smirks, nodding along. "I'll keep an eye on you, Puppet."

Tempting. I've not danced in so long. I finish my beer, getting to my feet when Jasmine waves me over again.

Adrian cuffs my wrist, his eyebrow raised. "You've not kissed me."

A wave of heat spills inside my chest. I love that about him. He has no trouble showcasing his feelings. Most guys avoid public displays of affection, but he's different: confident and affectionate.

"Kiss me," he urges, tugging my hand.

I bend down, pressing my lips to his, endorphins flooding my system.

Reality slaps me across the face when someone's arms snake around me from behind. Panic kicks in first, robbing me of rational thinking. I jump away, twirling around on my heel, my body rigid, heart pounding. A blond guy stands there, a beer in hand, a frown on his forehead when I shake my head. He empties half of the bottle, drunk and courageous as he takes a step forward, risking another rejection.

"No!" I yell, a touch too dramatic to the eye of a passive observer. "Find a different girl."

Either he thinks I'm joking, or the alcohol coursing through his system squanders his ability to comprehend what I'm saying because he grabs my hand again. I snatch it away, turning around. Even though I'm fleeing, I fight the rising unease, desperate to stop my past before it overwhelms me. The psychiatrist back in New York said I should face my fears and take opportunities... easier said than done.

With a deep, calming breath, I ignore my sinking heart, stomp my foot and turn back toward the guy. My shoulders tense painfully when he takes me by the arm, yanking me closer as if he knows I might change my mind again. A strong smell of booze, cigarette smoke, and heady cologne fans my face. I press my back to his chest, thinking it'll be easier if I don't see him. Nestling his face in my hair, he drapes one hand across my collarbones, inhaling deeply.

Don't panic. Don't panic. It's just a dance.

Not enough time has passed yet. I've not learned to deal with or control the fear that prickles at my nerve endings, overwhelming all senses. I wish I knew how to stop my mind from locking up. To stop my stomach from tying into a double knot. Unfortunately, I can't fool the fight or flight reflex when the guy's hands spread over my stomach in a possessive manner and then slide lower. I jump away, bile rising to my throat, every cell in my body brimming with dread.

"Oops, sorry," he cackles.

He's drunk beyond comprehension, hooded eyes unfocused as if he's not fully aware of what's happening around him. He sways on his feet, smelling like it's St. Patrick's Day, and cuffs my wrist cutting short the time I'm taking to decide whether I should stay or run.

Run.

"Let me go!"

"Oh, come on, let's dance."

Just when I free myself from his grip, a clenched fist shoots past my head, landing neatly on the guy's jaw. He barely held his own weight anyway, so one powerful punch sends him

folding down into a drunk heap at my feet. Blood gushes from his nose, turning his white t-shirt crimson.

I twirl around, looking for the owner of the fist, my pulse rioting until I lock eyes with a familiar face. Thomas stands closer than I expected to find anyone. And he's raging. His cinnamon eyes are fixed on the drunk, nostrils flared, hands balled into tight fists. I take an involuntary step back when his jaw starts working in tight circles as he bends his arm, winding his elbow back, ready to send his fist flying through the air again. But before he does, his eyes move to my face, and his whole stance changes before my eyes.

His muscles relax, the sharp edge to his features gone, replaced by two tiny wrinkles between his eyebrows. "You okay?"

I stare at him, utterly confused because he's not trying to touch me. Most people in his position would grab my arm or invade my space to make sure I'm okay, but Thomas keeps at a distance, waiting for my move.

The kiss he pressed to my hand in the parking lot flashes before my eyes first. The scene of us sitting so close at the back of Nick's house comes next. We spent most of the evening sitting side by side, close enough that I could make out the fragrant smell of his cologne. Since we walked into the club, he's kept his hand draped over the back of my chair. He even brushed his fingers along the nape of my neck a few times, trying to get my attention when it was time for a shot. Despite all that, I've not once had the urge to move away.

I'm not comfortable when my own brother comes near, but Thomas can invade my space as he pleases. I take a wary step forward, placing my trembling hand on his chest, curious if the fight or flight instinct kicks in.

It doesn't.

My eyebrows knot in the middle. Why am I not moving away? Why don't I mind him so close? He comes across as a guy who often loses control, taking pride in turning faces into pulp for sport. He comes across as a guy who's always in control, dominating every aspect of life.

Why am I not afraid?

"Thank you," I whisper, aware he can't hear me, but I think he read my lips.

His cheek brushes against mine, his lips touching my ear as he speaks. "Don't thank me for doing my job."

My stomach ties in knots again, but it's a pleasant sensation this time. An arousing one at that. A blush heats my face when he inches away. "Dance with me," I blurt out.

Something about his closeness puts my mind at ease. A feeling that's eluded me for months. It's addictive. I missed feeling safe, and I want more. I want him closer. I want to feel the weight lift off my shoulders as fear evaporates, even though I don't understand why my subconscious doesn't mind his closeness. J. Balvin's "Safari" seeps from the speakers, filling the club with a heated, Latino beat. My hips sway softly on their own accord while Thomas makes his mind up, taking his sweet time.

I used to love dancing. Problems lost their meaning when I lost myself in the music. Tonight, I want to feel free again.

Long seconds pass without a single word from Thomas. He just stares at me. I expect he'll shoot me down, but a heartbeat later, he straightens his spine, takes my hand, and laces our fingers as if he's done it a thousand times before. Instead of fear, sparklers light up my mind.

We squeeze through the crowd of sweaty bodies, stopping a few feet away from the DJ station, away from our friend's prying eyes. The music alone pushes away the grim memories that returned, thanks to the guy I danced with before. It doesn't work as well without Thomas, though. My hand still in his, he pulls me flush to his chest, and with that urgent touch, my past fades into a distant blur.

"Don't run," he says, lips brushing my ear again. "I won't do anything you won't let me."

I have no intention of running. Forfeiting the opportunity to feel *safe* goes against every instinct I was born with and those I developed while I fought for Adrian. I move my hand to his side, tracing his ribs with my fingertips, dazed by the heat radiating off him. A touch—so simple. So natural... so overwhelming without a jab of doubt seizing my every cell.

I'm drunk on his closeness, drunk on how good it feels not to fret when he grips my hip, moving the other hand to my back. He yanks me closer, his touch urgent, rushed, as if he needs me like I need him right now.

As if I anchor him the same way he does me.

His impulsiveness, skills, and the touch of his body against mine up the temperature around. Much time had passed since I let anyone touch me. I look into his eyes, matching his rhythm, and travel back to when I was just an ordinary girl before my life was flipped on its head.

I was never the strongest person in any room but strong enough to deal with life. Self-sufficient like most of my peers. Everything changed on the day of my eighteenth birthday. Since then, for three years now, I've fought to keep my head above the water. I've fought for every small, ragged, strained breath.

Now that Thomas holds me close, I fill my lungs with ease. It's almost painful. A delicious, wholehearted sting of oxygen surges through me after years of surviving on scraps.

The tempo shifts, the beat drops, and Thomas turns me around, pressing my back flush against his chest. "Close your eyes," he says, his lips skimming over my ear. "Imagine we're alone."

Strong hands rest on my stomach when the bass reverberates through my body. Thomas spreads his fingers, his hold possessive but fiercely protective at the same time. I close my eyes, handing over control.

A seemingly small change changes a great deal about how I experience the moment. The multi-instrumental beat that touches all senses is all I hear; Thomas's firm, warm body, is all

I feel. The delicate fluttering of a single butterfly's wings in my stomach turns into the fluttering of a thousand insects.

We move together, dancing, being. The back of my head rests in the crook of his shoulder, and Thomas moves his hand to gently clutch my throat. He dips his head, hiding his face in the crook of my neck, inhaling a slow, shaky breath.

And that's all I need to lose myself in the music and *him*. No wonder he's such a player. We met twelve hours ago, but I already have a hard time resisting his charm, although for a different reason than the herds of women he sleeps with.

Another Latin song plays next. We dance through that one and two more before Thomas rests his hand on my lower back, steering me through the crowd to our table.

"Where were you?" Nick asks, not giving us a chance to sit down before the interrogation begins.

"He offered to be my date at your wedding. He said he could dance... I don't buy a pig in a poke. I had to check he can dance."

Thomas scoffs, outstretching his hand over the back of my chair once more. "Satisfied?"

"You'll do."

"Who was that guy you KO'd before?" Scorpio motions at the crowd.

Thomas shrugs, handing me a shot. "No idea."

"Okay, so what did he do?"

"He didn't understand when Nadia said no. I think he needed the right push."

"Or punch," I correct, turning to him when he brushes his fingertips against my shoulder.

"You're tougher than you seem. I'll give you that." He points at my wrist. "Next time, shoot the asshole."

Nick and Mel hit the dance floor a moment later, and as if encouraged, Ethan gets up, holding his hand out to me. "Come on, cutie. Let's dance."

I've known him for five years. I know he's harmless, but

dancing requires closeness I have trouble handling. Still, after spending fifteen minutes with Thomas's arms around me on the dance floor, refusing Ethan might raise questions, trigger unwanted suspicion, and give Thomas the wrong idea.

"Oh... erm, yes, sure."

I wish men were quicker to catch on. If a woman heard me stumble over my words like that, she'd know I don't want to dance. She'd know I'm only rising from my seat out of politeness. Ethan's oblivious. Either that, or he chooses not to read into my words too much.

He leads me through the crowd, and for three whole songs, he breathes down my neck, touching my back while holding me too close for my liking. I inhale deeply, plastering what I hope is a believable smile on my lips, but I hate every second. I hate *myself* for not dealing with my issues better. And most of all, I hate Adrian because he messed me up so bad.

"I need a drink," I say once the third song ends.

"Yeah, me too. It's been a while since I danced. I should hit the gym more often to stay in shape," he chuckles, leaning close enough to make me uncomfortable. "Sit down. I'll get you a lemonade."

Thomas isn't at the table as I hoped. I'm jittery inside, shuddering whenever I recall Ethan's hands on my body. Thomas will chase away my demons without trying. Without *knowing*. Instead of sitting, I grab my purse and head outside, thinking I'll find him there, enjoying a cigarette. But he's not there. A few guys stand in a tight group, laughing and shouting. I stand to the side, fishing my cigarettes out of my bag.

"Did no one tell you Thomas is taken?" Alex asks behind me.

I spin around, finding her with her arms folded over her chest. "Taken?" I light the cigarette, inhaling a mouthful of smoke. "You mean he's dating someone?"

"Yes, *me*. I'd appreciate it if you'd stop flirting with him."

Either she's crazy, or I'm missing an essential piece of the puzzle from this picture. When have I flirted with him, exactly?

"I'm not flirting with Thomas, Alex. Excuse my ignorance, but how does your *relationship* work?"

"That's none of your business. What we have is special. I like you, Nadia. I really do, but if you mess this up for me, you will regret it. Just stay away from him, okay? It's all I ask."

Special? She's freaking special.

A psychiatrist's-dissertation-topic kind of special.

"Sorry, *sweetie*, but it's not like I can just stop seeing him. He's Nick's business partner and best friend."

She giggles, piercing my eardrums with that artificial, infantile sound. "I didn't mean *that*. Just don't get too close. Don't dance with him, don't sit next to him. Keep your distance, and I'll be happy."

Can she hear herself?

I open my mouth because she's being stupid, but I change my mind before I start an argument.

Not my circus. Not my monkeys.

The last thing I need is more drama. "Fine. Have it your way."

She sighs, curving her lips into a broad smile. "So, how have you been? How was New York?"

"I like London better, and I've missed everyone." *Not you, you lunatic.* I finish my cigarette in record time, heading back. One step inside, I bump into a firm, broad chest that smells familiar. "Really?" I ask, glaring at the ceiling, cursing fate for being rude. "Not funny."

Thomas frowns, his lips parting, but Alex speaks first. All she says is my name. The warning note rings clearly, turning my blood into red-hot soda water.

I grit my teeth, stepping around Thomas to leave them be. He has different plans, though. He takes my hand, halting me in place. The touch of his skin chases away the demons—ravens—infesting my mind.

"Come back out with me. I need company."

"I'll come with you, sweetie," Alex offers, bouncing on her

stilettoes like a child with too much sugar surging through their bloodstream.

"You don't smoke," he clips, not gracing her with one look.

I try to step away, but he holds me tight, his eyes boring into mine, waiting for answers to his unspoken questions.

"Let me go," I say. As if it's a magic spell, he does. "Please don't drag me into this. I don't want to be a part of whatever the deal is with you two." I spin on my heel, walking away.

Music rumbles through the speakers scattered around the room, and the bass vibrations shake the floor beneath my feet. Ethan and Scorpio are at the bar, probably ordering a few more rounds of tequila, and before they bring the shots over, Thomas and Alex join the pack.

She's close to tears, and he's annoyed, I think. His eyes narrow further when he sees me on the other side of the table, no longer occupying the seat beside him. It's absurd, but I'm equally annoyed by the unwanted separation. Thanks to him, this evening is not half as bad as I expected, but now that I'm robbed of his proximity, all I want is to go back home.

After finishing her Appletini two minutes ago, Amelia stepped over her daily liquor allowance and can no longer articulate nor control her limbs. Despite that, she still grabs a shot, so Nick decides it's best to take her home.

That's my way out. "Wait, I'm coming with you!" I squeal, taking my bag.

"No way," he says, searching through Mel's bag to retrieve a set of keys, which he then hands to Thomas, not me. "Get her home safely."

"I don't need a babysitter, Nick. I'm coming with you."

"It's not even midnight yet. Stay. Enjoy the night." He stamps a kiss on my forehead, exchanges a few words with Thomas, and steers Mel out of the club.

I'm left with Jane and Scorpio, furious Alex, pushy Ethan and the enigma that is Thomas.

Five

Point well made

NADIA

We stand outside the club, waiting for a taxi to become available, when Ethan plants a soft kiss on my cheek.

I stumble back. My eyes widen, and my heart is suddenly on its way out of my chest through my throat. He caught me off guard. He wasn't close enough to make me uncomfortable, and yet he stole a kiss. He's drunk, doing his utmost to pretend he's not.

It's not working.

"I'm going with them," he motions to Jane and Scorpio. "We live around the corner from each other. I'll see you next week, cutie."

"Sure." Or not.

It wasn't supposed to be a date, just two friends catching up. Ethan agreed, but he must've forgotten. The stolen kiss was his mistake. I no longer trust him.

There's also Thomas. Because I'm calm around him, I'm blind to anything else. Why should I deal with my past by myself

when a solution crossed my path and seems to want more from me than just friendship?

"I'll see you soon." Ethan leans in, ready to kiss me again.

Before his lips touch my skin, Thomas jerks him back. "They're waiting for you," he clips.

"Huh?" Ethan straightens his back, peers over his shoulder and then back at me. "Oh, right. I'll call you, cutie."

I nod, watching him stumble over his feet toward the cab. It's almost three in the morning. The cool evening breeze introduces goosebumps to my skin, and Thomas takes his jacket off, draping it over my arms, a cigarette between his lips.

"I wouldn't have guessed you're a gentleman, Mr Calix."

Okay, Alex wasn't wrong... I'm flirting. The moment the distance between us is less than a foot, everything else blurs, and Thomas becomes my focus point.

"I'm glad I surprise you."

He's full of surprises. Full of riddles I'm eager to figure out. Eager to find out what else he hides up his sleeves.

We sit on a bench, enjoying the clouds of smoke filling our lungs and the comfortable silence. It's been a while since I sat arm in arm with someone and not felt threatened. Thomas is an incarnation of my beloved diazepam. I wouldn't survive another day without the pills. There's nothing extraordinary about Thomas, save for his strong jawline and cinnamon eyes. Neither explains the influence he has on me.

People exit the club in large, drunken groups, shouting and laughing as they jump into the taxis waiting outside. I glance over my shoulder, hearing someone spew a whole litany of swear words. A dozen guys stand by the club entrance, shoving at each other. They're not the reason why my breath hitches. The guy I danced with earlier stands among them, swaying on his feet. He looks different now... as if he came face to face with an enraged Tyson. His left eye is swollen and purple, t-shirt stained with blood, and I think his nose is broken.

"Looks like he's having a rough night," Thomas says.

"It wasn't you?"

"You saw what he looked like when I was finished with him. He must've greeted another fist after mine."

No doubt about it. The longer I stare at him, the more I realise one blast couldn't have done that much damage.

"I guess he ended up picking on the wrong girl."

"You were his worst choice, baby doll. I wouldn't have left it at one punch if you didn't stop me."

"He wanted to dance with me, Thomas."

The corners of his mouth twitch. "I like it when you do that. When you say my name, you drag out the *s*."

"You change subjects like a bee changes flowers." I readjust his jacket. His scent alone soothes my senses, locking me in a protective cocoon. I hope I'll never change into a butterfly.

"You're tired, Nadia. You want to go home?"

"No, but I should."

Thomas laces our fingers, sending a shockwave through my system. It's a small, innocent gesture, but the touch of his skin soothes my haunted mind.

"Why did you trade places with Alex?" he asks once we take the back seat, and the driver sets the car in motion.

"I'm not allowed too close to you."

"Says who?"

"Says your girlfriend."

His nostrils flare. "I don't have a girlfriend."

"I know. You know it, too, but Alex doesn't."

"Why are you amused? It's infuriating; annoying at best."

"I just don't get it. I mean, she's obsessed with you! Not that she doesn't have the grounds for it because you are quite a something, but then again, you ignore her any chance you get. I don't understand how she can possibly not notice that. I guess what I'm trying to say is that she was always so down to earth, and now she's this brainless twinkie, and you're just a guy so—"

"Breathe. What does *quite a something* mean in your dictionary?"

"Was the compliment all you heard? Don't pretend you don't see how women undress you when they look at you."

"Do you?"

The low, husky tone of his voice hastens my pulse. He stares at me, waiting for words, but I can't recall the question, too busy containing the sudden rush of desire.

I swallow the chunky lump that just lodged itself in my throat. "Do I... what?"

"Do you undress me every time you look at me?"

"No." *Yes, but for different reasons than you think.* "So? Do all girls you casually sleep with act so brainless?"

"Most of them."

"You should choose them more wisely."

"I never slept with Alex!" he snaps.

At least he's no longer treating me with that low, raspy tone that turns my knees weak. "Figures. She's not a blue-eyed, blonde model type."

There's a short moment of silence, and then Thomas turns his body my way, his eyes not leaving mine. "Blue-eyed, blonde model type my ass." He weighs every word, his tone laced with a heavy note I can't decipher until...

My head spins.

Heart stops.

All senses apart from touch switch off when his lips catch mine. I want to dive into the moment and bask in the calmness he evokes, but my mind blares when I realise what he's doing.

I shove him away, my cheeks burning, blood boiling for two reasons. "What the hell, Thomas? I get it; you're trying—"

He shuts me up with another kiss.

This time, I back away faster. "Stop! I get it! You're not that shallow. Blondes aren't everything. Point well made."

He runs his tongue over his lips, one hand touching the side of my face, tracing its contour. "Stop fighting."

He leans closer, slowly, giving me time to decide. There are only two things I want—his lips and the calmness that comes as a package deal. I don't shove him away this time. I cling to him when his mouth comes down on mine, and his hot tongue teases my bottom lip, begging for more.

That's enough. The tall, armoured wall I've built around me over the past months crashes all around us. I give in like a leaf to the wind, parting my lips, letting him deepen the kiss.

A double dose of diazepam has nothing on Thomas. He's the most potent drug I've ever tried. Nothing can compare. I don't understand why; I can't find a single explanation, and I no longer care. Why should I? He eradicates pain.

His lips work with mine, the kiss soft, brutal, and demanding as if he waited a long time for me, this kiss, and my closeness. As if he can't get enough. He cups my chin, tilting my face up to his and his tongue slicks into my mouth. I have no strength to stop when the peace he offers is so important. We shouldn't kiss. We shouldn't want each other, but we couldn't care less.

The deepest, most intense desire is for the forbidden. Thomas is my forbidden fruit, just as I'm his. It escalates our craving to the point of fever. It's the simplest, most rudimental force on earth: lust in the purest form, a maddening need to feel our bodies fuse together.

I focus solely on him, lost in his touch. I want him. I want the irresistible serenity that comes with his proximity and the strength that follows suit. Adrenaline rushes through my veins as he climbs my thigh, digging his fingers into my skin with every inch he discovers. I gasp, sucking in a ragged breath, breaking the kiss. Thomas plants his mouth on my neck, and my skin breaks out in goosebumps everywhere he touches.

"Tell me to stop," he whispers, nipping my earlobe. His hands grip my hips, and he drags me onto his lap, his forehead against mine. "Say it. Tell me to stop."

If I could, I would, but I'm selfish. The consequences

might prove fatal if Nick finds out about this. I think a battle rages inside Thomas's head. I'm not his to take, but he wants me too much to stop.

Unfortunately, all I care about are *my* needs. I shake my head, letting him know I won't be the voice of reason.

"I'll burn in hell," he utters, glancing into the rear-view mirror. "Change of plans. 101 Queen's Lane. Fast."

I grab a handful of his dark hair, pull his head back, closing his lips with mine. A satisfied, low, primal growl bubbles in his chest as he digs his fingers into my flesh, deepening the kiss.

If I'll ever be tortured, asked how we got to his house, I'll die sifting through my memories, trying to recall the journey. Everything is a blur of raspberry lips and the firm grip of his strong hands all over my body.

The car stops outside a modern, all-glass house. Thomas glances at the embarrassed driver, his hands still on my hips, under my skirt. "Come back in an hour," he says. I draw a line of open-mouthed kisses across his neck. "And a half." I bite his earlobe, sucking gently. "Don't bother," he mutters, squeezing my thighs. "We'll call."

Thomas lifts me into his arms the moment we're out of the car. My legs wrap around his hips tightly, hands on his neck, lips working their way across his jawline as he carries me across the hallway and up the stairs.

Before I gain any perspective, he has me naked on his queen-sized bed. His pupils grow every time he looks me over with hungry eyes, passion and lust painted all over his face. My head rings, pulsing with an intense head rush. He yanks his t-shirt over his head, watching me in awe, then kicks his trousers off and crawls over me. He kisses his way up my stomach slowly, tasting every inch of my skin as he skims his nose up the valley of my breasts, inhaling deeply.

I love having his big, toned body over me; how small, precious, and safe I am even now that he's caging me in his arms. Even when his movements and touches are almost predatory. Each stroke of his hands on mine is deliriously, pleasantly possessive. I gasp when he moves to one side, flicking his hot tongue over my puckered nipple.

"Oh God," I utter. "Don't make me wait, Thomas..."

I feel him smile against my skin. "So impatient. I want you soaking wet before I get in there."

He traces a tiny circle, driving me crazy with the simplest touch. A touch I've never experienced. A touch that ignites my senses in the most arousing way imaginable.

"Mission accomplished. In, Thomas. I want you in."

With a low, almost pained groan, he moves his hand up, up, *up* so slowly, cupping my breast, teasing the tip between his thumb and forefinger, his tongue toying with the other. I squirm, muscles in my abdomen contract, and the torturous delay drives me insane. God, the buildup is so unnecessary... I don't want foreplay. I want him closer. More. Everything he can give me. Every ounce of peace his big body hanging over mine evokes, filling my mind with addictive bliss.

I weave my hand through his hair, but he pins it back down with his. "Please, Thomas. Enough."

"Look at me," he says, parting my thighs with his knee as he nestles himself between my legs, guiding his thick, buzzing erection to my slick centre.

Our eyes lock, and he drives into me hard and fast, as if being inside me is all he wants. I bite his shoulder, scratching his back with my free hand, but he pins it down too, holding me hostage under his weight.

I never want to break free.

I'd let him consume me whole if he'd stay where he is and never let go. I struggle to take him in, to take in the overwhelming, surprising pleasure. This isn't what I'm used to.

It's too much. *He's* too much. How he makes me whole is too much, and how I never want him to stop making me whole

and normal is by far the biggest *too much* in the equation. But it's perfect in all its imperfection.

"You feel amazing," he breathes against my lips, pulling out to thrust harder. "I never wanted anyone so much in my life."

"You have me now." I struggle against his tight grasp around my wrists. "Let me touch you."

He lets go of my hand, and I touch his face, enthralled by the look of him as he nestles his cheek against my palm, driving into me at a hastened but tender pace.

"You're beautiful, doll." He hooks his elbow under my knee, raising it to his ribs, each thrust scooting me up the bed a little, my boobs bouncing, back arching. "I want your eyes on me when you come."

"Shut up," I hiss, searching for the high. "*Please.*"

A smirk lights up his face a split second before he dips his head, reviving my lips. His tongue strokes mine while his cock strokes a sensitive spot inside me. With every move he makes, I rise closer to a spectacular release. Our bodies seem on fire, and I struggle to keep quiet, or relatively quiet at least, taking out the tension pulling taut inside me on his back and the sheets, but it's useless. I cling to him, trying to set the pace with his rhythm, but all I can do is drown in the intense pleasure.

God, he feels amazing...

"Don't hold back, Nadia. I want to hear you," he commands, holding onto my hip, hitting the right spot over again—and just like that, I'm coming. Everything clenches and tightens as Thomas prolongs the orgasm, burying himself in me up to the hilt. "That's it, that's it..." he chants, pinning my trembling leg to his side. "Eyes, Nadia. Eyes on me."

It's not easy holding his gaze when my body vibrates, over-powered by a soul-shattering orgasm, but I do, mesmerised by the awe painted across his handsome face, parted lips, and the abyss of his black pupils. I can't contain my moans any longer, writhing under him as the overwhelming release sets me free for the first time in months.

"I'll get addicted to seeing you like this very fast," he says. "You need to come for me again."

As soon as my body stops trembling, Thomas sits up, his back against the headboard. He pulls me with him, holding me close, our bodies almost fused together as he claims my mouth, holding me by the neck.

I wrap my arms around him not to miss one second, then press my lips to his forehead, trembling all over. "We're in so much trouble..."

"That's why we'll make the most of this." He tucks the loose strands of my dark hair behind my ears. "You're in charge, doll. Ride me." He eases me down on top of him, holding my gaze. A barely audible *ooh* is all I manage, digging my fingers into his shoulders. "Was that a good *ooh*?"

"Yes, definitely a good *ooh*. I've never done this before, so you need to—"

He stops moving. Stills beneath me as his muscles bunch under my fingertips. A look of quiet, menacing thunder clouds his face. "You've never had sex? You're a *virgin*?!"

"No. No, no, no. I'm not. Of course, I had sex. I just... I was never on top before." I tentatively touch his chiselled chest. There's not an ounce of fat on him, all corded muscle but not bulky and disgusting. Healthy, sexy, nothing more than a hint of six-pack rippling down his abdomen. I find that entirely too enticing. I've always preferred the suggestion of muscles over bulging, veiny pecs and abs. He holds my gaze as I explore, tracing the hard lines. "If you want to enjoy this, you'll have to help me out a little."

He exhales a long, loud puff of air, closing his eyes briefly. I straddle him, his cock deep inside me, stretching me in the most delectable way. I wait while he makes his mind up, and just when I think he'll push me away, deeming me not experienced enough for his taste, his eyes fly open, a new sense of

determination shining through the anger that was there moments ago.

"Don't rush," he says, gripping my hips. "Back and forth. Back..." He pushes me away until just the head of his cock teases my entrance, "...and forth." He yanks me closer in a rough stroke, filling me again. "Back and forth."

I mimic his moves, cautious at first as I gain confidence. His dark, hooded eyes tell me I'm doing this right, and I settle for an urgent rhythm, reading into the signs his body sends when his grip on my hips tightens.

God, this is *perfect*. Not only do I feel him inside, but I stimulate myself by grinding over him, my orgasm looming close by once more.

Another *ooh* slips past my lips. Thomas snakes one hand around my shoulder blades, pressing me closer. He hides his face in my neck, grazing his lips over my pulse as we frantically move together. He nips my earlobe, tearing another moan out of my lips, a bit louder and more satisfied.

This is so good. I've never dominated before. I had no idea what I was missing.

Thomas holds onto my hip with one hand, adjusting my pace to his preference, but soon enough, I don't need his help. The rhythm of his body is enough. I lean in, stealing a kiss, claiming his mouth the same way he did mine. I bite and suck his lower lip, earning a strained, satisfied groan. The pleasure coursing through me stacks up, threatening to topple over.

"Again," he demands, smug and arrogant, a mixture of plea and promise in his voice. His head hits the headboard, and he cups my ass, sliding me back and forth faster until my body takes his gestures as an order. "Remember, eyes on me, baby."

I dig my nails into his shoulders, fighting the instinct to throw my head back. The oncoming orgasm flashes with black spots on the backs of my eyelids, turning me inside out with pure ecstasy.

Thomas pushes me back, my hands locked in one of his, far above my head. I'm flat on the mattress again, and he's still inside me, manhandling my body until I'm right where he wants. He pulls out and pushes back in, filling me to the brim, determined to wring out every bit of pleasure from me. He seals my mouth with a demanding kiss, and I cry out, moaning into his lips, the orgasm like a bolt of lightning coursing through my veins. If he makes me come like this again, I might come apart at the seams.

He grabs the underside of my thigh, pulling up to spread me wider. "You'll ruin me," he whispers, pushing in one last time before he tenses, coming with a low growl, his dark, hooded eyes on me.

I feel his cock throb, swell and twitch inside me, triggering an aftershock of my release. I hold him close, kissing his neck and jaw until his grip on me loosens. I'm feeble and drained, but I've never been this satisfied.

Thomas slowly moves away, easing his cock out of me as he sits back on his calves. He rubs his face with one hand looking down at me. "I shouldn't have touched you." There's no regret playing in his voice. Quite the opposite: he sounds pleased with how the evening ended.

A dreamy smile spread across my face. "No, you shouldn't have, but I'm glad you did."

"So am I." He grips my hips, yanking me a little closer and touches the inside of my thigh, travelling north to gently brush his fingers over my swollen, slick folds. "Three, was it?"

I chuckle at his smug smile. "Is that a record?" It's a rhetorical question, one I never want him to answer. "Either way, I know why you worry... don't. Nick will never know."

"I'm *not* worried, doll." He pats my thigh, dipping his head to lick my nipple, then seals my lips with a quick kiss.

He gets to his feet, holding onto the full condom, strolling over to the bathroom. Once the door shuts behind him, I close

my eyes, reliving the intimate moments.

Sex with Thomas is a very different experience to what Adrian got me used to. He was an utterly romantic, mellow lover—dimmed lights, candles, music.

Thomas is the opposite. A hurricane. Intense, eager, passionate. He took me like I was his to take. I may not be a virgin, but in many ways, Thomas claimed my firsts tonight. Sex with him is new and exciting. I want more: more of him and more of the strength he carelessly, unknowingly offers.

The air smells spicy, heady, and sweet like sex, betraying what the walls around me had witnessed. My knees remain weak, as does the rest of my body, but my breathing returns to normal after a few deep, calming breaths.

A small clock on the mirrored bedside table reads twenty past four in the morning. Dawn is not far away, but for now, moonlight sneaks inside through an open window. I order a taxi and get dressed. I consider waiting for Thomas to say goodnight, but he's taking too long in the shower, and I'm falling asleep standing, so I simply leave.

Six

All over her

THOMAS

I wasn't ready to lose my shit like this. Not now, not ever. When Nadia's within my reach, my brain short-circuits. She's a magnetic field jinxing my wiring. Knowing I'm the only person whose touch doesn't send her into an anxious frenzy, I'm confused, proud, and fucking fuming.

Someone triggered that response.

Someone *hurt* her, and even though I met her less than a day ago, the thought of anyone hurting Nadia drives me wild. It helps that her hands didn't tremble when I held her; her eyes didn't show signs of fear when I kissed her. She's at ease around me. A strangely satisfying and confusing thought. All I saw in her dark irises when I pushed deep inside her was perfect calm. It must be what drew me to her most—that she trusts me more than anyone, that she's not afraid of me.

Instead of lying in bed with the only girl I want to just lie in bed with, I'm under a stream of ice-fucking-cold water. Nadia wreaks havoc in my currently missing brain. Saying I'm

perplexed would be the understatement of the century, but as we entered an intimate, sexual relationship, I'm not that worried.

Time is the answer. The more time we'll spend together, the faster I'll get used to her effect on me, and the sooner I'll riddle out her behaviour. Apart from grief, there's more that torments her mind... and I'd be willing to bet my arm that her ex-boyfriend is the reason.

I spent the last three years stripping my life of meaning. It was the only way I could think of to fix the mistake fate had made. While I won't flush my resolutions down the drain just yet, I discovered a new part of me tonight. A part that wants to see where the thing between Nadia and me is heading.

After all, the blooming obsession could simply be a temporary indisposition on my part...

I drape a towel over my hips as I walk out of the bathroom, ready to sleep. The clock on the nightstand shows four fifty-five, and the sky outside, painted by sunrise, turned blood orange while I took an extra-long shower. I lie in bed for the first few minutes, certain that Nadia's using the master bathroom. Cool, morning air breaches the room through the open window, ruffling the curtains, and the soft rustle is the only sound I can make out. For another minute, I listen closer, trying to make out other sounds, but all I hear is my breathing.

The house is oddly still. Silent. I flick on the nightlamp, walking out of the bedroom. The door to the master bathroom out in the hallway stands open, the room empty. I check every room upstairs before I make my way downstairs.

She's not there, either.

She left.

She used me and left.

How rude! I almost burst out laughing before I realise it's not fucking funny. I'm losing my goddamn mind because of this girl, and she one-night-stands *me*...

Truth be told, I had it coming. I deserved that. Still, how

fucking rude? And how fucking insane that I want her even more? If it weren't for her temporarily living under the same roof as Nick, I'd go after her. She needs to know one night won't cut it. At least not with her.

Am I being needy, or what?

Yes, yes, I am. I'm also too tired to think of ways around that little speed bump. It's not like her disappearance changes anything, and I can't blame her for walking after what she must've heard about me from Amelia. The playboy tag she undoubtedly pinned to me was a perfect fit until today.

One day.

It took Nadia *one* day to own my ass.

***

Mel suffered from a severe hangover after the party, and I had to fill in for Nick at the office on Saturday morning while he stayed home, nursing his fiancée. He had a meeting scheduled with the manager of our brightest star—Aaron James.

That guy is a golden goose. We signed him two months after setting up the label. Ever since, all his singles have topped the charts, and both his albums have won Grammys.

I dragged my ass out of bed three hours after I fell asleep and then spent most of the day at the office. Gareth, Aaron's manager, left the meeting pissed off around lunchtime. I refused ninety percent of his idiotic requests. He'll call Nick, asking him to reconsider, but that one thing about our partnership works perfectly—if I say no, he backs me up and vice versa.

Gareth's bad luck that Nick stayed home today. If he had dealt with him first, he would've left the meeting in a much better mood. Nick's softer than I am. He cares more than I do.

At four p.m., I make my way over to his house, a lame excuse for my visit at the ready. Admitting that I want to see Nadia equals suicide, and it so not a good day to die.

Scorpio calls when I'm halfway there.

"Morning sunshine, how's your day going? Fancy a pint or ten later?"

"Morning? Evening. I'm on my way to see Nick, but—"

"You mean Nadia. Fuck me, mate, you got it bad."

"But I can drop by yours later."

"Yeah. Do that. Jane's at her mother's. She won't be back until tomorrow. I would tell you to take Nick with you, but you've got some Nadia talking to do, mate. It's best he doesn't bloody hear it."

Ditto.

The alluring fragrant smell of Nadia's perfumes targets my nose once I set foot inside Nick's house ten minutes later. My mind drifts back to last night. Her soft gasps resonate in my head, taunting me as they did all day long. Her naked, trembling body beneath me flashes before my eyes. The picture is engraved into my brain for-fucking-ever. Feeling her walls clench around me when she came, moaning softly was, hands down, the best minute of my life.

I want more. I want her to come on my cock again. And again. And then some.

Nadia's at the kitchen table with my best friend, whom I stabbed in the back last night while taking his sister as if she's mine. They peer up, eyebrows raised in silent questions.

I look from gorgeous Nadia to her not-so-gorgeous brother. "You didn't give me the demo we talked about."

Thank God for small favours.

Nick opens his laptop. "I've got a few we could check. Got time?"

"Set it up." I move my attention to the true reason behind my visit. Meeting her eyes has me right back in the hot seat. "You coming out for a smoke, Nadia?"

She grabs her cigarettes from the table, rising to her feet. I watch her hips sway when she walks outside, and I visualise touching her the same way I did fourteen hours ago. Desire pools in the pit of my stomach, radiating over me like an electric impulse fashioned out of desire.

Once we're outside, I'm all over her.

In my head, that is.

Nadia sits on the make-shift bench, inhaling a mouthful of smoke. God, I want her lips on mine...

"May I ask why you're staring?" she asks.

"Why did you leave?"

She tries to stifle a laugh. "Why? I doubt you wanted to cuddle, and I was exhausted."

A satisfied smirk crosses my lips, but Nadia shoots me down fast.

"Not thanks to you, though, so lose the grin."

"Next time—"

"There will be no next time."

It takes me a disgraceful amount of time to understand what she said. I don't want to let the meaning of her words in.

She's joking, right?

Shit... I don't think she is. She's far from amused.

What the actual fuck?

I hadn't once considered one night might be all she wanted. It seemed as probable as Nick giving me his blessing to fuck her. How is it that the one girl from whom I want more than one night is the one and only girl who wants just one night from me?

Talk about irony.

I clench my fists, staring into her eyes, hoping she'll take it back, but she remains indifferent... she means what she said. She's not screwing with me.

Well, she is, or was, but... argh, fuck it. You know what I mean.

She lowers her voice, glancing around to make sure Nick's not eavesdropping. "I won't be one of your regulars."

"I don't have regulars," I bark, my jaw working in tight circles. "So you just wanted one night?"

"I didn't give it much thought last night, but today I know you and I are a bad idea, Thomas." She drops her gaze to her hands, rolling the cigarette between her delicate fingers. "I'm not made for a purely sexual relationship. Right now, I'm not made for any relationship." She takes a drag, puffing out her cheeks, eyes sad. "I want us to be friends... we both know it won't happen if we add benefits to the equation."

There's more to that decision than she lets on. She avoids my gaze like every liar. I bet she doesn't want to sleep with me because she doesn't know why she feels at ease when I'm around.

You and I both, baby doll.

I'm out of my element here more than she is, I'm sure. I can't begin to understand why she makes me feel things I blocked for years. I can't block Nadia.

I couldn't even try because she snuck up on me like a trojan horse and wrecking-balled my defence walls before I realised that she's a threat.

"I think you're a decent guy despite what I heard. Last night was fun, fulfilling, and enough."

"Fulfilling?" I ask, clutching at a straw. "I'm just getting started, doll. You don't know the meaning of fulfilled. Not yet."

She watches me for a moment, her eyes darkening with every second. "Tempting, but I'll pass."

To stop myself from throwing a tantrum worthy of a spoilt brat, I clench my jaw so hard my teeth start to crack. She doesn't want me, and I want her even more.

Go figure.

She's turning me into a psychopath with *pussy-whipped* tattooed across my forehead. This is fucking ridiculous. She's not even my type. Yeah... that argument won't work. I've slipped too deep into the madness universe.

The battle's lost, but the war rages on. This isn't the time to wave a white flag. This is the time to retreat and regroup before hitting again. It's time to put some distance between us—six miles.

I get up, ready to leave, when I remember that the letter Nadia wrote to her father is in my jacket pocket. "By the way," I say, glad my tone doesn't betray how unhinged I feel. "You left this in my car yesterday."

Nadia glances at the letter, her complexion bleaching faster than I can blink. She snatches the paper, getting up, paler than pale. "Did you read it?" She presses her hand to her forehead, then covers her mouth, the pale skin greenish now as if she's ready to double over and puke.

What the hell is happening?

She takes one weak step forward, swaying on her feet. That jolts me out of the trance. I jump to catch her, wrapping my arms around her middle, keeping her upright. Her heart beats so fast that I feel her pulse everywhere. She fists my jacket, resting her forehead on my chest, breathing in through her mouth and out through her nose.

"Don't tell Nick. You *can't* tell Nick, Thomas. Please. I'll do whatever you want. Just promise you won't tell him."

Two lines crease my forehead, but not because of what she said. She's been in my arms for seconds, but she's nowhere near panic level anymore. She's calming down, breathing no longer erratic, her pulse slowing down. She's no longer trembling, but I'm not about to risk letting her go.

"I haven't read it." I kiss her head.

Shit. I *kissed* her head... that can't be good.

Her eyes give nothing away when she inches back. Not a single clue what those few pages filled with her handwriting hold. What secret is she so desperately keeping? What made her this vulnerable?

"I swear," I continue, seeing how my voice calms her further. "You said it, Nadia—I do have some decency." Not much, but whatever I have is hers. "Are you okay, doll?"

She nods, her cheeks no longer white as kneaded dough.

"I'm sorry. I should've known you've not read it."

"Because you trust me?"

"Because you wouldn't look at me the way you do."

Way to pique my curiosity. She takes the Zippo out of my hand, holding the letter above the flame. We sit, silently watching the orange flames consume her secret. Soon, the black, burnt pieces fly away, leaving a burning hole in my stomach—the need to *know.*

"Have you told anyone apart from your father?"

She frowns, unhappy I'm asking a question. "I don't want to talk about it."

What a shame that's all I want to talk about. "It didn't take much to convince you I hadn't read it."

"Don't," she says quietly. I expected her to grow more annoyed, but she's growing sad again. "I'm grateful you respected my privacy, Thomas. Don't stop now."

She throws the cigarette butt into an ashtray and marches back inside without a sideways glance my way. I hang my head low, taking a long drag. I must be a masochist because the shit I just witnessed does nothing to convince me she's not worth the hassle. Whatever her problems are, I want to help her forget.

Seven

Full of shit

THOMAS

A remote hits my head.

"Time's up, mate," Scorpio chirps. "You've been eyeing the wall for half an hour. Spill it. Who pissed in your Cheerios?"

I gulp the rest of my beer, opening one more. Looks like I'll be taking a taxi home. "How bad will it look if I smash Ethan's face?"

"Depends on whether you use your fist or a baseball bat." Scorpio chuckles. "But seriously, why do you want to smash his face? Is he still all over your girl?"

This isn't the first time he called Nadia my girl, but the first time the idea of having a girl doesn't make me flinch.

"She doesn't want me."

Scorpio narrows his eyes, touching his index finger to his upper lip. "Right... so you think it's Ethan's fault. Am I close?"

"Quit goofing around," I seethe, massaging my temples. "I'm serious."

"Okay, okay. Chill." He brings his hands up in surrender.

"Go on. Why do you think it's Ethan's fault?"

"Why else wouldn't she want to sleep with me again? She one-night-standed me. Can you fucking believe it?"

"Whoa!" He tears himself out of his seat. "Hold your horses. You bagged her?" He awaits confirmation, and once I nod, his face turns red. "You *fucked* Nadia? How stupid are you? You can have every girl you want, but you go after the one you... wait a minute." He pauses, tapping his fingers on the bottle.

"I swear, if you drum "Bohemian Rhapsody", I'll break your finger."

"Did you say she doesn't want you? Does that mean you bloody do?"

I throw my head back, closing my eyes. "I don't know. There's something about her."

"Blimey! You *want* her? You want to be with her? Hold her hand, kiss her head and all that crap?"

"Don't get ahead of yourself. I didn't say I want her for longer. It's just... one night doesn't cut it."

Who are you fooling?

"You never bag them twice, mate. Either she has Kamasutra committed to memory, or you're full of shit."

Maybe I am full of shit. Maybe I consider introducing emotions to my life. Hell, maybe I even want more than meaningless sex—and I want it, whatever the fuck *it* is, with Nadia, despite her obvious issues. When I had her close, I didn't want to let go, and since that has *never* happened before, I should at least check where this goes. One more night is the bare minimum that I need to check if my newfound humanity is here to stay.

"I'm not the guy for her. You know I'm not, but I want another night or two. I'll be done after that. I'll move on. You know I'm right. I'll get bored as always. It'll just take longer this time."

Not what I think, but Scorpio doesn't need to know I lost the plot.

He scoffs, leaning forward, eyes spewing fire. "That's why

you should stay away from her. I'm not fucking around, Thomas. This once you're right—you're not good for her. For different reasons than you think, but still not good. You're messed up. Trust me here, I know you."

That stings.

Somewhere deep, I thought he'd object and tell me I can make things work with Nadia, but hey! What are friends for?

"I know you better than you think," he continues. "I know that even though it's been almost four years, you're still hung up on Adam's death. You do everything to detach yourself from life."

Adam was my best friend, my brother by choice. He had his life planned with the woman he loved. We were three months away from leaving the Army when a letter from Claudia arrived with the pregnancy news. It was the happiest moment in Adam's life and the happiest I ever felt because everything that affected him affected me as strongly.

An hour later, we drove out of the base in full body armour. James was with us; the three of us were inseparable since we set foot in the Army base twenty-one months earlier. The field was a bloodbath when we got there. James got shot when we jumped out of the truck. My knees gave in, but Adam pulled me out from the open. If not for him, I'd be dead.

We ducked behind a wooden building and threw two grenades at the enemy line. Adam got shot when he peeked around the corner. Two hours after learning he was going to be a father, Adam was shot. Gunfire never stopped while I held his head on my lap, trying to stop the bleeding. He made me swear I'd take care of Claudia and the baby. That I'll always be there if they need help.

Tell her I love her. Tell her I'm sorry, Thomas, tell her she's the best thing that ever happened to me.

His words woke me up at night for months. Guilt and regret feasted on my brain, tormenting me every day.

I should've died out there. Not Adam. *Me.* I had nothing,

no one I cared about, no one to go back to. Adam had it all...

Three months later, once my deployment ran its course, I drove straight to Claudia's house, still in full uniform. She was six months pregnant by then, expecting a baby girl. She had never seen me before, but Adam told her a lot, and when I showed up, she clung to me for hours, crying and cursing fate. I couldn't agree more.

Fate played a twisted game, killing the wrong guy.

As time passed, she got her peace. She forgave fate for taking Adam too soon. She forgave me, although she never said she blamed me.

I never forgave myself.

I don't deserve a full life. I don't deserve happiness or anything remotely close to what Adam had with Claudia because it's not right. Not fucking fair.

For three and a half years, I've been perfectly content with my choices. Perfectly happy spending my time with Claudia and Maya—my way of compensating for Adam's absence. I never once considered setting my life on a different track; never questioned my decisions or why I'm damned; never considered that maybe I made it out alive that day for a reason.

Scorpio sets an empty bottle down, bringing me back to reality. "Tell me I'm wrong, Thomas. Tell me you don't think you should've died out there instead of Adam. You blame your-self because you think his life was more precious than yours."

"It was."

"Bullshit. Do you think Adam would approve of who you've become? What happens if you reverse the situation? Would you want Adam to waste himself like you do?"

I hate Scorpio's condescending tone. I hate the pity mixed with anger shining in his eyes. I hate it because he's right. Adam would roll in his grave if he knew what life I've led since he died. He wouldn't want this for me. He'd kick my ass for not following my gut, and then he'd nail Ethan to stop him getting in my way.

Adam's life was more precious than mine, filled with people he loved and cared about. My life back then, just as now, is nothing more than quick fucks and endless hours at the office. I've never had anything I'd look forward to... until I kissed Nadia.

Maybe there really is a reason why I'm still breathing.

Maybe she's the reason; the chance for redemption.

Maybe we're supposed to save each other.

Eight

Too little, too late

NADIA

"I heard Ethan asked you out." Amelia smiles from the other side of the kitchen table on Monday morning. "I'm glad. He's a good guy, Nadia. I don't think he took his eyes off you once all evening."

No, he didn't but considering what happened later, Ethan's relentless efforts to win me over were the last thing on my mind. I glance at Mel weighing my options. I want to tell her about Thomas, but I'm afraid of what she'll say... and that she'll tell Nick.

He *can't* find out.

Not for my sake. I can handle my brother, but I don't want him and Thomas to argue. A long time ago, Amelia could keep a secret. Hopefully, the engagement ring didn't change that.

"If I tell you something, will you promise you won't spill the news to Nick?"

That piques her curiosity immediately. She holds out her pinkie like she used to in high school. "Promise."

"I... uh, I slept with Thomas."

Her eyes widen as excitement takes over, heating her cheeks. "No way! Oh. My. *God*! How? Why? I mean, you're a brunette!"

"You don't say. I don't know why. It just happened."

Liar, liar.

I know exactly why we ended up in bed. I could've stopped Thomas before we got that far, but I took what he offered, consequences be damned. Unfortunately, as far as truth-telling goes, Mel won't get the behind-the-scenes insight. I can't tell her *why* without explaining where my reluctance to be touched or the paralysing fear Thomas eradicates came from.

I dive back to the intimate moments we shared, and the memories alone make me swell inside. I've not been this content in a very long time. I almost forgot what it feels like.

"We were on our way home, bantering about Alex, and he kissed me. Before I knew it, we were in his bed."

"I can't believe you!" she squealed, then drew her eyebrows together when a different thought pushed out the excitement. "I told you he's a playboy. He won't date you, sweetie."

"I don't want that. All I wanted was him, Mel. You've no idea how good he is."

Or how he controls my emotions, eases anxiety, summons peace and brings me back to life like some mind-controlling Marvel superhero. Whichever one that might be.

"Oh, okay," she mumbles halfway through chewing a big bite of an apple. "Good for you then, I guess. Although I still can't believe it. You're the complete opposite of his type."

"Looks like we both needed something different. I got what I wanted. You could say he ruined me for all my future boyfriends. No way anyone can top that."

Because there's no way, I'll find another guy who'll be an antidote to the disease eating me alive.

"He looks like he knows his stuff," Mel admits. "While we're on the subject—what did Alex want? Did she throw a jelly fit?"

"A jelly fit?" I chuckle. "I've not heard you say that in ages.

Definitely a jelly fit. She thinks they're a couple. She told me I should stay away from him."

"From who?" Nick appears in the doorway with a briefcase. "Who are you supposed to stay away from, sis?"

"Thomas," Amelia supplies, smiling when Nick pecks her forehead. "Alex issued Nadia with a restraining order."

"I'm with her on that one." He grabs a bottle of water and snatches the car keys from a bowl on the counter. "I'm off to work, but I should be back in time for the catering company meeting." He pecks Mel again and then kisses my head before marching out of the house.

I don't need to ask why he thinks it would be wise if I stayed away from Thomas. Nick's an overprotective older brother, and he doesn't want Thomas to use me.

Too bad it was the other way around, and too little, too late.

***

The meeting with the catering company hired for Nick and Mel's wedding lasts so long that Nick arrives bang in the middle despite coming home shortly after four o'clock. He promised he'd come earlier, but I doubt he tried very hard.

Not that I blame him.

If I could, I wouldn't show up either.

Hannah, the agent, is fed up with the future bride but remains professional, handing out endless menu options for two hours straight. All for nothing because the monster bride didn't take a liking to any of them, and we're currently making a new one from scratch.

"I'm not sure if ice cream is such a good idea. It'll be warm, the desserts will melt..." she whines, her eyes glassy, tears pooling in the corners.

Nick outstretches his hand over her shoulder, pulling her closer and plants a firm kiss on her temple. I'm not sure who he's trying to calm down. He's about ready to burst into flames, and he only arrived half an hour ago.

"What about a traditional apple pie?" Hannah offers.

I'm sure she imagined suffocating the future bride at least a dozen times by now. In my head, I'm holding Amelia down to speed things up.

Overall, it takes over five hours to put the menu together. When I think the nightmare is over, Mel calls it the first draft, saying she'll think about it some more. If Nick was upset that he wasn't included in the wedding plans, he surely regrets ever offering his help now.

Once Hannah leaves, he pours himself three fingers of neat whiskey while Mel moves to the living room so she can catch up on some drama series. I join my brother in the kitchen with a cup of coffee and a book.

"Can we talk?" he asks, breaking the comfortable silence.

I look up from *And Then There Were None* by Agatha Christie. A part of me wants to run because his face betrays the topic. Instead, I set the book aside, marking the page before I close it, offering Nick my undivided, even if reluctant, attention.

"Sure. What is it?"

He closes his laptop, sipping his whiskey as if needing a moment to gather his thoughts. "I want to know what happened between you and Adrian."

I tilt my head back, staring at the ceiling and once again hoping to find strength in the sky-blue colour. "I won't go into details, but it didn't end well. I just couldn't stay there any longer."

"What do you mean by didn't end well?"

His reaction to that one sentence is all the confirmation I need if I had any doubts about whether he should know the truth. There's no reason to drop the bomb on him for the sake of honesty. I accepted what had happened. I don't need him digging up the dirt again, uncovering still fresh wounds.

"We had a big fight and realised we're not good together

anymore. Adrian changed, Nick."

"I just can't get my head around it." He squeezes the bridge of his nose the way he always does when he's trying to keep his cool. "You were perfect together, sis. He loved you like crazy. What did he do?"

"It doesn't matter. I had my reasons to leave him. Can't you just trust me?"

He sighs, defeated. "I trust you. I'm just worried, okay? Promise you'll come to me when you're ready to talk."

It's not about being ready, but there's no point in explaining that to Nick, so I just nod along.

"And one more thing... Thomas."

"Don't start. Don't warn me, Nick. Mel already told me everything on Friday. I know; he's a player."

"You like him?" He cocks an eyebrow, studying me with narrowed eyes.

"I do like him. He seems nice."

Like doesn't paint the picture. I like him the way you would a new friend, but in terms of the other side of the coin, Thomas himself doesn't matter at this stage. Anyone who'd calm me down the way he does would quickly become someone without whom getting up every morning seems even harder than before.

And that's why I refuse to spend one more night with him. He might unknowingly be helping me, but it's nothing more than a temporary fix like the pills I'm addicted to. I don't want Thomas to be another addiction.

"Nice?" Nick laughs, not a trace of amusement in that sound. "That's the least fitting word to describe Thomas. He's not nice, sis. He's cautious, tight-lipped, and downright rude. He's got a short fuse, and he can be vile."

I cross my hands, feeling somewhat defensive. Nick's not being fair. "And here I was thinking you two were best friends."

Nick smirks, ignoring the sarcasm. "We are. Thomas is difficult, but I like him a lot."

"So you're telling me he's a plague to discourage me?"

"Kind of... I saw him on Friday, Nadia. He's different around you. I'm not sure if he's acting protective because you're my sister or if I'm misreading him, and he's actually possessive because he wants to fuck you, so I am warning you. Don't be fooled. You're worth more than a guy like Thomas."

"Thank you. Duly noted, but don't worry about me. I did okay for two years in New York, and you weren't there."

Another lie.

I cried myself to sleep more times than I can count, wishing Nick would come over to help me.

My cheeks heat as shame washes over me because he looks as if I slapped him. "I'm sorry, that came out wrong. Just... try to understand I'm not your little sister anymore. I make my own decisions, and I know what's good for me."

"You think Thomas is good for you?" A vein throbs on his temple, threatening to burst.

"That's not what I said. He's a player, and I'm not looking to get hurt. Just don't act like I'm still a helpless little girl."

Or else I'll never find the strength to keep going.

"I'm trying," he says, gathering his things. "I'll be upstairs in my office; I have a few contracts I need to look through." He rounds the table, leaning over to kiss my head.

Once he leaves me alone, I start reading again but don't manage half a page before Mel enters the kitchen, no longer stressed. On the contrary, excitement spills out of her ears.

"We've got the bridesmaids' dresses fitting tomorrow, but we should go shopping afterwards. I bet you need a dress for your date with Ethan."

"It's not a date."

"Yeah, yeah." She waves me off. "But it won't hurt to have a new dress at the ready, right?"

"We're going to play pool. I'm not wearing a dress."

Truth be told, I'm not sure if I'll go through with that *date*.

Ethan's nice, but he wants more than I'm willing to give.

"Oh, bite me." Mel rolls her eyes. "We're going shopping. I'll relax, and you'll buy a dress. Please. For me?"

Puss-in-boots cute eyes coupled with the pleading tone of her voice... I don't stand a chance.

"Great!" She claps, apparently seeing the white flag I'm waving in my head. "If you won't wear the dress for your date with Ethan..." she whispers, glancing around, "...maybe Thomas will rip it off you."

I'm hot, bothered, willing, and ready just like that...

Nine

Pity the fools

THOMAS

Time. I gave Nadia time to think about what had happened between us. I know she'll be thinking about it because I can't fucking stop. I even dream that I'm touching her. We're good together. Sex was unreal. Surely she must've noticed.

I gave her Monday, Tuesday, and I'm determined to keep my distance until Friday, by when she should miss me. Too bad it's only Wednesday... I hoped she'd give up sooner.

I sit with Nick in his office, munching takeaway lunch, when Amelia calls. He answers, putting her on the loudspeaker so he can continue stuffing his face with chicken teriyaki.

"Hey, how about we go to the cinema tonight?" She hits the horn. "You moron! Watch where you're going!"

"Yeah, sounds good. What time?"

Mel's outburst comes as no surprise. She's neither a good nor a patient driver. "We've got the dress fitting soon, and I'm taking Nadia shopping. We should be back home by six."

"Shopping? If you want her to buy a dress for the wedding,

there's no way you'll be back by six."

"No, it's just date-dress shopping today. Shouldn't take long."

Nick stops chewing. "Date-dress?"

"She's going out with Ethan, remember?"

My stomach somersaults back. She's going out with the Jerk? Fuck. I assumed she was trying to make me jealous when she agreed to go out with Ethan.

She really doesn't want me, and time won't fix that...

I push the food aside, marching out of Nick's office. No way I'll listen to Mel babble how she thinks Nadia and Ethan might hit it off. If it was up to me, a brick wall would be the thing Ethan would hit... with his head... pushed by my hand.

I need to get laid. Fast, so I tell my brand-new, tall, blue-eyed, blonde assistant Marie to stop by my office at five o'clock sharp. She beams, running her long, pink nails over her bottom lip. She knows why she's being summoned after hours, and by the look of her, she's more than willing.

Don't get too excited, sweetie. You won't enjoy it.

Women in the industry know my game, and fifty percent of the blondes falling at my feet do so *because* they know. Some hope they'll change me. They think they're special enough that I'll want to settle down. Others are more realistic and just hope for a record deal. Few are in it for fun.

Nick barges into my office a few minutes later. He collapses in the chair across from me, eyes focused on the view outside the windows behind my back.

During our business partnership, we've developed a little routine. Nick likes getting things off his chest, but he always waits until I ask the questions. I play along. Whenever he comes over annoyed or bothered, I close my laptop, push the paper-work away and start the conversation.

It's always one of two things. Either Amelia or work. Not today, though. This time he's all bent out of shape because of his precious little sister.

84

You and me both.

"Care to share?" I ask, pumping my fists. I don't want to talk about Nadia's upcoming date. I don't want to think about it, but Nick won't leave until he vents.

He squeezes the nape of his neck, pushing a short, exasperated huff past his lips. "She's going out with him."

You don't fucking say.

What the hell does the Jerk have that I don't? Can I buy it? Because I'll buy it. I'll buy ten of it.

"I don't want her to go out with him!" Nick whines. "She should work things out with Adrian."

She should work things out with me.

Adrian is history. A memory, but Nick needs more time to accept the facts. That, however, isn't my problem. My problem is the *Jerk*. My problem is Nadia heading out with him after she slept with me. After she shot me down, claiming she's not cut out for any relationship right now.

Friday night was fucking perfect! I've never got such a kick out of making a girl come, but with Nadia, I didn't give a damn about my release. Watching her writhe beneath me, lips parted, eyes closed... I couldn't get enough.

I can think of just two reasons why Nadia doesn't want me again. One—she likes Ethan. There's obviously no hope for me if that's true, so let's pretend that's not an option at all, and number two is the real reason—she still thinks of me as a player. And since players are always assholes, she has me all figured out, right? Kind of, but I'm not my usual self around Nadia. I don't really know who I am when she's close, but I like the guy she awoke on Friday.

I want to sleep with her again, but that's not *all* I want. That girl obviously drives me crazy, and I want to check what we can make of it.

"Why is she going out with him?"

Nick rolls his eyes. "He asks her."

Like brother like sister.

"No shit. I'm asking why. Does she like him? Did she say anything?"

"If you want me to let her make her own choices, then spare me. I know I can't forbid her, but Ethan's *not* the guy for Nadia, Thomas. Adrian's the guy. Ethan's weak; he wouldn't know the first thing about taking care of her." Nick rests his head on the back of the chair, eyeing the ceiling. "I used to know everything about her. I didn't have to ask what was going on, but she's different now. I know something is wrong, but she's been shutting me out since she came back."

I can relate. Nadia's definitely hiding something. It bothers me too, but I have no right to ask. Besides, if she didn't let Nick in, she won't tell me shit.

"I've not asked Nadia about Ethan yet, but Mel's being weird about this, too," Nick says, pulling his lips in a thin line.

"Weird how?"

"I don't know. I told her I'm not happy Nadia's going out with Ethan, and Mel said I should be happy it's Ethan and not, for example, *you*." He walks over to the window, his shoulders sagging. "Why would she mention you?"

My question exactly. "Mel tried to set them up since Nadia said she's no longer with Adrian. I guess she brought out the big guns to convince you he's good for your little sister."

He's not. This once, Nick is one hundred percent right. Ethan's a pussy, and Nadia... Nadia is not a low-maintenance kind of creature. She's irritating, irrational... fucking irresistible.

"Maybe," he sighs. "But there must be something there. Mel wouldn't mention you out of the blue." He turns toward me, arms folded across his chest. "Is there something I should know about?"

A hot sweat washes over me, and I shake my head a firm *no*. I'm only partially lying. There's nothing going on between us. Not anymore.

"She's my sister, Thomas. She's off-limits to you."

The speech. Well, a condensed version, but still. He should've thought about this sooner.

"I know. She's not a girl you nail and run." I bite the inside of my cheek, keeping a smile in check. "She's a girl you fall in love with."

"Damn right she is."

A moment later, he closes the door, leaving my office a little calmer. Unlike me. I spend the afternoon working my ass off to stay distracted. Not that it's working particularly well.

Nick comes over again to say goodbye a few minutes before five. He's been avoiding me all afternoon, sensing my pissed-off mood and an even worse attitude. I'm sure he has no idea what my problem is, but from experience, he knows it's a good call to stay out of my way when I'm barking orders and banging doors.

Marie doesn't bother knocking two minutes after Nick leaves. She props her back against the door, her blue eyes roaming over my chest as she pulls her dress up, showing off long, ivory legs. "You wanted to see me," she purrs, crossing her ankles while tracing the curve of her hip with a pen. That's my permission. The green light allowing me to take whatever the fuck I deem fit.

I cross the room, not daring to slow down or—God forbid—stop and think. I know my mind well. It'll change the second I hesitate. "It won't take long."

The seductive smile stretching her dark-pink lips tells me she thinks I'm kidding. Nah-ah. Five minutes is all I need to spin her around, pull her dress up, do my thing, then fire her ass once I readjust my pants.

Before I can grab her waist, she rocks on her heels, pushing away from the wall, and rests against me, forcing her tongue inside my mouth. Not how I planned this, but whatever. I can spare thirty seconds for a warm-up.

Marie grabs my jacket, yanking me closer until I press her

against the wall with my body. I don't like how she caresses my arms, so I catch her wrists, locking them in a tight grip. She moans, biting my lip, but I don't like that, either. It's different and not good different compared to how Nadia nipped my lower lip. The sounds Marie's making annoy the living hell out of me too. They're nothing like Nadia's sweet gasps.

Focus, Thomas! Marie spreading her legs.

Nadia's smile. The sweet, zesty smell of her perfume. Long, dark-brown hair blown out of her face by the wind.

Marie spreading her legs.

Nadia's delicate body. Her laughter. The way her hand fits into mine with our fingers interlocked.

Marie spreading her legs.

Nadia's full lips. Her taste. Her trembling beneath me. Brown eyes, looking at me with nothing short of serenity.

"Get out," I clip, breaking away from the blonde bimbo.

I clench my fists, chest heaving. Anger hangs over me like a storm cloud, threatening to unleash unrivalled chaos.

Marie narrows her eyes, her cheeks pink, lips parted as she pants, breathless after a thirty-second kiss. She closes her mouth, then opens again, a fish out of the water.

I only have enough self-restraint left to wait twenty-seven seconds before I'll toss the first thing I can get my hands on, so I stop Marie before she tries to word a less-than-bright question.

"Get the fuck out, or I'll fire you before you say *what.*"

She stands there, frozen as if thinking I'll drop the act and get back to making out. Not today. As much as I wanted this to be an act, it sure isn't. Cold-blooded fury consumes me whole, my mind like a ticking bomb.

Marie reconsiders, shoots me a *you're fucking nuts* look, and retreats out of my office, wobbling on her seven-inch heels.

For fifteen seconds, I listen to the rhythmical, rushed clicking on the marble floor as she hurries down the corridor. When I can no longer hear anything other than my rapid heartbeat and the sound of my blood boiling, I let my emotions take the stage. Trashing my office takes three minutes.

I stand in the middle of the room, frowning at the mess. My desk is upside down; documents litter the floor. A painting I put my fist through no longer hangs on the wall, and my laptop's screen is cracked in four places. To top it off, I probably broke my hand when I hit the wall.

Good job, Thomas. Way to stay cool.

I stand by the window, my breathing erratic as if I just ran a marathon. I guess the meticulous effort I put into destroying my office like some unrestrained psychopath is close enough to running a marathon. Or maybe a sprint.

Jesus, I'm losing it...

Losing it over a girl. A girl who's not any prettier than the herds of blondes spreading their legs at my sight. A girl who's not even my type. Brunette, small boobs, and short, to put it nicely. Yet she's the most beautiful girl I've ever seen. Flawless, delicate, hypnotising.

I grip the windowsill with both hands, looking out to London's city centre. Thousands of people live through their problems right before my eyes. They look like ants from where I stand, but each one of those ants has a mind, a life, and a problem that keeps them up at night. Whether it's love-related drama, work-related drama or some other drama, everyone has issues. Until recently, I pitied the fools who dwell on one thing. It's neither healthy nor smart. I'm done pitying now that I understand the mechanics. I've been obsessing over a petite brunette for the past five ridiculously long days.

Like hell I'll be the guy who loses his shit over some chick.

She's just a girl, for fuck's sake. Remember how I said I like the guy she awoke? My alter-ego of sorts. Well, scratch that. I don't like the guy anymore. He's unhinged.

For the next ten minutes, I coach myself not to lose my shit over Nadia ever again. Her name enters my mind, summon-

ing a picture of her face and her beautiful brown eyes staring at me, ripping my chest wide open.

Beautiful brown eyes that belong to a girl who's not mine and won't be mine. The girl who brings out the best in me with one fucking touch.

A girl who doesn't want me.

A wave of agonising frustration hits me square in the jaw.

Yeah, excuse me while I lose my shit again.

Ten

Guilty as charged

NADIA

I hope I'll never get married. Watching Amelia panic every step of the way is scarring me for life. If this is what brides turn into while planning their weddings, then I want no part of it. She'll turn grey soon, worrying about the tiniest details and weeping whenever things don't go according to plan.

A meeting with the band closes week one schedule.

Week *one*.

There are six more to go, and I'm not sure I can handle Amelia's craziness that long.

After a few failures earlier this week, i.e. the florist struggled to locate roses in the specific colour—magenta pink—Amelia chose; the bridesmaids' dresses required corrections, and the handmade invitations had the wrong colour bows attached, we hit the jackpot with the band.

The lead singer was more than accommodating throughout the meeting, agreeing to everything Mel said before she finished her sentence. He knows who the groom is, so I bet he's hoping

to land a record deal if things go well.

Whatever the reason, I'm grateful. Thanks to him, Mel's in a great mood, which means she's not whining now that we're browsing furniture I might buy for my flat.

The decorators finished last night, and I convinced Nick it was time I move out. He's not overly happy about it, though. Especially since I don't even have a bed yet, but after much convincing, he caved. He even promised he'd help me move.

"Look!" Mel runs further into the furniture store, stopping beside a swing chair hanging from the ceiling on a thick, silver chain. "Buy it! Imagine reading a book, *swinging* in your living room!" She claps once, her smile slipping when I shoot her a sceptical look. "Buzzkill," she mutters, moving toward the dining room section. "You need a table, babe. Speaking of tables, how about a housewarming party tomorrow?"

"No, the place is empty. You want us to sit on the floor? Even if we could furnish the place by tomorrow, it's Saturday, and Ethan's taking me out. We'll have the party next weekend."

"Buzzkill!" she says louder this time. "Again, while we're talking dates... what's the deal with you and Thomas? You guys had a fight?"

Ugh, she just had to open her big mouth! I've been doing so well ignoring his existence until now. "How is that related to my date with Ethan?" I huff a heavy sigh. "We didn't fight. Why? Did he say something?"

She shrugs, all nonchalant, as she examines canary-yellow plastic chairs. "He's not said a word, but he hasn't been around this week. Usually, not a day goes by without him coming over. He's avoiding you, Nadia. I wanna know why."

"Ask him." I walk away, noting down the pick-up locations for the table and chairs.

Amelia follows, careful not to push over kids running among the shoppers. "I'm asking you."

"As I said, we didn't fight." I lower my voice, my cheeks

heating a touch. "I told him I won't sleep with him again, so maybe that's why he's not been around."

"He wants you *again*?!" she yells, summoning everyone's curious attention. "Sorry," she adds, pulling an apologetic face.

If looks could kill, she'd bleed out right here, in the middle of the sofa area. I move along, glancing around, hoping that something will catch my eye.

Mel trails behind me, her excitement palpable in the air. "How about this one?" She points at a dark green corner sofa, then grips my arm, steering me away until we're mostly out of view, hiding between wardrobes. "Why didn't you tell me he wants you again?"

"I don't know; I didn't consider it headline news."

"It is! He *never* sleeps with any girl twice, Nadia. Not only are you completely *not* his type, but he still wants you when he already had you! He's breaking all his rules!"

She acts as if Thomas grew a second head. No longer than five days ago, she told me I'd be better off staying away from him, and now she acts like she's ready to shut the door behind us.

"So? What will you do? I can tell you regret saying no. You've been daydreaming all week."

I cross my hands, glaring at my reflection in the mirrored wardrobe doors. I sure look pathetic lusting after Thomas, thinking about the mindblowing sex twenty-four-seven. I must look even more pathetic to Mel. At least I know that sex isn't what I want most. It's just a surprisingly pleasant bonus. All she knows is that we had sex, and I want more.

Yeah, pathetic.

"If you don't mind that it's just sex, why did you tell him no? I mean, I want you to find a decent guy, but if Thomas's bad boy charm is what you want, go ahead. I swear I won't tell Nick."

That's the problem. Thomas's bad boy charm is all I think about. I miss his lips, his touch and how normal I feel when he's close.

My pills still work the same, but comparing the calm they evoke to the calm Thomas does, it's clear I'm not taking enough diazepam. I can't take any more... Stopping the meds was my goal, but instead, I'm diving headfirst into a different addiction.

"You're obviously trying to heal a broken heart, so I'll forgive you," Mel winks, touching my arm.

"You're wrong. This isn't about Adrian."

Liar, liar.

It is about Adrian, but not in the way Mel thinks. I'm not trying to heal a broken heart. I'm trying to regain my peace... Thomas just makes the task of forgetting my past much easier.

Mel cocks an eyebrow, a hidden *yeah, right* in that gesture. "Whatever you say. What will it be then? Round two with Mr Calix? What's the worst that can happen?"

"Nick might find out. I can't... I'll only dig myself into a deeper hole. I'm already head deep, anyway."

"Okay, fine. Ethan it is. I guess he'll get friend-zoned tomorrow big time."

That he will.

***

Ethan got friend-zoned before we left my flat. He said he understood when I told him I'm not looking for a relationship, but I could tell he was disappointed. Maybe even slightly annoyed. Still, he agreed tonight isn't a date.

I can't fault the guy. He's intelligent, handsome, polite... sugar, spice and everything nice, but he lacks chemical X.

We spend the evening playing pool at his favourite bar, drinking Coronas and not really talking much. Ethan lost interest, no longer acting overly polite.

I kicked his ass, winning eight out of ten games we played. Pool is definitely my game. We had a table at home when I was growing up, and I played against Nick every day. Whenever he won, he made me serve him food. I made him stay up all night watching movies together.

"I hope you had fun tonight," Ethan says, stopping the car outside my building a few minutes past nine o'clock. "Maybe we can do this again sometime."

It sounds forced, like he's hoping I'll get out and leave him be. Incredible how fast a man can change from a decent guy to an a-grade a-hole. We've been friends since I started high school, but apparently, that doesn't mean much now that he realised I don't want more than friendship.

He doesn't even want that.

"Sure," I say, even though we both know it's a lie. "I'm throwing a housewarming party next Saturday. Come by around five."

His face lights up with a genuine smile. Maybe he doesn't know I was only being polite...

I wait for whatever he'll say, an uncomfortable silence buzzing around us, magnified tenfold when his gaze drops to my lips. A cold shiver slides down my spine, and my mouth turns dry. I'm glued to my seat, too stunned to form a coherent sentence. I should've because Ethan takes my silence as consent, closing the distance parting our lips. My heart picks up the rhythm, bruising my ribs and threatening a coronary.

I'm not normal. My reaction isn't normal. I want to cry because I'm so helpless. So paralysed by the thought of Ethan touching me. Memories bombard my mind, fuelling the growing unease when his warm breath fans my face. I flinch and jerk away, forcing him to retreat.

"I'm sorry." He looks away, staring out the windscreen. There's nothing apologetic about that *sorry*. "You said no dates, but I like you, cutie. I've been waiting for my chance for years."

"That doesn't mean you can ignore what I said earlier. I was honest, Ethan. I'm not ready for more than friendship. I just got out of a long relationship. Considering how long we've known each other, I thought—"

"The problem is," he cuts in, "I don't want to be your friend. I never did. We were just unlucky. There was always something or someone getting in the way. Now, we're on the same page. Both single. I know you might think it's too soon to start something new, but I'll make it worth your while."

Huh... does he really think he can coerce me into dating him? Or better yet, guilt me into kissing him? Good luck.

"We're not on the same page. I'm sorry I misled you. Goodnight."

I exit the car, closing the door softly even though I'd much rather slam it hard enough to shatter the window.

Great. Just great. As if I'm not dealing with enough shit, Ethan adds his two cents. I watch him drive away until he turns right at the end of the one-way street.

I take my phone out, dialling Mel's number as promised. She made me swear I'd call once I was back home.

"Don't tell me you're done already," she answers, sounding annoyed. "What happened? Oh, wait. Can I put you on speaker? Nick wants to know too."

Of course. Why wouldn't he? Every sane, mentally stable brother is curious about his sister's love life. Not.

"Yeah, sure. Go ahead."

At least this way, he'll hear the story from me instead of getting Mel's twisted version.

"Okay, fire away," Mel says. "Why are you back home early? Because you are, aren't you? He didn't leave you alone at the bar, right?"

I enter the building, my heels clicking happily, echoing throughout the empty corridor. "No, of course he didn't. Did you really think Ethan could just ditch me? I'm home early because he's not happy with me. He's pissed off, actually. We both are, so call it even."

"What did he do?" Nick growls. I can easily imagine the menacing frown marking his forehead right now.

"Nothing I should be upset over. He's a guy who waited five years to take me out."

I enter my flat, my shoulders sagging. I forgot how messy this place is. Cardboard boxes, shopping bags, my suitcases tucked away under the stairs... I should spend the evening getting this general mayhem under control, but I'm not in the mood. Still, with no other plans, I might as well get busy.

"That doesn't tell us much," Mel clips, huffing down the line. "Was he pushy? Did he offend you? What happened?"

"Did he offend me?" I chuckle, balancing on one leg, taking my shoes off. "I'm not thrilled that the guy I've known so long only acted nice because he wanted to fuck me, but I won't say I'm offended. Annoyed? Yes. Maybe even upset because I got all dressed up, and I'm back home already."

What a waste of pretty makeup.

"Should I be concerned? You don't sound good," Nick says, his voice louder as if he moved closer to the phone. "Should I come over?"

"No, I'm fine. I've got twenty boxes to unpack, so I'll stay busy. You're welcome here tomorrow. I could use help getting this place in shape."

If there's one thing Nick hates, then DIY is it, but Mel agreed to come over tomorrow afternoon, and she'll drag him along despite his protests.

I cut the call, changing my mind about unpacking. The undeniable mess can wait a few more hours. I plug in a large Bluetooth speaker I bought earlier and then search my playlists for something that might lift my mood.

Music has been ever-present in my life during the last few months, drowning out my screaming mind. "Take Shelter" by Years and Years fills the silence twenty minutes later once the speaker finally pairs with my phone. Standing by the kitchen island, I sing along, swaying to the music, lining up the evening pills on the countertop. I start from the smallest, stalling until

the chorus starts so I can dance my way across the kitchen to the sink. When I finally swirl around, I freeze.

Thomas leans against the door frame, arms crossed, dark eyes looking straight into mine. He takes two steps, cups my face, and seals my lips with a hot, demanding kiss. I give in, taking handfuls of what he offers, soaking up the positive emotions that arrived with him. He pulls me closer as if all he needs to stay sane is me.

I can relate, but *what the hell?*

I brace against his torso, fighting my heart as I push him away, but the gesture lacks resolve. Thomas grazes his teeth along my lower lip, then skims his tongue over mine, his hold on me growing tighter.

With every passing second, I'm losing sight of what's right. I shouldn't use him like this. It's not fair. I push harder, taking a step back.

"What are you doing? How did you get in here?"

An explosive mixture of lust and anger glimmers in Thomas's cinnamon irises, raising the temperature inside the flat by a few degrees. If it were anyone else watching me the way he does right now, I'd panic, but fear is absent when Thomas is present.

"Kissing you. The door was open," he hisses. "Did he touch you?"

Again, *what?*

If the look of him doesn't prove insanity, his tone dispels any doubts.

"Who?"

"Ethan!" he snaps, then fists his hands, taking a deep breath along with a step back. "I asked if he *touched* you."

My first reaction is to slap him, but I'm a coward. Just because I slept with him a few hours after we met doesn't mean it's my regular play. Thomas simply offers more than anyone else, hence the rush.

"Don't ask questions you know the answer to."

He takes a step forward, and I take a step back. One, two, and one more before he backs me against the kitchen island, his eyes roving over my body. I think he's checking that I'm not hurt, that Ethan hasn't done anything against my will.

"Don't make this harder, baby," he pleads. "You sounded upset over the phone."

"You were at Nick's just now?"

"Yeah. You said Ethan wanted more than just a date. I'll ask again—did he *touch* you?"

It seems as if he's waiting for confirmation so he can hit Ethan without consequences. He shouldn't act possessive, but knowing he has my back puts me at ease.

"No, he didn't. You're smarter and more perceptive than any of our friends, but right now, you're acting clueless."

"I know you wouldn't want him to touch you, but some guys don't wait for permission."

I roll my eyes. "You should know."

"Guilty as charged. The difference is, I know you don't mind *me* kissing you. You don't mind *me* touching you."

The pull is mutual. We both feel it equally strong.

"I told you there won't be another round."

"I remember. I just don't understand why. You want me, Nadia. I'm the only one you're not afraid—"

"Doesn't it scare you?" I cut in, crossing my arms.

"That you trust me? That you're not anxious when I'm close? It's intriguing, not scary."

"It should be. You're wrong, Thomas." I spread my fingers over his hard pecs, forcing him to step back.

He does. He knows acting against my will won't do him any favours. I lead him outside, taking a seat on a metal chair on the terrace, and pull my knees to my chin.

"I don't want *you*. I want the strength that comes when you're around. I'm not sure what, but *something* about you calms

me down. When you're here, my issues fade away, blurring so much it feels like things that happened a few weeks ago happened in a different lifetime."

I chance a glance his way. He stands by the wall, surrounded by a thick, grey smoke cloud, staring at the sky. He's silent, either waiting for me to keep talking or wondering what the hell is wrong with me. I already said too much. A simple *no* would've sufficed, but he makes me want to talk. Vent. Scream my truths before they turn me inside out.

"I can't do this," I continue. "I'm addicted to pills, Thomas. Many different pills... I don't want you to be my new addiction. I can't use you to get my life back on track. It's not fair. I should do it alone, or else I won't ever move on."

It takes another minute before he reacts. He throws the cigarette into an ashtray, readjusting his jersey. "Point well made," he fires my words right back at me, a defensive, arrogant expression on his face. "I'll let myself out."

A sad, tearful chuckle is my only answer when he leaves. A sad, tearful chuckle that morphs into pathetic whimpers when the door closes behind him. Ten minutes later, I'm curled into a ball on my bed, crying myself to sleep, praying I didn't just make the biggest mistake.

Eleven

Rebound case

THOMAS

Kill me.

Kill me now.

Better yet, kill whoever the fuck thinks it's okay to call me at eight o'clock in the morning, three hours after I crawled into bed drunk off my goddamn mind.

After I left Nadia's flat, I hit the club. All I needed was one drink to get over her—one drink to forget that she knocked me off my feet.

At least, that's what I thought.

One Corona made it clear I needed much more than one drink just to take the edge off the overwhelming disappointment. Drinking my sorrows away might've not been the best coping mechanism, but I had no idea how to handle my emotions. I never handled shit like this before.

I sat by the bar for hours, pouring Coronas down my throat, scouting the room, searching for a girl I could fuck in the men's toilet, but every time a potential candidate arrived,

Nadia's face flashed before my eyes, and my ass remained glued to the seat.

Her words replayed in my head, flaring my anger.

"I can't do this. I can't use you to get my life back on track. It's not fair."

I wanted to scream, *"Use me! Use me, goddamnit!"*

Another sentence she spoke poisoned my thoughts all night, regardless of my intoxication.

"I don't want you."

I sat there, downing one bottle after another, until I felt sick. Ten pints will do that to a man. The upside was the drunken state—it numbed the pain, masking shame and regret that swept over me the second I left her sad and alone.

The most disturbing image I ever witnessed—Nadia's eyes filling with fresh tears, her secrets, scars and vulnerability on display. Why she shot me down was understandable, and I must admit she's a tough girl. If I found a way to erase the negative feelings that've accompanied me since Adam's death, I wouldn't walk away.

The biggest problem? I found it. Nadia is it. She's my way. My road to redemption, but she wants to face her demons alone, and we're both losing out.

Too drunk to stand straight, let alone drive, I needed a ride home, so I called my personal taxi driver—Scorpio. Clever guy that he is, he brought Jane so she'd drive my car back home. Annoying prick that he is, he didn't pass the opportunity to twist the knife.

"You know what you feel right now?" he asks once I tell him what Nadia told me.

"I sure do. I'm pissed off. Fucking confused."

He shakes his head. "You're humiliated, Thomas. First time in your life, you've been rejected."

Know-it-all.

Nadia makes me want to change and do better. I built my hopes up based on one night and enormous ego, and I finally got what I deserved after years of treating women like blow-up dolls. Karma's a bitch, always arriving at the least convenient moment.

I bang my hand over the nightstand, looking for my blaring phone. Eyes closed, I swipe my thumb across the screen, setting the phone on the side of my face, then tuck my hand back under the warm duvet.

"I need a favour," Nick says, skipping the well-mannered *good morning.*

I remain silent; my loud, pissed-off breathing is the only greeting he deserves.

"Nadia called..."

I sit up, and Nick's voice trails off when the phone slips off my face, landing on the floor.

Yep, I'm *wide*-awake hearing her name.

The aroma of stale beer coming from, well—from me, makes me cringe. I pick up the phone again, squinting, so my eyes will adjust to the bright sunlight breaching the room through the balcony doors.

"...I'd appreciate it if you'd help her," Nick finishes whatever he was saying.

"Help her with what?"

It doesn't matter; I'll help her with anything, but I don't like not knowing. Regardless of how much her words last night hurt, I'm jittery inside, knowing I left her alone and upset. If I can make her life more bearable by helping, then count me in.

Nick lets out an exasperated puff. "Did you even listen to me? I asked if you'd help Nadia put together a dining table and chairs. It was delivered flat packed. She rang, asking for a screwdriver. She'll poke her eye out if left unattended, and you know I'm not a DIY expert, either."

"Runs in the family?" I drag myself out of bed, still half-drunk, when I stand, and the room spins.

"I guess. You got time? I can call Ethan if you're busy. Or maybe Scorpio. I don't really want Ethan alone with Nadia after last night."

Neither do I.

"I'm up. Nothing better than DIY on Sunday morning."

Nick laughs, says *thanks*, then cuts the call. I hit the shower, scrubbing off the stench of beer, smoke, and sweat.

My reflection stares at me when I'm taming my hair. I look like shit—pale, ashen skin, dark circles under bloodshot eyes. Cold water, toothpaste, three painkillers—damage control at its finest. It helps with the smell and the banging headache, but my eyes betray I drank too much last night. Way too much.

Twenty minutes later, I leave my house with a set of tools. My hands shake as I grip the steering wheel. I've never been this self-conscious. Halfway to Nadia's flat, I'm talking myself out of turning back...

What if she doesn't want my help?

What if she puts me out the door?

At least I'll know I tried.

She doesn't want more than friendship, but she's still Nick's sister. She's not going anywhere, which means I'll see her around. I should get used to the bitter aftertaste of rejection. My own thoughts drive me fucking livid. I met her a week ago. One week and a multitude of emotions I never expected to feel pound on my mind like a drum.

Getting through traffic takes me twenty minutes. London just wouldn't be London without traffic. I'm not far away when the hands-free system activates, and *Claudia* flashes on the dashboard. My eyebrows knot in the middle. She never calls this early. Muscles in my shoulders tense, and the intense worry settling over me burns whatever alcohol still courses through my bloodstream.

"What's wrong?"

"Paranoid much?" she chirps. "We're fine, babe. I'm calling

with an invitation. Brunch next week on Sunday? I'll cook."

An involuntary grimace twists my face. "Please don't. I'll bring the food. Italian, okay? What's the occasion?"

"I'll cook," she says firmly. "Hold o—"

She doesn't finish before her voice is replaced by a different, much cuter one. "Thomas!" Maya exclaims. "Are you coming? I have new puzzles!"

I smile, relaxing as the familiar warmth fills my insides like hot air fills a balloon. "Good morning, sunshine. How are you?"

Maya giggles. She always giggles, and I absolutely love that sound. "I'm okay. When will you come?"

"I'll come next week. I'll take you somewhere nice, so your mummy can cook in peace."

"Yes! Oh! Can we feed the ducks with Uncle Nick?"

"Whatever you want."

Maya's the only girl who can mess with my head. The only one allowed to walk all over me. There's not much I'd refuse her. Quite frankly, I can't name a single thing. If Claudia hadn't protested, I would've bought her a freaking pony for her birthday last year because she whispered, *I love you, Thomas*, before she asked.

"I'll see you soon, sweetie; put mummy back on the phone."

I don't expect she will. Maya always hangs up when she's done talking. I redial, and by the time Claudia answers, after most likely chasing Maya around the living room to retrieve her phone, I'm parking outside Nadia's flat.

"Sorry, I can't get her to stop doing that," Claudia sighs. "She's been bugging me to call you all week."

"You should've. I'll always find time for her. I'll take her out on Sunday, and you'll cook in peace. Maybe without distractions, you won't kill me with whatever you're making."

"Ha. Good one, Thomas. I'll have you know I'm getting very good. You'll love what I'll make, and you taking Maya out is actually great. She's hit that age when she wants to help and

by help, I mean cause chaos." She inhales a deep, shaky breath as if bracing for something unpleasant. "You asked what's the occasion... I want you to meet someone. Please be nice, okay?"

Cue in another cold shudder. More alcohol evaporates while I'm almost fucking ablaze with anger. "*Someone?* Who's *someone*, Claudia?"

"Someone I've wanted you to meet for a while now," she says quietly, her tone full of hesitation. "His name is Richard, and he's very important, so, *again*, be nice, please."

"You're *dating* this guy? Are you serious?" No fucking way. *One shitty piece of news at a time, please.* "What about Adam? What about Maya? Does she know him? Does she like him? Who the fuck is this guy, Claudia?"

"Can we talk when you come over? This isn't a chat I want us to have over the phone."

The disappointment in her voice hurts me more than I anticipated. She's right. We should talk face to face so I can change her mind. She's Adam's girl. Richard can't touch her. He'll have to go through me first, and *good fucking luck, mate.*

"I'll see you on Sunday. Make sure Maya's ready."

I make a short pit stop at a nearby coffee shop, drink one espresso on the spot, and order two black coffees to go.

Claudia and Richard are pushed to the back of my mind when I climb the stairs to Nadia's flat. She takes the stage. Everything else blurs into an unimportant blob.

Last week I would've been excited to spend time alone with her, but today excitement evaporated, leaving behind a sense of dread. Somewhere in my deranged mind, there's still hope that she's changed her mind.

I enter her flat without knocking—an involuntary habit. I'm greeted by a strong smell of turpentine. Music plays from a large portable speaker tucked under the stairs, but I don't recognise the song. Calm rhythm and half-whispered, half-sung words create an intimate, sad atmosphere.

I should've knocked.

I regret barging in uninvited even more when I enter the kitchen, finding Nadia holding a glass of water and a palm full of pills. Half a dozen orange prescription bottles litter the countertop: diazepam, citalopram, paroxetine. I can't even pronounce the names of the others.

"What are you doing here?" she asks, pushing the meds aside.

White, black and grey splatters of paint stain her hands and clothes. She's put her hair up in a messy bun and a few loose locks, smeared with more paint, surround her doll-like, dirty face. A speck of black marks her cheek, and a bit of grey stains her forehead. She's so fucking beautiful...

She swallows the pills, washing them down with water, avoiding my gaze. If not for her red, puffy, dull eyes, I'd consider her artistic attire the sexiest look she has worn so far.

"You were crying," I say, the realisation like a punch in my throat.

"You were drinking," she retorts, accepting the takeaway coffee I push across the countertop. "I asked you a question, Thomas. What are you doing here?"

I clear my throat, annoyed by the sudden coarseness. "Nick called. He said you need help."

She rolls those big, sad eyes, places her glass by the sink and starts scrubbing the paint marks off her delicate hands. "You could've told him you're busy."

She grabs a bottle of olive oil, pours a hefty amount over her hands, and scrubs with the hard side of the sponge, flaring her skin.

"I'm not busy." I drop the toolbox on the tiled floor. "But you sure look like you had a busy morning."

"I felt like painting," she admits, a little less hostile. "Too bad the convenience store down the road only stocks small sets of oil paints. They're a bitch to wash off."

"There's an art supply store in the city centre."

She scrubs harder, her skin redder by the second. "I doubt it's open at midnight."

"You went shopping after I left?" I can't watch any longer. I take the sponge off her, splashing her hands with cool water. "You'll peel your skin off. C'mon. Show me what needs doing."

"Nothing. I told Nick I needed a screwdriver, not helping hands. I can manage. Go home, Thomas. You look like you should spend the rest of the day sleeping."

She rejected me—fine, well, not *fine,* but I can't change her mind about that. What I won't accept is her pushing me away when she already said she wants us to be friends.

"I'm not saying you can't. I'm sure you wouldn't poke your eye out, but I'm here now. You might as well take advantage of helping hands."

Considering all the boxes and the overall mayhem in the flat, she does need help. She's just too proud to ask, as if letting me help will somehow make her weaker.

She pulls her lips into a line and then turns around, marching straight into the living room. The white wooden floor is mostly covered by flatpacks. A large, bottle-green corner sofa and a black coffee table might be the only ready-to-use furniture around.

"No bookshelves? No TV unit?"

She motions at more flatpacks stacked under the window. "Nothing comes pre-assembled these days."

"You got more anywhere?"

"Yes, every room."

Looks like I won't be going anywhere else today. I shimmy out of my jacket, rolling the sleeves of my jumper. "We'll need more coffee, doll."

She frowns when I tear open the first two boxes. Instead of arguing or convincing me that she'll put the furniture together herself like I expect, she touches her small hand to my arm, taking me outside for a smoke.

"Watch your step." She looks over her shoulder. "It's wet."

I halt in the doorway, looking at the enormous canvas that lies on the balcony floor—at least six feet long and three feet wide. Four water bottles anchor all corners, stopping the masterpiece from flying with the wind.

It really is a masterpiece. Hauntingly beautiful. Harsh strokes in the background, dark colour palette. What grabs the attention immediately is a girl with sweeping long hair, dressed in a white, flowy dress. She's arching at the bottom of the canvas as if she's falling. Thin, shimmering strings are tied around her hands, feet, middle and throat, all held by two large hands painted at the top.

"I had no idea you're so talented," I admit, struggling to look away from the girl in the painting, her eyes closed, dark hair flowing in the air. "It's amazing."

"I like how it turned out, but it'd be better if I had a stretched canvas. I'll get it stretched tomorrow."

I glanced at the painting again, shaking my head. "Don't. It's perfect like this. Where will you hang it?"

"Nowhere. It'll be stored in Nick's attic like all others."

"Why? This should be displayed, Nadia. How about the wall behind the sofa?"

She studies her work, a shadow crossing her face. "I don't think I can stomach seeing this every day."

I'm no connoisseur. The art around my house was either a gift, or I bought the pieces because they fitted the décor. Looking at Nadia's painting, I see what's there—a human puppet; a girl controlled by someone's hands; harsh lines, dark colours; a sad, creepy vibe.

Thinking about what she told me and what I figured out based on her behaviour, I can't shake the feeling the painting portrays her deepest fears. It's a self portrait...

"Is that you?" I point at the girl in a white dress.

White means innocence... not sexual in this case. Nadia's not a virgin. This is a different kind of innocence, I think.

Whatever happened between her and Adrian wasn't her fault.

Nadia nods, inhaling the smoke and peering up to meet my gaze. "A puppet," she whispers, her voice weak, and my heart fucking cracks. There's so much torment in her eyes. So much hurt. "That's what Adrian called me." She straightens as if gathering her courage. "I thought about our conversation last night. I lied when I said I don't want you. I do, but..." She motions at the canvas, "...Adrian still has a hold on me."

"So, you want me, but you're still saying no?"

She puts the cigarette out, walking back inside. We sit on the sofa, and Nadia tucks her feet under her bum. "I might feel strong when you're around, but sex won't fix me, Thomas," she mutters, cheeks pink. "*You* won't fix me. I'm not any better today than I was before we ended up in bed. You're like those pills I take, just stronger... and I want to stop taking them. When have you ever seen an alcoholic recover after switching from beer to vodka?"

"That's a lousy comparison. Whatever your problems are, I think you'd work past them faster if you'd let me help."

A sad smile crosses her lips. "What's in it for you? I mean, I'm not that good in bed. Why are you volunteering as my rebound case?"

I rest my elbows on my knees, sipping the hot coffee, scanning the endless cardboard boxes. Nadia's opened up to me a little, and she deserves an explanation for my sudden change of character. "We're not so different. We're both trying to leave the past behind. I'd be using you too... I liked the guy you awoke in me last week. He was decent, relaxed, and looked forward to the next day. I've not felt that way in years."

"You *are* a decent guy. I told you I didn't want you last night, yet you're here to help... speaking of which—we should probably get started."

Twelve

Not-so-light bedtime reading

NADIA

Week two of wedding preparations proved more demanding than week one. Each day brings us closer to Mel's start date as the Marketing Assistant at C&G Records, which means she'll no longer have time to recheck every detail ten times over.

Thank God.

She's obsessing over things no rational person would care about, driving me insane. Every evening I crawl into bed exhausted, hoping it'll mean a good night's sleep, but exhaustion doesn't keep Adrian away. I stay awake for hours, reliving the best and worst times. Once sleep takes me, I wake up soon after, drenched in sweat and even more tired.

Every rational cell in my body knows casual sex won't help me deal with the past, but the *what-ifs* remain. Thomas's touch works like magic, offering much-needed peace.

The night we had sex was the first night I slept longer than two hours since the nightmare began six months ago. The fake calmness lingered throughout Saturday—more than I managed

myself armed with dozens of pills. I've been fighting the urge to show up at his doorstep ever since, twelve long days. He deserves better than being my distraction.

Thursday is the least demanding day in Mel's schedule. She didn't plan anything for the afternoon, so I use the opportunity to visit someone I should've visited as soon as I came back from New York.

Two takeaway coffees stack one on top of the other, I walk through the tall, wooden door into a modern foyer. A reception desk stands proudly in the centre, the same receptionist still sitting behind the counter. Not much has changed here during the past two years. The same Ficus stands in the corner, at least a foot taller now. The same soothing lavender-scented candles burn on a side table.

What did change is the décor. A red carpet has been replaced by a dark wooden floor, and an obscure magenta wallpaper has given way to dove-grey paint.

"Nadia!" Daphne coos, a small, sad smile twisting her lips. "How have you been, love? I hoped I'd never see you again."

"Thanks." I smile, knowing she means well. "I hoped never to come back, but here I am. Is he available? I've not made an appointment, but—"

Daphne holds out her hand. "Don't worry about an appointment today. He's got the afternoon free. I'm sure he won't mind seeing you. Go right in. We'll catch up when you're done."

Clutching my handbag packed full of prescription meds I brought home from New York, I knock three times and enter once I hear *come in*. Not much has changed here, either. James sits at his desk, a banana in one hand and a pen in the other. Light hair frames his overworked, tired face lined with first fine wrinkles. He peers up from the papers on his desk and stops chewing.

"Hey," I say, raising the coffee cups slightly. "I brought your favourite. Half-caff, half-sweet, non-fat caramel macchiato," I recite, proud I remembered his order.

James swallows hard, dropping the half-eaten banana in the bin, watching me as if he's seeing a ghost.

"Nadia, you're the last person I expected to see today. Come in, take a seat. How have you been?"

I hand him the coffee, settling into a comfortable position on the sofa where I spent two hours every day, six days a week after my dad died. It's weird being back here, right where I started... relying on psychiatric help again.

"When did you come back?" he asks, sipping the steaming macchiato. "God, I've not had one since you left."

I point to my tall, extra shot, extra-hot, extra-whip, sugar-free vanilla latte. "Neither have I."

The high-maintenance coffees are an odd ritual. We came up with those orders during one of the many hours we spent here together. Trying to relax the atmosphere and get me to talk, James told me a story about a barista who always misspelt his name on the coffee cup, driving James mad. He must've done that on purpose. James isn't exactly difficult to spell.

I suggested we make the barista's day a touch harder. We came up with the most ridiculous orders to annoy the guy, but the coffees turned out amazing, and we made them a part of our daily routine.

"You're not here to catch up, are you?" he asks warily.

He's not good at hiding emotions. In a way, I'm glad he's affected by my visit. I'm glad he's a little sad seeing me back here because it means he cares.

Our relationship was never truly a professional one. Yes, I'm the patient, and yes, he's the doctor, but I always thought of him as my confidant. No one else knows as much about me as he does.

I shake my head *no*, taking out the prescription bottles before I hand him a black folder. "I came back two weeks ago. I hoped a change of scenery would help, but I'm not making much progress. The longer I'm without him, the stronger the

need to go back. I don't want that. I can't go back, James... I need help."

He grabs the first prescription bottle, reading the label. "I assume this is no longer about your father." The more bottles he checks, the deeper the creases on his forehead. "Please don't tell me you take all of them. It's too much, Nadia."

"Sometimes, it's not enough."

He pushes three bottles my way. "Anxiety meds, anti-depressants, sleeping pills. Even those three together are too much. Especially since the doses are so high. Why do you have so many pills?"

I shrug, picking my nails. Shame prickles my eyes because I'm a mess. I've been a mess for years, and I'm tired of failing. "None worked. None took the edge off, so I kept asking for something stronger."

"And you kept the old meds just in case? Nadia, you *can't* take them together. I don't even want to think how badly this has damaged your health. Do you want to tell me what happened? Why did you need the meds? What changed? You were doing better before you left."

James is the only person who has my full, undivided trust. He earned that during months of therapy. It took three weeks before I spoke the first word and three more before I told him about my father's death. He's my last resort this time, too.

"I can't... it's too much too soon." I push the folder across the table. "Some not-so-light bedtime reading. Those are my psychiatrist's notes from New York. His business card is there too. He said you can call him if you need more information."

James skims the pages, probably looking for keywords or phrases to get an idea of my newest issues. More sadness clouds his eyes. Maybe that's the wrong way to look at this, but I'm glad I'm not just another day at the office; just another patient he can bullshit.

"I..." he looks up, meeting my gaze. "I need time to read

through this, but I might not be the best person for this job. This requires a very specific approach."

"What does that mean?" Anxiety makes a reappearance. Here I am, ready to take a step in the right direction, only to find the road is closed? No. No way. He's my only chance. Without his help, I'll never find a way out of this pitch-black tunnel. "You won't take me back?"

He sets the folder aside, resting his elbows on the desk. "Of course I will if that's what you want. I'll do my best, Nadia, but I want you to get the help you need, and frankly, I don't think I'm equipped..." He leans over his desk. "There's a woman, Samantha Johnson; she specialises in cases like yours. She's absolutely brilliant. I could call her, explain the situation, fax her the documents—"

"I don't want anyone else. I trust you, James. You know my history; you—"

"Hey," he cuts in, reading my mood perfectly. I'm rambling, growing more agitated by the second. He knows he should stop me before I wind myself up too bad and end up crying. "You want me, and you're getting me, but please, think about letting Samantha in. She could join our sessions, a silent observer. She's the best—" He snaps his mouth shut because now he's the one rambling. With a deep breath, he calms down, his features softening. "I hate seeing you struggle again."

What stops me from letting in someone other than James is nothing but good old shame. After all, despite what Adrian did, I stood by him. I knew I shouldn't, but I did it anyway, trying to protect him. I weaved a security blanket around him, fuelling his addiction instead of holding him accountable.

The worst part? I don't regret that half as much as I regret leaving. He deserved better than he got from me...

"You can consult her if you need guidance, but I don't want her here." I reach to grab the pills, but James stops me.

"I can't let you have those back. Not all of them." He pushes

anti-depressants my way. "That's all you're getting until I see your lab results."

"B-but..." I stutter, my hands trembling, stomach wringing out like an old rag. "I need the sleeping pills too. Please, I won't sleep without them. They hardly work, but I get two or three hours. Without them, I won't sleep at all."

"I wish I could, but without reading the notes and seeing your lab results, I don't know which meds you actually need and which ones do more damage than good." He clicks a few buttons on the keyboard and then hands me a blood work request form once the printer spits it out. "Get this done asap."

"I'll get it done today," I assure him, my voice small.

"Come back first thing on Monday. I'll have the results back by then, and we'll get to work."

Monday morning is eighty-nine hours away. Eighty-nine hours without diazepam or fluoxetine. Eighty-nine hours of flashbacks, sleepless nights and maybe even panic attacks.

James gets up, rounding the desk. He looks ready to touch my shoulder the way he always did at the end of our sessions, but he quickly changes his mind, recognition flashing across his face. He must've recalled what he read in my file.

"Stay occupied. Keep your head busy while you're off the meds. Try ASMR at night. It helps some of my patients."

Dark thoughts loom nearby, waiting for the remnants of fluoxetine to leave my system. Good thing my flat requires TLC before the party on Saturday.

Maybe it'll be enough to keep me occupied.

Thirteen

Sex, what else?

NADIA

Seven vials of blood lighter, I enter my flat, feeling lost and out of place. The Puppeteer painting hanging behind the sofa summons Adrian.

"This is nice," Adrian scrutinises my outfit when I open the door to my dorm room, "but not appropriate. Get changed."

I cock an eyebrow. "I thought we were going to the cinema. You keep quoting old Pacino movies."

"You caught that? I'm impressed. Well done, but we're not going to the cinema, so please swap the sweater and jeans for a pretty, modest dress."

"If you think I'll go to see you fight—"

He takes my hand, spinning me around until I'm facing my room. "Get changed and stop guessing."

"Fine. I'm intrigued." I close the door in his face, shimmy out of my jeans, and pull on a tight, green dress with puffy sleeves. There's nothing bold about it other than that it's backless.

When I open the door again, Adrian glances at me from his casual lean against the wall across the narrow corridor. He sizes me up, then twirls his finger, silently asking I do a one-eighty.

A small smile curves my lips. He's refreshing. In equal parts confident and adorable. If not for his determination, we wouldn't be going out tonight. I didn't come to New York to date, but Adrian's been downright stubborn the past month. Asking me out a few times a day, utterly unaffected by being rejected time and time again. It worked. After four weeks, I caved. Dimples in his cheeks and his almost black eyes watching me with delight helped him get a yes when he asked again yesterday.

I spin around, listening to him exhale slowly.

"Better?" I ask.

"Better, sexier, and I love your back, Nadia. Really. If you can love a body part, then I love the spot just below the nape of your neck."

"You're mad."

He bows, offering me his arm. We exit the building, where a black limousine waits, taking three parking spaces. I glance at Adrian when the chauffeur opens the back door.

"Please don't tell me you're rich."

He presses his finger to his lips, touching the spot on my back he's already in love with.

"Patience isn't my strength," I mutter, looking out the tinted windows. We're driving across campus, heading toward the main road.

"I thought so." He takes my hand, lacing our fingers. "That's why you won't have to wait long. We're here."

The limousine stops on cue. We're parked outside the Performance Arts building... three hundred yards away from my dorm. The chauffeur opens the door again.

"Thanks, man. We're square," Adrian tells the driver, helping me out of the car.

I'm pretty sure the two vertical lines on my forehead will forever be etched into my expression after tonight.

"Curious?" he murmurs into my ear. "Come on, it's almost time."

"Time for what?"

"For the show."

He pulls me toward the door, then down a long corridor, deeper into the building. We pass small groups of people, mostly children before we reach a set of tall, double doors. Adrian hands two tickets to the boy standing there, lacing our fingers as we enter the theatre. Eighty percent of the seats are occupied by children, and I'm frowning again when we take our seats at the back of the room.

I expect many things. Colourful houses, castles, maybe the hut of seven dwarfs, or the scenery worthy of the ball where Cinderella lost her shoe. I'm all wrong, though. Standing on the stage is a huge... stage. We're about to watch a puppet show. I burst out laughing. I've not laughed for months, but I can't help it. Adrian looks at me, his dark eyes gleaming with joy, and I know that making me smile was his priority tonight.

I glanced at our hands, fingers still intertwined, and then look into his dark eyes. Following my heart, I lean over, pressing my lips to his. He doesn't skip a beat, taking my face in both hands, gently pulling me closer, his lips eager but calm.

"This is the best date I have ever been on," I admit, inching away.

"Yes, it is." He steals another kiss before pecking my nose. "I love seeing you smile, Nadia."

The lights dim as a cheerful melody fills the air. I've never seen a puppet show before, but I can't tear my eyes off the stage. Adrian's more focused on me, watching me beam until my cheeks hurt.

An hour later, the lights come on again, and the actors and organisers flood the stage. Kids applaud, but Adrian doesn't let me join in. We slip out of the room through the back exit. He rests his back against the wall outside the door, pulling me close. His lips catch mine slowly, but my body reacts with a flood of intense heat filling my chest.

"It's been a month," he says. "I kissed you twice. We've been on one date. How too soon will it be if I tell you I'm in love with you?"

I'm speechless, recalling the last month full of smiles. I didn't think I'd ever smile again, but thanks to him, I'm smiling every day.

"This guy crossed the line, and he didn't even blink," I quote Pacino from Insomnia. *"You don't come back from that."*

Adrian laughs, kissing my head. "You are impossible. You're mine.

And I'm in love like a teenager, Puppet."

"Puppet?"

*A smug smile crosses his face. "You were so immersed in the perform-
ance, yet you didn't notice that one of the characters looked like you?"*

"Which one? The princess?"

"No. The one who wore a green dress like yours."

"The witch?! I look like a witch?"

"You're the most beautiful witch I've ever seen, Puppet."

I adored that pet name because it mattered. It reminded
me of our first date, his resolve to make me smile, and his
unyielding adoration. For a long time, he did all he could to
pick up my pieces whenever I fell apart.

And then he was the one who made me fall apart.

I take an ice cube out of the freezer, hoisting myself onto
the breakfast bar. The ice cube melts while I stare at the wall.
The grounding technique clears my head enough that I remember I should stay occupied. A three-door wardrobe was delivered
last night, so with a cup of green tea and a screwdriver Thomas
left behind, I head upstairs, determined to put the wardrobe
together and unpack my clothes before the day ends.

An hour later, all parts are neatly lined in the order I'll need
them. Too bad I'm ten inches too short to get things done... a
chair is no help.

Surrounded by parts, cardboard boxes, and foil packets full
of screws, I sit on the floor, wondering how to go around the
problem. Calling Nick, or better yet—Thomas would be the
easiest choice, but they're still at work. Asking Thomas has a
few more perks than just helping hands. His presence is a good
substitute for diazepam, but I'm not struggling enough to rid
my inhibitions yet.

A brilliant idea pops into my head—work smart, not hard.
I get to work, putting the wardrobe together horizontally. That
works and only takes me three hours. It must be a record.

The last step—standing the wardrobe up against the wall doesn't go so well. It's heavier than I expected, and I can't lift it far enough. After thirty seconds of back and forth, the wardrobe wins. The doors break out, but the frame stays in one piece, collapsing on top of me.

"Ouch."

I glance at my watch, massaging my sore back. Nick and Thomas should be home by now, so I find my phone, dialling my brother.

"Hey, sis, what can I do for you?"

"You can give me Thomas's number."

He clears his throat, his voice changing from cheerful to reserved. "What do you want his number for?"

"Sex, what else?" Sarcasm covers my words. A low chuckle that isn't Nick's resonates in the background. "Let me guess," I say, my cheeks burning. "You're still at the office, and Thomas is there too."

"And he can hear you."

"Good. Hey, Thomas. I assembled my wardrobe, but it's too heavy, and I can't stand it up. Could you please, please, *please* come over?"

"You had me at *sex*, Nadia," Thomas says, still amused. "I'll be there soon."

Nick growls, huffing into the receiver. "Not funny."

"Your paranoia isn't either. And Thomas? Bring tools. The doors snapped off. I'm not sure how to fix them."

***

Thomas enters my flat twenty minutes after my call. He didn't knock again. Hasn't even shouted *hello*.

I expected him in full suit seeing that he's coming from the office, but he's wearing jeans and a plain, white t-shirt—far less intimidating than a three-piece designer suit. Much sexier, too.

"I'm glad you changed your mind." He motions at the Puppeteer painting, proudly displayed behind the sofa.

"Face your demons," I say, handing him a cup of coffee.

"That depends. What do you see when you look at it?"

"A girl who gave up. A broken, scarred mess."

"I wouldn't say you gave up." He sits in the wing chair, eyeing the painting. "You know what I see? Your strength. You're fighting despite everything that torments you."

I consider his words, my heart swelling three sizes. One simple sentence turns my world upside down. Until now, I considered myself a victim, but the truth is I'm a survivor. Many would consider me weak for sticking by Adrian this long. People wouldn't think how much courage I needed to fight for him the way I did despite what he put us through.

"Thank you." I smile a rare, genuine smile. "I didn't think about it like that."

He moves his hand, touching my thigh, digging his fingers into my flesh. Calmness washes over me, the anxiety nothing more than mild static at the back of my mind.

"Change the negative into a positive, baby. You're not a mess. You're lost. You're dealing with your issues alone, but keeping secrets doesn't take the weight off your shoulders. It adds more." He stands, taking his cup. "Come on. I hate to say this, but we need to start. I'm playing poker at Nick's in an hour, and I can't miss that, or else he'll come here, breathing fire."

I follow him, but before we climb the stairs, Thomas grabs my phone from the kitchen island.

"Next time, call me when you need help. You don't have to be self-sufficient, Nadia." He saves his number in my contacts. "I'm under *A*."

"*A for* arrogant?" I tease.

"*A* for all you need, doll."

"I don't need you."

He smiles, ignoring my harsh tone. "Agree to disagree."

Fourteen

Cross that bridge

THOMAS

Mel argues with Nick when I arrive for the housewarming party. I heard her high-pitched shrill all the way outside.

"What's that about?" I ask when Nadia greets me in the hallway.

She doesn't mind me entering her flat as if I own the place. Good, because I'm not about to change my habits.

Dark circles surround her eyes, clearly visible despite her best effort to hide them under makeup. She's pale, her skin almost ashen, vulnerability shining in her dull, brown eyes. I don't think she slept last night.

"Bachelor party," she says, eyeing the big box I set on the floor and taking my jacket off. "He told her you've planned a night in Amsterdam. She's not happy."

I catch her hand when she turns to join the party. "Are you okay?" Stupid question. She can't fucking fool me. I know she's not okay.

She squeezes my hand tighter, shaking her head a firm *no*. "Bad dreams."

The urge to wrap her in my arms strikes me out of nowhere. This must be the first time I ever considered hugging a girl other than Maya or my mother. Nadia steps back before I can try, though. She turns on her heel, entering the living room. I hang my jacket over the staircase railing even though there's an old-fashioned coat hanger by the door. Jerk's jacket is there... *great.* More *cutie* all evening.

"There, make a good use of this." I hand Nadia the large, heavy box I brought—a housewarming gift.

She wrinkles her nose, shaking the box hard, clearly amused. "You bought me tools? Does that mean you no longer want to be the first point of contact when I need a screwdriver?"

I shake hands with the guys and lean over the girls, letting them kiss my cheek. "No. If you need tools, you call me. Stop guessing, Nadia. Open it."

The gift isn't random. No, I thought hard about what to get her, and I bought something meaningful, something that proves I paid attention from the start—a set of art supplies.

I never realised how much shit was needed to paint. The art shop was half the size of Ikea. The ceiling-high shelves were full of endless art supplies...

For twenty minutes, I gawked at a shelf stocked with red paints. They all looked identical, but since they had different names like burgundy, crimson or flame, they had to differ somehow. How many reds are there, exactly? Isn't red like one fucking colour?

Apparently not. At least fifty different shades stood on the shelves. There were even more greens than reds, not to mention blues. Who the hell comes up with these idiotic names, anyway? Parrot green? Midnight blue?

What the fuck? Midnight is black, end of story.

After half an hour of growing more paranoid, I called my mother. I should've done it sooner. She knew exactly what I should buy.

Nadia takes unnecessary care unwrapping the orange wrapping paper before she places the box on the floor. A genuine smile touching her eyes is all I hoped for, and I get it when she peeks inside, taking out a set of acrylic paints, brushes, a few stretched canvases in different sizes, and an easel that requires assembling.

Still smiling, she wraps her arms around my neck, pecking my cheek. "Thank you."

"You're welcome. There's one more canvas in my car, but you'll get it if you promise to paint something for me. Choose what you like, but I want her..." I point at the girl she painted a few days ago, "...to be in it."

"We have a deal," she beams. "I'll get you a drink."

While she's in the kitchen, I grab the easel and take a seat by the table, ready for more DIY.

Amelia's eyes burn holes in my face, her lips in a pout. "Strippers, booze and weed in the European sin city! Why the hell do you think it's a good place for a stag do, Thomas? Why would you take my husband there?" At least she waited until I sat down before the hissing commenced.

"All the things you just said. Relax, we'll behave."

At first, I kept the location a secret, but Nick's been getting on my nerves, asking about the details ever since he asked me to be his best man. I caved last week. He's far too excited to let Mel boss him around... I think. He's devised a foolproof strategy, preparing the answers to every possible question Mel might ask. One thing he overlooked is that sharing the location with his future bride will come back to bite his ass.

Amelia sure won't let him off easy. She looks at Nadia, who comes back with my drink—vodka on the rocks—and sits beside me, close enough that our shoulders touch. "Whatever plan you had, forget it. We're going to Barcelona."

I smirk, securing the easel with three screws. Not the sturdiest design...

"No way in hell!" Nick snaps.

It's too late, though. Mel eyes him with an *in-your-face* kind

of smile. The only way she'll let this go now is if Nick decides to ditch the Amsterdam idea.

And we all know that won't happen.

"Why don't you work this out in bed?" I say when Nick opens his mouth again.

He downs his drink, changing the topic. "I almost forgot. We're throwing a party the Friday before the stag do. Aaron's album went platinum within a week. You're all invited."

"Aaron Young?" Nadia asks, her eyebrows meeting her hairline when Nick nods. "You signed the guy, and I only now find out? He's amazing."

"And so handsome," Jane says with dreamy eyes.

The party kicks off with a sexual version of *Truth or Dare*. Within five minutes, the game became my all-time favourite. First, Scorpio humiliated himself by performing a striptease. Then Amelia confessed she always wanted to kiss a girl and every man's fantasy came true when Jane kissed her.

Yep, definitely my favourite game.

I grab a pink card from the pile for Nadia. "Truth or dare?"

"How many vetoes do we get this time?" she asks Mel.

"One as always. Why?"

"No reason. Truth, please."

I glance at the card. "Where do you like to be kissed most?"

She ghosts her fingers along my neck, starting below the ear and travelling south until she stops at my collarbone. "Here."

I'll remember that.

She takes a blue card, and I answer before she asks.

"Truth, baby doll."

Everyone stares at me instead of Nadia, and I need a few seconds to realise my mistake. The endearment wasn't inaudible... *oops. My bad.*

Nick's face turns red, his temper flaring. "*Baby doll?*"

"Small, delicate, pretty." I play dumb, ignoring his agitation.

He should get used to this. I'm nowhere near done pursuing

his little sister. The long-term plan is simple—make her mine, which is why I have to plant the seeds in Nick's mind right away.

He grits his teeth, eyes drilling a hole in my face. "Yes, she is, but she's not your groupie."

"Tell me something I don't know."

See? Baby-steps.

"How many women have you slept with?" Nadia reads the question jumping in at the first opportunity to break the tension before shit hits the fan.

Nick sure looks ready to burst into flames, but he cackles at Nadia's question, shooting me a dirty look. "As if you remember." He turns to Nadia. "Too many to count, sis."

"One," I say, watching him fall silent. "I *slept* with one. I fucked a lot."

The moment my glass empties, Nadia's up on her feet to get me a refill. Ethan watches her every move like some psycho rapist, pissing me off. I open my mouth, but before I can tell Ethan to stop looking at her, Scorpio kicks me under the table.

A short text message follows suit.

Scorpio: Keep your shit together!!!!!!!!!!!!!!!

Any fewer exclamation marks, and I'd think he's joking.

"That's nasty!" Ethan hollers, eyeing Nadia, who's trying to reach a bottle of vodka from the top shelf. "How did you do that?"

No *cutie*? Finally.

I turn around, curious what got him so alarmed, and I fucking freeze. A purple bruise the size of my hand marks her lower back, flipping my stomach. I get up to examine the bruise further, but Nadia shoots me a tiny, reassuring smile.

"It's nothing," she says, pulling her blouse down. "I lost the battle with my wardrobe."

"The three-door wardrobe in your bedroom?" I ask, handing her the vodka. "It's a miracle your bones are intact."

We keep playing, going around the room twice before the first veto is cast. Nick picks a card for me because Nadia's making drinks in the kitchen once again. He tosses the card on the table, nostrils flared, jaw clenched.

I chose truth last time, so now it's time for a dare. Whatever the card says must involve Nadia or Nick wouldn't be glowing red again. The card lands by Scorpio's drink, and he leans over, checking what the fuss is about. Good thing Nick can't see the smirk taking more real estate on his face with every word he reads. He also can't see the wink Scorpio sends my way, or else... I'm not sure what, to be honest. Nick can't land a decent punch to save his life, but I think he'd try.

"Kiss all single girls," Nick snaps, fisting his hands. "I'd rather you didn't, Thomas." He stares at me.

I stare right back as if it's a game, and the first one who looks away loses. I'm not losing this. No fucking way.

"It's just a game, chill out, mate." Scorpio pats Nick's back, prompting him to look away from me.

Winner, winner.

I glance over my shoulder when Nadia's heels click on the wooden floor. I'm going to win this girl over one kiss at a time. She's still torn between what she wants and what she needs— *wants* to heal without help but *needs* my help. Despite what she says, I hope *needs* win, even if it means she'll be using me as a distraction. I won't mind. Hell, I already volunteered, and I've not changed my mind. If I can be close to her, even if we'll only have sex, I'll have time and the opportunity to turn our relationship into more.

She sits down beside me. "Veto."

Again, she could slap me, and I wouldn't know the difference. No explanation, not even a glance my way. She's so fucking confusing she makes my head spin. I swallow the vile, disgusting lump lodged in my throat, acting cool. No big deal...

Jesus Christ. It *is* a big deal. She keeps shooting me down, and I keep crawling back. *Pussy-whipped.*

Another round goes by while I ignore the godawful rejection drumming on my mind. Music plays as background noise while we watch Ethan try his worst pick-up lines on Jane. We also get a too-detailed rendition of Mel's worst sex. I can't *un*hear that. Ever. Despite the *veto*, my arm still rests across the back of Nadia's chair. I ghost my fingers over the nape of her neck, watching goose bumps break out across her smooth skin.

What did I say? Confusing as hell. She doesn't want me but reacts to all the faintest touches, contradicting her words.

She turns to me, vulnerability no longer as prominent as when I arrived two hours ago. Her eyes are still sad, but she's calm because I'm close. A sense of pride inflates my chest.

"Break time?" she asks as if reading my mind. "Come on."

We head outside, Nick's gaze follows our every step, and I feel it on the back of my skull as if he's holding a gun to my head. He's right not to trust me, but I'm a bit pissed off that he thinks I'm not good enough for Nadia. We've known each other for a long time. He *knows* my lifestyle thus far was a conscious choice, not who I am.

"So, a kiss is too much?" I ask, leaning against the wall. "It's just a game, Nadia. You made it clear we're not happening again. I'm not happy about that, but I respect your decision."

"*Just* a game," Nadia scoffs, shaking her head. "*Just* a kiss, right? Not for me. I wish you'd stop pushing. We're not cut from the same cloth no matter what you say."

She steps closer, utterly oblivious that she's drifting toward me. She's fighting a lost battle.

"I'm trying not to push, but I don't understand why you don't just give up. You want this. You want *me*."

"I won't be a selfish bitch, okay? I won't use you. It's not right." A shadow crosses her face, and she shakes her head, dismissing the last three sentences. "I... I'm afraid I won't let you go when the time comes," she whispers, staring into the distance.

I curl my fingers under her chin, tilting her head. "We'll cross that bridge if we get to it, baby."

"If? What do you mean *if*?" Her eyes dart to my lips.

Fuck this girl.

She'll break me in ten different ways.

"You assume I'll be the one who'll want out first. You're afraid I'll move on before you recover. What if you're the one who'll leave first? Stop overthinking the future and focus on the present, Nadia. Let me in." *Let me help. Let me show you how good I can be for you.*

Because I can be good. For her, I'll be the best version of me there ever was.

Two lines mark her forehead, and God, I hope I struck the right chord. All she has to do is take the first step, and the rest will fall in place. I'll make sure it does.

Ethan bursts through the door, startling us both. We weren't here just now. We were alone, locked, unavailable to the outside world, but that moment's gone.

A smile taking half of Ethan's face slips when he glances between us. Nadia's mere inches away from me, my fingers still curled under her chin. I drop my hand when she steps back.

"C'mon, cutie, I have a dare you're a part of."

"I'll be right there," she says, inhaling a cloud of smoke. Ethan gets back inside, and Nadia closes her eyes briefly, pushing the smoke past her lips. "And now, I regret using my veto on you."

So do I. Whatever Ethan's dare, it involves touching. Most likely kissing. So far, all dares were intimate, so it's safe to assume his isn't any different. No way I'll sit back and watch the Jerk get anywhere near Nadia. Possible scenarios play before my eyes... not one ends with Ethan's face still intact.

"You can use my veto," I say, pinching the ash of my cigarette. "You better do. For his sake."

"You have no right to act possessive, Thomas. What I do is my decision alone."

I catch her wrist when she turns to leave, then twist our hands until our fingers are interlocked. "Maybe you're right. Then again, I had no right to touch you and look where we are. Don't act surprised when I hit him if he touches you."

I almost want Ethan to make one false move. That way, I could justify my right hook breaking his nose.

Nadia snatches her hand out of my grip, marching back inside. I follow. The atmosphere is thicker now than before we left. Nick sits with his arms folded over his chest, watching Ethan's every move. Mel's sending warning glares in Nadia's direction, and Scorpio's eyes are on me as if he's anticipating a shitstorm.

He knows me well.

And Ethan? Ethan can't contain his excitement, fidgeting like an impatient child.

"So? What's the dare?" Nadia asks.

Nick's jaw tightens, and he shoots me a look I can't quite decipher. One thing is clear. After Ethan and Nadia's date, Nick no longer wants Ethan to adore his sister.

"He has to fish an ice cube out of your cleavage using only his mouth," Mel says, sounding apologetic, eyes on me instead of Nadia, as if my reaction will tell her more.

I guess she knows about the night Nadia spent with me. Good thing she can keep a secret from Nick.

"Thomas let me use his veto," Nadia says, casually sipping her drink. Casually only to an uninterested observer because I see her hands shaking.

The song we danced to the first night at the club starts playing quietly. My mind floods with how her petite body felt pressed against mine as we swayed to the rhythm. The sweet smell of her perfumes. How she relaxed under my touch.

She steals a glance my way, and I know we're both thinking about the same moment.

"Nice try, but it doesn't work like that, cutie." Ethan fishes out an ice cube from his drink.

My temper flares when he stands, showing off his pretty teeth. Same ones he'll be picking off the carpet if he takes one more step.

"Sit," I snap. "She said *no*."

"Oh come on!" Jane cuts in, rolling her eyes. "What's the big deal? We all play by the rules, Nadia. You're out of vetoes, and you're not having Thomas's. Get up and get on with the show."

"Fine," Nadia huffs.

My stomach sinks for just a second. A blinding wave of anger is quickly replaced with ease when she turns my way and fastens her soft lips on mine.

Finally.

Jesus...

Finally.

I weave my hand through her hair, pulling her closer, kissing her back with everything I've got as my tongue skims hers, teasing, tasting, devouring the cute doll as if I'm starved.

I am. It's been too long. I've imagined kissing her every day for two weeks. This is my one shot to remind her how good we are together, and I'll make the most of it regardless of who's watching. I bite her lip, slow down, and deepen the kiss, swapping eagerness for intimacy. She fucking melts under my touch, plays by my rules, and adjusts to my pace.

I close her lips, moving away even though all I want is to sit her on my lap and not let go, but we're not alone.

She's once again perfectly content. Even the dark circles under her eyes look lighter somehow. Harry Potter can kiss my ass. I don't need a fucking wand to perform magic tricks.

"You taste sweet, baby doll."

She bites back a smile, turning to Ethan. "I believe that's my veto reinstated, so... *veto*."

He doesn't comment, too dumbstruck to get a word out. I chance a glance at my best friend, expecting to see steam coming out of his nose, but his face is void of emotions as if the last minute never happened. He reaches for a pink card to read Mel's dare.

Fifteen

So sorry

NADIA

"How the hell am I supposed to convince Nick now that there's nothing going on between you and Thomas?!" Mel hisses, throwing plates into the sink.

She's helping me clean up now that Ethan, Scorpio and Jane have left, but honestly, I'd rather she leave too. I'm physically and mentally drained, barely holding up after two sleepless nights. I sure won't get much sleep tonight, either. Every time the room falls silent, memories press down on me. Thomas brought me back from my head a dozen times already, helping while not even trying. I'd be much worse if he weren't here, and that makes keeping him at a distance ten times harder.

I don't need Mel's nagging on top of everything else.

"There *is* nothing going on," I sigh, pouring Ethan's drink down the drain. "Stop overreacting."

"It's been two weeks, and instead of his interest dying out, it's growing. I see how he looks at you! So does Nick, by the way. He's not blind!"

The digital clock on the oven shows twenty past one in the morning—not the best time for arguments. Not the best time for guests, either. I should've called off the party when James confiscated my pills, but I thought company would help the time pass faster.

Convincing Mel she's wrong might be a Sisyphean task with a few drinks in her system, so I leave just as Thomas enters the kitchen. *May the force be with you.*

Nick's not helping. He sits at the table, polishing the last of the chicken salad, his eyes heavy thanks to the five drinks he poured down his throat. He pats the chair beside him, silently asking me to sit, his head swimming. Can't they just leave already? Reluctantly, I sit. Dodging his nosy questions might be easier now that he's slurring his words, no longer thinking clearly.

"You're so smart," he mumbles, leaning closer. His warm breath, a mix of whiskey and chicken salad fans my face. Lovely. "You know that, right? You're so smart, sis. You can't fall for his bullshit. Please don't. He'll hurt you. He'll make you cry, and I'll have to kick his ass, and I'll lose my best friend."

"You should get some sleep, Nick. You're wasted."

His unfocused gaze roams my face before he lets out a long, heavy breath, massaging his temples. "You like him. If he weren't such a whore... if he could take care of you the way you deserve... God, sis, I'd do *anything for* you, you know? Just trust me here. Thomas doesn't deserve you. Whatever went wrong between you and Adrian you can still fix it!"

One sentence.

One word.

One *name* and the walls I've built around myself while Thomas sat beside me all evening come crashing down like an avalanche, knocking me out of breath. The impending doom spreads, probing at my stomach, poking my heart that triphammers the same way it did every time Adrian came through the door, crazy in his black eyes.

"Where were you?" Adrian asks when I enter our small apartment off campus. He's at the breakfast bar, his pupils dilated, breathing shallow. I frown. His grey t-shirt is drenched in sweat, cheeks flushed, hands trembling as he lifts a beer to his lips. It's not even six in the afternoon. "Why are you drinking alone?" I leave my bag by the door, crossing the room. He's pale, despite the red cheeks, shuddering ever so softly. "Are you feeling okay, baby?" I touch his forehead. Instead of feverish, he feels oddly cool.

He grabs my wrist, squeezing hard. "I asked you a question. Where the fuck were you all this time? It's late!"

I step back, my eyes growing larger. Something is definitely wrong. He's never spoken to me like this before. "I bumped into Katie after lectures. We went shopping. Why are you so mad? I sent you a text. Did you check your phone?" He tears himself out of his seat, swaying on his feet.

I grab him by the waist, holding him up even though he's twice my size. He shoves me away, nostrils flared, jaw set tight.

I look past him, scanning the countertop to see how many empty bottles are there, but something else grabs my attention, and my complexion blanches, matching Adrian's.

A small grip seal bag full of yellow pills has my heart rate soaring, beating out of my chest so fast it's painful. I look at Adrian again, hoping against all hope that he didn't take any, but the symptoms are there: enlarged pupils, unjustified anger, sweat, trembling...

I was offered one of those pills by a freshman two months ago at a frat party. I stood outside, smoking, while Adrian was inside, celebrating a fight he had won. Ty brought Adrian's hoodie out for me just as the freshman pulled the pills out of his pocket, holding them out for me. He ended up with a broken nose, split lip, and a death threat courtesy of Ty.

"Don't ever take that shit," he told me when the poor freshman ran away, bleeding. "They call it Angel Dust. It's hallucinogenic. It'll mess you up like nothing else, girl."

Angel Dust, or its official name, PCP, claimed its first victim on campus three weeks later. A girl jumped out of a third-floor window.

According to her friends, she was convinced she could fly.

"You're high?!" I cry, snatching the foil packet off the countertop. "Why did you take it?" I run to the bathroom to flush the pills down the toilet. Adrian's heavy footsteps close behind me. "God, baby! Why? What the hell happened?! We need to get you to the hospital." I rip the bag open, but before I tip it over, Adrian twists my wrist, steals the bag, and swallows one more pill.

"You're such a fucking liar!" he booms, shoving the bag in his pocket. "I know you were with Ty all day! You're fucking him, right? You fucking cunt!"

That's not Adrian. He'd never say anything so hurtful. Adrian loves me. He trusts me. He knows there's no one but him. This guy towering above me is not my *Adrian. I shove him away, ducking under his arm, and rush back to the living room, falling to my knees.*

"Nadia!" Nick slams his fists on the table.

I crash with reality, my mouth dry, tears looming close by. I grab an empty crystal glass, grounding myself the only way I can without raising questions. I focus on the glass.

Firm, cold.

Smooth.

Round.

Heavy, empty.

Sedatives work faster, better and longer than any grounding technique ever invented, but I don't have any...

"What?" I ask once the cacophony of my thoughts dies down and my heart rate slows. "I'm sorry, did you say something?"

Playing dumb never worked on Nick. He saw me on the verge of a panic attack and during one after our father died. Hopefully, he's too drunk to connect the dots tonight.

"You switched off, Nadia. You switched off like you used to when Dad died. You're still shaking!"

Sometime during the last minute, he must've sobered up. He looks just as worried as Thomas, who now sits on my right, his eyes not leaving my face, body leaning toward me as if ready

to catch me. I want to climb onto his lap, close his lips with mine, and have his arms around me.

"This has gone too far," Nick continues. "I can't help you until you tell me what went wrong! You're a mess again, Nadia. What the fuck happened? What did Adrian do?"

I set the glass aside, placing my hand on his shoulder. At the same time, I catch Thomas's hand out of Nick's view. If not for Thomas, I wouldn't touch my brother while he's so exasperated.

I wrap my fingers around Thomas's, seeking some semblance of peace. Short-lived, but peace, nonetheless. I hate using him. I know I'm being selfish, but fear forces me to grab the one thing within reach that will help. Thomas does exactly what I hoped he would. He lets me feed off his strength, intertwining our fingers as he strokes my knuckles with his thumb—a non-verbal agreement.

"What happened is irrelevant," I say, my muscles relaxing while Thomas holds my hand. "You're right. I am a mess, but I'm getting help, Nick. Soon I'll be back to my normal self."

The sad part is that I'll never be the same again. That's impossible. Too much has happened. Too much has changed.

"Help?" Nick gets up, pacing the room. "What are you talking about? What *help*?"

I let go of Thomas's hand before Nick notices. Enraging him further won't do me any favours. Too bad I've not noticed Mel standing in the doorway. Her eyes jump between Thomas and me, her lips in a tiny pout.

"I'm seeing James again," I say as Nick walks back and forth, his hands clasped over his head.

"Yeah, because that worked so well last time," he scoffs. "He's not the right doctor for you. I know you trust him, but you weren't much better after six months of therapy."

"It's not magic, Nick," Mel interjects. "These things take time. I mean, it's been fifteen years since my parents abandoned me, and I still struggle sometimes."

Nick disregards his fiancée, turning back to me. An enlightened gleam shines in his eyes. "Did Adrian cheat on you?"

"No!" I snap before taking a moment to think.

It would've been the perfect explanation. Nick knows cheating is the one thing that could destroy my relationship with Adrian beyond repair.

Cheating killed my father. Dad would still be alive if our mother hadn't slept with that asshole on my eighteenth birthday.

"Then what did he do?!"

The answer stops at the tip of my tongue. I swallow hard, not letting the heated moment ruin my brother. "If I'm ever ready to talk, I'll come straight to you, Nick. I promise, but now is not the time."

I glance at Mel, motioning my chin at the door so she'll take Nick home before we argue, but her features pinch, and I know she's not siding with me this time.

"You should tell us. You're keeping a secret for no reason. You won't move forward like this, Nadia. You're making this hard on us, too. I can't stand seeing you so fucking sad."

A pang of disappointment jabs my mind. She's the one who should understand the reluctance to share traumatic events, and despite that, she's still pushing. Cornered by the two most important people in my life, I'm left with no choice...

"I'm going to bed," I say. "Let yourselves out. Goodnight."

A minute later, I gently close my bedroom door, sliding down until my bum slaps against the floor. My composure is an illusion, a defence mechanism designed to protect everyone but me. Silent tears drip down my chin; the sense of failure, a mindless detachment, clutches my heart like a wet, wrinkled hand, squeezing hard, stripping my flabby, unstrung mind of the firewall. More memories seep through the cracks of my bruised psyche, and the second the door to my flat closes with a theatrical bang, I crawl into my bed. I fist the sheets, crying like I haven't cried since Nick told me Dad died.

An all-gone feeling turns me inside out. I've been fighting this intolerable imprisonment in nothingness for months, fighting to feel, care, forget... but not tonight. Tonight, I let the pitiful, barred darkness consume me whole.

I let every hurt I've experienced bleed me dry because I'm too tired to fight again.

For months, I suppressed the negative emotions and consequently failed to process what Adrian did. Heavily medicated from day one, helping *him* through the addiction, I didn't think about *me*.

I fall to my knees, rummaging through my bag, looking for my phone. Adrian snatches my cell, sending it flying across the room. He grabs my arm, and his long fingers dig in hard, bruising my skin as he shoves me against the wall with all his might.

My head bounces off a picture frame, shattering the glass.

Tiny pieces slash my skin.

Warm blood drips down my back.

"Stop!" I cry, punching his chest. "Let me go. Please, baby, you're high. You're delusional. Let me get help!"

"Help?" He grips my neck, clasping five fingers around my windpipe. "You mean Ty?!" He squeezes harder. Hard enough to cut off my air supply. "He's not getting anywhere near you. Never again. You're mine, Puppet. You're only mine. Say it."

I nod, clawing at his hand, my lips parted, but oxygen doesn't reach my lungs. Tears blur my vision. I'll say anything to calm him down.

"I'm gonna kill that son-of-a-bitch if he even looks at you."

Adrian loosens the grip, and his attitude changes as if a switch has been flipped inside his restless mind. I cough, pumping air into my lungs when aggression fades from his face. His eyes hood over as if his system is crashing. He takes a few rickety steps back, then stumbles down the hallway. A loud thud follows when he collapses on the bed.

I don't move, still, flush against the wall as blood drips down my neck. My heart beats so hard I can hear it over my ragged breaths and almost inaudible whimpers. A long, loaded moment passes before I regain the feeling in my legs, my body stiff as I slide to the floor, shaking like an uncoiled spring. I don't know how long I stare into the distance, listening to Adrian's loud, steady breaths before adrenaline zaps my nerve endings. I crawl across the floor, picking up my phone. The screen's cracked, but it still works. I dial Ty's number, crawling into a corner.

"Hey, girl. What's up?" His voice brings a wave of intense relief, and my whimpers become more audible. "What's wrong, Nadia?"

"Adrian's high," I whisper, hugging my knees. "He fell asleep now, but—" I whimper, clawing at my neck where I can still feel Adrian's fingers as he choked me. "He lost it, Ty. Can you come? I'm scared. I don't know what to do."

"Hold on." Doors slam in the background, and gravel crunches under his feet. "I'm coming. Get out, okay? Wait downstairs. I'll be there in five minutes."

His car springs to life, roaring like a wild animal a second before the line dies. I tiptoe across the room, my legs like cotton candy. Careful not to make a sound, I close the door behind me with a soft click.

Ty arrives when I'm halfway through a cigarette, trembling in the cold January air like a frightened kitten.

"What happened?" he asks, crossing the sidewalk. He stops two feet away, colour draining from his face. "Fuck. Did... shit! Did Adrian do this?" He points at my neck, taking two more weary steps, and curls his fingers under my chin, tilting my head to take a better look.

"I don't know what got into him," I say, the choked-back sobs threatening to unleash now that Ty's here, keeping me safe. "He acted insane. I've never seen him like this, not even during our worst fights."

He cups my face briefly before hiding me in his arms. It lasts just a second. "Shit," he clips, spinning me around, his right hand stained with blood. "What the fuck did he do? Get in the car, Nadia. I'll grab your things. You'll stay with me tonight."

Adrian calls Ty around noon the next day, screaming down the line so loud that the speakerphone isn't necessary. The sheer panic in his voice sends shivers down my spine. "Is Nadia there with you?!"

"Yeah, she's here." Ty drapes his arm over my shoulders, pulling me to his side.

"I'm coming."

Before Ty can answer, Adrian cuts the call. My body tenses and fear blooms in the pit of my stomach, spreading to all vital organs.

"He should see you," Ty says, holding me closer. *"He loves you, Nadia. He'll never touch drugs again when he sees how he hurt you."*

We wait in silence. Each second stretches like bubble gum. Five minutes later, the door to Ty's apartment bangs against the wall.

Adrian rushes in, halting three feet away from me. *"No,"* he mutters, his eyes filling with tears. *"No, no, no..."*

A bizarre memory steals my attention—the image of my father shedding a few tears at his mother's funeral. I was only six when Nanny died, and I don't remember the funeral well, but my father's tears are etched into my brain. For years, I've been convinced that men cry square tears. It's absurd, but now that I see normal tears rolling down Adrian's cheeks, I realise square tears aren't possible.

He grips his hair, tugging hard, then clasps one hand over his mouth, falling to his knees. *"I'm so sorry, Puppet."* He holds his hand out to take mine. My first thought is to run, but the self-loathing painted across his handsome face convinces me otherwise. Seeing me hurt, knowing he did that, breaks him in ways only a man in love can be broken. *"Please,"* he whispers, swatting the tears away. A futile attempt. More keep coming. *"I'm so sorry. I love you so much, Puppet. You know that, right? Nothing matters more than you. Please, please don't leave me. I'll never take that shit again. Just... please don't leave me. I can't be without you."*

"You scared me." I swallow the lump in my throat, taking his hand. *"Promise you won't ever do that again."*

"I swear, Puppet. I swear on my mother." He moves my hand to his head, so I'll stroke him as he hides his face in my lap. *"I'm so sorry. I can't believe I hurt you."* His voice breaks, tears wetting my jeans, and he hugs my legs tighter. *"I won't ever do it again. I promise."*

Ever lasted three weeks. Then a vicious cycle began—

drugs, bruises, apologies. We were stuck believing he could change. That he could stop... that I could help him. We were deluding ourselves, hoping for better days, which were never to come.

Sixteen

Again, then again

THOMAS

I hand the taxi driver a twenty-pound note, exiting the car the minute Nick and Mel's taxi disappears behind the corner. There's no way I'll leave before I check on Nadia. She looked so fucking broken even before Nick started the interrogation about Adrian yet again.

He's oblivious to the severity of Nadia's issues. Consumed by the need to find out *why* she left Adrian, he doesn't notice the small things—how anxious she is, the torment in her eyes, the pills she swallows like candy and that she hardly lets anyone touch her. The list goes on, but somehow, I'm the only person who pays enough attention. The only one who sees her scars run deeper than anyone can guess.

I climb the flight of stairs, entering her flat. I'm actually a little scared of what I might find. I don't think I'll handle it well if she's crying. The place looks like we left it ten minutes earlier—silent and dark if not for the soft hue of LED lights coming from the kitchen.

Nadia stands by the breakfast bar, face wet. Anxiety radiating off her demolishes my composure. She's so fucking frail, holding a glass of water, a box of paracetamol on the countertop. The door closes behind me, and her head snaps in my direction, cheeks white, eyes big, full of tears.

I take three steps. A fundamental change happens before my eyes: her shoulders sag, a powerful, choked-back sob shudders her frame, and she runs out of the kitchen, crashing into me like a small, fragile wrecking ball.

"Make me feel something else," she whispers, hiding her face in my chest, fisting my jacket. She inhales deeply, shuddering all over. "Please, Thomas... make it go away."

My stomach twists in knots as I wrap my arms around her, holding her close, kissing the crown of her head. "I've got you, baby. I won't let go. You're safe."

Eyes closed, she presses her lips to mine, digging her fingertips into my neck and forcing me closer. I can taste her salty tears when she sweeps her tongue over mine, pressing herself flush against me. I want to hold her until the worst is over, but the urgency of her touch betrays that she wants more than cuddling. More than my arms wrapped around her on the sofa.

Much more.

She's vulnerable and scared, and my chest squeezes at the thought of giving her what she wants. I grip her wrists and push her away, regretting the decision when her bottom lip quivers.

"Don't do this," she whispers, more tears spilling down her white cheeks. "You said—"

"I'm not saying *no*, Nadia." Not by a long shot. This is me summoning all the decency that hides inside me somewhere. "If you want this, if you want *me*, I need you to say it."

I need consent. Verbal admittance, or else I'll forever worry I took advantage of the situation. That maybe I misread her intentions.

She peers up, holding my gaze. "I want you just as much as I need you right now, Thomas. Take me to bed... please."

She speaks with such conviction and strength that her words could wipe out a small city. She's pushing her scruples aside, surrendering to the selfish part of her character. She's putting herself first, and I couldn't be fucking prouder.

She trusts me to make her pain go away, and I won't let her down. I close her lips, backing her against the wall. The chemistry between us amplifies, escalating our craving to the point of fever. She's relaxing, fucking melting under my touch, no longer shuddering. No longer afraid.

I am.

I'm afraid to break away in case this turns out to be a dream, but the way I react to her proximity is definitely real. My fingers disappear in her hair, the kiss deep, urgent, *desperate*. Nadia slides my jacket down my shoulders, tugging my t-shirt next.

This isn't me taking advantage of her.

This is her using me.

And I let her.

I'd let her use me as a ladder so she could climb out of the ditch she's in. The two-week-long struggle comes to an end. I've got her in my arms, ready, *willing*. The anticipation skyrockets. My heart pumps blood faster. Desire spills under my skin like a drop of ink in a bowl of water.

I grip her thighs, lift her off the floor, and climb the stairs as she kisses a line along my neck, her breathing shallow.

"I want you exhausted," I say, dropping her on the bed. "I want you panting my name, baby doll." I yank my t-shirt off, then slide her skirt down her smooth legs, kissing the inside of her thighs. "Already wet," I breathe, grazing my nose higher. "God, you smell so good."

"Thomas, please." She raises the top half of her body and grips my hair, forcing me to crawl higher. "No experiments. I want you in right now."

"Experiments? Are you saying you never came on a man's lips? No one tried to taste you?"

Her cheeks heat, nice and pink. It's surreal. Mere moments of our closeness are enough for her torment to give way.

"You've been dating the wrong men. You've no idea what you've been missing. I'll show you how good it feels."

"Not tonight. Please, I need—"

"I know, *in.*" I pull her blouse over her head. "Close."

I want to dive between her legs and lick until she comes, but patience is a virtue. There will be time for checking how sweet she tastes. Tonight, she dictates the rules, and whatever she wants, she'll get. Tonight, I'm her personal fuckboy.

Within seconds, we're naked, and I let her feel the weight of my body on top of her. The closer I am, the calmer she seems. The feeling is mutual. I've not been this quiet in my head for years, but when she's under me, there's no buzzing. No noise. No thoughts rushing about at a hundred miles an hour.

I settle between her thighs, boxing her arms with my own, holding her close. A small, content sigh slips past her lips, not a trace of unease tainting her beautiful face.

"Remember the drill? Eyes on me when you come, doll."

"Do you ever stop talking?"

I nip her ear, driving into her with one urgent thrust, earning a satisfied moan. "When you make those sweet little noises."

Three hundred and forty-eight hours passed since I last felt her, but I missed the petite brunette as if it's been an entire goddamn century. She yanks me down by my neck, bruising my lips with demanding kisses. With every thrust, every kiss and every touch of my hands on her body, she gives into me more. Every time her lips part in a soft gasp, my efforts double.

She's locked between my arms, my hand on her waist, the other on the mattress. I'm pumping in and out, hitting that one important spot inside her, the rhythm of our bodies growing hastier the closer she gets. Her nails dig into my back, drawing long, angry lines down my shoulder blades.

"What did I say keeps me quiet?" I ask, wrapping her leg

around my waist so I can sink in deeper. "I want to hear you."

With each satisfied sound coming from her lips, I feel like I can move things with sheer willpower. She's surreal. So fucking perfect my chest squeezes like a sponge.

She's writhing beneath me, rising higher, closer to the all-encompassing orgasm, but this time I'm smarter. I won't let her come so fast. I don't want this to end, and I'm afraid I might fucking burst the second she'll start pulsating around me. She has to remember this. How good she feels when she lets me close. How peaceful. She needs to long for that peace and, consequently, long for me.

"Not yet, baby." I slide out when she's seconds away. "You made me wait *two* weeks."

Her eyes widen. "Are you punishing me?"

Not now, not ever.

"In the end... it'll taste like a reward. I promise."

She calms down slowly, squirming with every kiss I stamp on her neck. Good thing I've got all the time in the world. I rock back into her when she stops trembling, but it doesn't take long before she's right there again, poised on edge, ready to be tipped over.

I stop again.

Then again.

And again.

Just when I think we can play until dawn, Nadia cups my face, tracing her delicate fingers along my jawline, watching me with those large, brown, unbe-fucking-lievable eyes.

"Thomas... please." She strokes my cheek, squeezing her thighs together. "Please, enough."

Everything around us explodes like hundreds of confetti cannons the second I lean over her, thrusting harder and deeper to give her what she wants.

I'd give her everything she could ask for.

Every. Fucking. Thing.

Seventeen

Food poisoning

THOMAS

"I want an ice cream!" Maya giggles when we park outside Claudia's house after spending four hours at the zoo. She already had two ice creams, a doughnut, and pink cotton candy.

One day she'll become the most powerful woman in this country. No doubt about it. She's only three, but she already knows how to manipulate people.

Or maybe it's just me being utterly weak wherever she's concerned. One sad face, and I crawl out of my skin to make her smile again. Hence too much candy...

Nadia has a similar effect on me. Stronger, probably. She fell asleep last night while I took a minute to clean up in her en suite. I should've left then. Obviously, I didn't. I crawled back into bed and cuddled her into my chest for over an hour, stroking the line of her spine, basking in how fucking right it felt to just hold her close.

"You know I rarely say no, but this time I have to. Your mum wouldn't approve. It's almost lunchtime."

Maya giggles, hopping out of the car, hands outstretched within a second so that I'll pick her up. I do. I always carry her around. I should've dismantled the car seat first, though. It's damn near impossible to do that with one hand.

Maya drapes one hand over my neck, pulling a sad face. "Please don't go home."

I take the car seat out, closing the door with my knee. "I'm not going. You said you'd show me your new puzzles, and your mum spent all day cooking, so I'm in for food poisoning."

We both know Claudia's not a good cook. Even Claudia knows, but she keeps trying. I have to say she's getting better—no-need-for-an-ambulance-on-speed-dial better.

"Mummy!" Maya yells when we enter the house, and Claudia emerges from the kitchen. "Okay, well, Thomas took me to the zoo! I saw zebras, lions, monkeys and, and..."

"Hippos," I whisper.

"Hippos and tigers, elephants, birds, snakes!" She bounces up and down where I set her on the granny chair.

Claudia's décor makes me nauseous. A blue leather sofa is pushed against the wall by a green recliner from the nineteen-forties—neither vintage nor retro—just old. Fucking ghastly. It smells funny too—like sweat, dust and old people.

The room resembles a second-hand furniture shop. An oval pine coffee table, a glass bookcase, and a rather sad-looking plant in the corner. Nothing works well, but what makes me cringe most is the pink carpet with a floral pattern.

Claudia frowns, ghosting her fingers over Maya's yellow dress. Well, it was yellow when I picked her up. Now it's grey and stained with every sweet thing she ate.

"I'm not even going to ask," Claudia huffs. "Maya, go up-stairs, put a different dress on and wash your hands." She moves her eyes to me. "You want coffee?"

"No questions? No lecture? You won't even ask how many ice creams I bought her?"

"Too many, but that's not important." She puts the kettle on, resting against the kitchen cabinets. "Be nice to Richard, okay? He's important."

And the award for *The Fastest Way to Trash Thomas's Good Mood* goes to...

"Is he? More important than Adam?"

"Don't be like this. You know Adam will always be a part of me, but he's gone, Thomas. He's not here anymore. I'm trying to live, okay?" She bites her bottom lip, chewing hard. I know what that means—she's holding back tears. "I want you to meet Richard. I hope you can approve."

I rub my face, easing the frustration and wiping away the guilt gnawing at me now that she's almost crying. "I don't think I can, Claudia. I can't fucking stand the thought of you with another guy. You're Adam's girl. This isn't right."

Anger sparks a fire in my mind at her imminent betrayal, but a wave of sympathy washes over me when she wipes her eyes, extinguishing the flames.

"I'm still Adam's girl. I'll always love him, and Richard knows that. I just... I don't want to be alone anymore."

"You're not alone. You've got me."

She bites back a pathetic chuckle. "There was a time when I thought we could make it work. I thought we'd end up together, you know?"

I cock an eyebrow, uncomfortable with the mere idea. "You wanted... *me?*"

The thought of us together never entered my mind since I've known her. Claudia's like a sister I never had. Dating her is out of the question.

Fuck that. It was never *a* question.

She shakes her head, picking her nails and avoiding my gaze. "I don't know. You're great with Maya. She loves you, and at some point, I thought being with you would be sensible. Safe." She looks up, smiling softly. "I got over you quickly, don't

worry. I know it'd be too messed up. *We* are too messed up, Thomas, but I want to be happy, and Richard makes that happen. It doesn't mean I forgot about Adam. I never will, but I'm trying to move on because I know Adam would want that."

She's right. Adam wouldn't want her to dwell on the past. As much as I want to, I can't give her everything she needs. She has the right to find happiness.

I pull her into my arms. "Just promise me one thing."

"Anything."

"Promise you'll take things slow. Promise you'll be sensible with this guy and that you won't forget about me. I can't lose you."

She knots her fingers around my nape, pecking my cheek. "I'll always need you, Thomas. *We* will always need you. And I have been taking it slow with Richard. We've been dating for a few months, but he only met Maya last weekend."

"Does she like him?" I ask, feeling all kinds of nauseous.

"She does. I'm sure you will too." She smiles, pressing her cheek to my chest. "She likes him, but she loves *you*."

I don't need more than that.

A knock on the front door stops our conversation. Claudia wipes her face, heading out of the kitchen. I tense at the sound of a male voice like a guitar string on the verge of snapping.

Thankfully, Maya comes back first. She pushes a chair close to mine, making herself comfortable, her little hand poking my side with a giggle. The broad, cute smile puts my mind at ease. She does love me, and if I keep making time for her, she'll never forget me.

Claudia enters the room, followed by Richard, and I calm down further. I expected a guy like Adam—big, broad, lethal, but Richard's the opposite. He's the type every father or brother would approve of at first sight—well-groomed, well-dressed, completely harmless. He walks in slowly, fidgeting once he stops, his back straight as he meets my gaze. He shrinks, paling a touch, which tells me that he cares about my opinion and that, in turn, means he cares about Claudia a great deal.

Despite the obvious nervousness, he extends his hand for me to shake. "Richard Stanley. Call me Rick."

"Thomas Calix. *Don't* call me Tom."

Whenever someone calls me *Tom*, I picture Sir Tom Jones, hear "She's a Lady" and have a tiny mental fit, which is why Nick enjoys calling me Tom when he wants to piss me off.

And he often does.

"Claudia told me a lot about you," he admits, looking over at Maya. "Hey, Maya. Mummy told me you went to the zoo."

"Yes! Thomas took me! I saw zebras and lions, monkeys, hippos and tigers and elephants, birds and snakes!"

This time she's using her fingers to count. All the way home, she recited ten animals on repeat so she could tell Claudia what she saw. Now, with eight fingers up, she glances at me, her little mouth in a pout.

"Penguins, and—"

"And cheetahs!" She bounces in her seat, beaming like only kids do.

We spend a few hours talking and eating the roast Claudia prepared—the best meal she's cooked to date. Richard's easygoing, well-spoken and polite. Besides my loyalty to Adam, I'm out of arguments against their relationship.

Claudia walks me out, leaving Richard to clear the table with Maya as his assistant. "Thank you." She climbs on her toes, kissing my cheek. "It means a lot that you tolerate him."

I hang my jacket at the back of the car. "You were right. Adam wouldn't want you to dwell on the past."

"He wouldn't want you to do that either."

I heard that before. Nick said it, and so did Scorpio, but I never listened. I only let myself believe the words now that Claudia spoke them. Her opinion matters most. "I'll remember that." I peck her forehead. "Call me if you need me."

The irony of the past two weeks crashes down on me when

I pull out onto the main road. I've finally allowed myself to see past Adam's death. I considered leading my life back to normality after spending almost four years convinced that I don't deserve it, but the girl I want to sort out my shit for is a mess. After I saw her meltdown last night, I can't shake the feeling I might not be able to help her.

So, I do the one thing every self-respecting man would do in my position—I visit someone who always knows best. Someone who has an answer to every question. Someone who can flick the light on at the end of the maddening, dark tunnel I've been trying to navigate since Nadia entered my life.

That someone is my mother.

She's the only person who can tell me what the hell I'm supposed to do now. Years ago, when I was a little boy, she had Band-Aids. Now, she's armed with advice.

The clock on the dashboard shows eight p.m., but I'm always welcome at my parents' house regardless of how late or early I show up. I park outside the oversized mansion and smoke a cigarette, gathering my thoughts. I step inside, greeted by soft classical music reverberating through the vast space.

I guess my father isn't home. Alistair Calix doesn't enjoy Tchaikovsky or Bach. My mother, on the other hand, loves great composers. It's funny how people with different backgrounds and interests find their way together. My mother, Monique, was born into a wealthy family. My grandparents were the London elite, hanging out with the aristocratic crowd.

Alistair was raised in a small town outside of Manchester, in a room he shared with three brothers. But he was bright. Brighter than ninety-nine percent of his peers. His brains secured him a place at one of the most prestigious universities in the world—Cambridge. He met my mother on campus; as he always says, it was love at first sight. Thirty years later, they're still in love as if they met last month.

The sound of music leads me to the library located in the

east wing. Yep, the house is so large it has wings. The soothing melody grows louder with every step I take. My mother stands by the far window, a glass of red wine in hand, surrounded by rows of ceiling-high bookcases.

She looks over her shoulder, smiling softly. She doesn't say a word, though, as if she knows words aren't what I need just yet. I wrap my arms around her middle, resting my forehead on her shoulder, breathing in her tangy perfumes.

There comes a time in every man's life, when after years of teenage rebellion, he appreciates his mother like never before. My time came three and a half years ago when I came back from the Army. My mother was the only one who didn't tell me that the pain of loss would go away. She didn't console me. Instead, she let me grieve and stayed by my side throughout all stages.

"I saw Maya today," I say, eyes closed. "We spent the day at the zoo, and then... I met Claudia's boyfriend."

"Boyfriend?" she asks, turning around. "I sense you don't like him."

"It's not that," I huff, following her to the kitchen. "I just never expected Claudia to date."

I fill her glass with sweet, red wine and make myself a drink—vodka with ice.

Mum scrutinises my face, eyes narrowed as she sips her wine. "That's not why you're here."

She's good. One look at me, and she knows I'm stalling.

I rest my face in my hands, shaking my head. "No. It's not." How am I supposed to explain the mess without confessing what kind of a jackass I've been for years? She raised me better. She raised me to respect women and take care of them, not use them as a distraction from the pain ripping my chest wide open. "I met someone."

I don't have to see Monique to know what her face looks like right now, and surely, when I drop my hands, gripping the crystal glass, she's stunned.

"Who is she?" she asks, aiming and fucking failing at a casual tone. A hint of poorly concealed excitement rings loudly.

"Nadia. The one you helped me pick out a gift for the other day. She's Nick's sister. My business partner slash best friend's sister." I down half of the drink, my hands shaking. I may be a confident man, but telling my mother about a girl isn't something I ever thought would happen. Not in my wildest dreams. I rake my hand through my hair, squeezing the nape of my neck. "I don't know what to do. I'm losing it, Mum. She's going through some things. I'm helping the best I can, but she doesn't want more than help. Half the time, she doesn't even want that."

A broad smile taking half the width of her beautiful face is not the reaction I hoped for. She was supposed to comfort me, give me advice... not laugh at my misery.

Way to kick me when I'm down.

I finish my drink, getting up for a refill.

"Didn't she come home two weeks ago?" Mum asks, her voice dripping with amusement.

Nice one, Mum.

"She did. Why?"

"*Two* weeks, Thomas."

I grind my teeth. "Yes. Two. I hope you're going somewhere with this."

She laughs softly, rolling her eyes as if dealing with my ten-year-old self. "Sweetie, you just met. If she's going through things, help her, and wait until she's ready. She knows nothing about you. These things take time, honey. You can't expect her to fall in love with you after two weeks."

That.

That is why I came here.

I smile, twisting her words to fit the situation. Nadia knows a lot about me, well, not me, the playboy I used to be. She knows next to nothing about the guy I am without blondes or the guy I was before life dealt me shitty cards. Maybe she doesn't want me because she thinks all I can offer is great sex.

Maybe she needs time to get to know the real me.

Hope returns, flooding my chest with a warm, fuzzy feeling. "I love you." I kiss her cheek.

"Care to tell me more about the girl who has my son so disturbed?"

Where do I even start? I'd like her to meet Nadia and see just how mesmerising she is. There are already so many things I like about her it'd take hours to list every single one.

"She's like quickly progressing cancer, Mum. She's invading my whole goddamn world."

Eighteen

Breathe in

NADIA

Thomas enters my flat on Sunday evening. No knocking as per usual. He finds me on the couch, smelling a cup of peppermint tea—another grounding technique. I've been alternating between different ones all day.

"I didn't expect you to come back," I say, eying the hint of his muscles visible under his long-sleeved white t-shirt.

"Why didn't you?"

I drink a small sip, inhaling some more. "I thought you'd change your mind about friends-with-benefits after last night."

"Yeah," he drops his keys on the coffee table, draping his jacket over the back of the couch, "don't count on it. Whatever your issues are, you're better when you're with me. I'm better when I'm with you, so let's quit running around like we don't give a shit and just agree that we'll use each other."

I'm done fighting. Done denying myself the help he carelessly offers. Last night should've scared him off; he should've reconsidered now that he witnessed my meltdown. He clearly didn't. He wants to follow me into the labyrinth of my issues, and I'm too weak to stop him.

"We need ground rules," I say when he sits beside me.

"Okay." He tugs my hand until I straddle him. "I can think of one—no more dates with Ethan or anyone else for that matter. I won't share you."

"Done." I dip my head, kissing his soft lips, the smell of his spicy cologne engulfing my senses. "No questions. No guessing. No pushing. And Nick can't find out."

"Deal, but you don't pretend you're fine if you're not while you're with me, and you call me when you need a distraction."

So, all day every day?

"Careful what you wish for. I'm off the meds. Hence the meltdown last night. If James doesn't have a prescription ready for me tomorrow—"

"Then you'll call me, and I'll make sure you don't have to smell peppermint tea to feel safe."

"How do you know that's why I do it?"

"Told you you're not the only one who has issues." He pats my thigh, sliding me off his lap, then stands, pulling me with him. "Turn around." He forces my back against his chest. "Do this if I'm not here when you need me."

"I don't need you," I snap on autopilot.

"Keep lying to yourself." He takes my hands in his, moves the right one to the side of my ribcage, close to the heart, and clasps the other on my right arm. "Close your eyes."

I do, lacing our fingers when he hugs me tight.

"Now breathe in," he whispers, inhaling in sync with me through his nose. He taps his index finger over my knuckles four times before exhaling through his mouth. "Remind yourself who you are. Where you are." He dips his head, pressing soft, open-mouthed kisses along my neck. "Then recall this moment—my lips on your skin; the sound of my voice; the way your body relaxes under my touch." His hold on me loosens,

and his lips work their way across my jaw.

I turn around, fisting his t-shirt. "One more rule. Don't hope for *more*."

He grips the hem of my sweater, pulling it up and over my head, exposing my plain, black bra. "I'll take whatever you give me, baby, and I'll make the best use of it for us both."

***

James retained most of my meds. All he gave back was diazepam with clear instructions not to abuse it. He prescribed me new anti-depressants, a handful of vitamins and another handful of whatever else my body's short on.

I take eight pills every morning before I rush out to take care of tasks Mel sends every evening. She started working as a Marketing Assistant at the record label on Monday and no longer has time for the outstanding wedding tasks. It's actually a blessing. Things get ticked off the list as *done,* not *pending* now that she's not interfering as much.

Under different circumstances, I'd hate the fast-paced days, but running all over London keeps me distracted and off diazepam until Thomas takes over the role of an ad-hoc anaesthetic every evening.

Today is Friday. Day eight since James confiscated my meds. Day eight without alprazolam, diazepam, temazepam and a few others. All I have are anti-depressants and a still unopened box of diazepam. I'm overusing the grounding techniques and Thomas's body to make sure it remains unopened.

My phone rings when I emerge from a coffee shop near James's office. I've got a half-caff, half-sweet, non-fat caramel macchiato in one hand and an extra shot, extra-hot, extra-whip, sugar-free vanilla latte in the other. A bag over one shoulder, two folders under my arm, and a bag filled with two hundred and fifty fandango pink organza gift bags for wedding favours dangles from my wrist. I'm yet to pick up two hundred and fifty of each: personalised, handmade lollipops, test tubes filled with loose-leaf tea and wooden puzzle pieces engraved with A&N. Oh, and *obviously*, I'm the one who'll assemble the gift bags.

I growl, halting in my tracks, trying to move things around and free one hand so I can fish my phone out of my bag. I place the latte over the macchiato but drop the folders. My exasperation kicks up a notch. Careful not to spill the coffee, I kneel on the pavement, set everything aside, then shove my hand inside the bag. The phone stops ringing the second I grab it.

"Hey!" Mel chirps when I call her back. "I know you're busy, but could you please meet the band straight after your therapy session? They want to make sure they're prepared."

"I'm supposed to finalise the menu today," I say, collecting my belongings.

"No worries, I rescheduled. Hannah will meet you at two."

"Two? Jane's coming over at four." She kindly offered her help when I mentioned the two hundred and fifty gift bags.

"Hold on a sec," Mel says. A voice I know so well sounds somewhere in the background, clear enough that I know Mel has me on loudspeaker.

"You got the posters for The Crooks?" Thomas asks her.

"No, I don't, but they were delivered yesterday. Check with Nick. Sorry, Nadia, yes, I know, but the meeting won't take long. I'm sure you can make it home before Jane comes."

I rush across the road, glancing at my wristwatch. Ten past nine. *Surprise, surprise—you're late.* "That would be true if I had a car. I'm relying on public transport, Mel. I still need to pick up the lollipops, puzzles and tea today, and I'm already like a packhorse."

"Oh," she gasps quietly. "I'm sorry, I didn't think this might be too much..." She sniffles, close to tears. I can't wait until the wedding is over and I get my best friend back because that mess on the phone just now is *not* her. "It slipped my mind that you don't have a car, sweetie."

"Don't worry. I'll get it done." *No* will reduce Mel into tears, so I don't have much choice. "I'll just cut my therapy session short today. Text me Hannah's number, please."

"Thank you," she breathes down the line.

I cut the call balancing both coffees in one hand while tucking the phone away. By the time I enter James's office five minutes later, the coffees have gone cold. "Sorry I'm late. It's been a busy morning."

Intense too. Thomas couldn't keep me company last night but showed up this morning at twenty to seven, demanding to use both my shower and me.

"No problem," James says. "What are we talking about today? You want to tell me more about your busy morning?"

Since we restarted the sessions last week, I've been gathering the courage to tell James about Adrian. So far, we've talked about everything that surrounded my two years in New York, but Adrian's name hasn't yet been mentioned.

Every day I wonder how to tell James about the abuse I suffered at the hands of the man I loved, and I realised something disturbing: every imaginary conversation about Adrian I hold in my head starts with assuring James that Adrian is a good person. That he loves me. That he's the only reason why I stopped mourning my dad. I make him sound blameless. I come up with excuses and keep repeating over again that Adrian only hurt me when high. *Never* sober. Sober Adrian is a personificationof every girl's dream boyfriend.

The demarcation my mind creates scares me more than the possibility of Adrian showing up and battering me again. I can't connect sober Adrian to what he did while high. I can't admit that sober Adrian is the same person who made every one of my breaths painful after he broke my ribs.

I glance at James, hoping he can help me erase the line I drew between my Adrian and the drug addict. "No." I squeeze the cup so hard that the lid pops out of place. "I want to tell you about Adrian now."

A soft knock stops me from saying anything else. Daphne enters with an apologetic smile. "I'm sorry, but someone's here to see you, Nadia. He says it's important."

I frown, annoyed that my brother dares to disturb my session, but it's not Nick who waits in the reception. Thomas stands by the door, a three-piece suit hugging his tall, muscular frame. Daphne ducks behind the counter, offering us a false sense of privacy.

"What are you doing here?" I ask.

"I heard you need a car." He holds out the keys to his BMW. "Pick me up when you're done."

I cock an eyebrow, glaring at the keys. "You're lending me your car? Haven't you heard stories about women drivers?"

He cuffs my wrist, pulling me in. A soft, delicate kiss follows. "You're not a stereotypical woman, baby doll."

"But—"

"No buts. You're not bailing on therapy to accommodate Mel's every whim. Don't worry about the gifts, either. My assistant will pick them up. Now, say thank you, kiss me, and get back in there."

"Thank you." I close my fingers around the keys. "Why do I feel like this shouldn't be part of the deal?"

"Because you need more time than I do to accept the facts."

Cue in another frown. Another question waits on the tip of my tongue, but I'm not ready to hear the answer. Thomas knows the rules, but sometimes his actions betray that I'm the only one holding onto them for dear life.

"How will you get back to the office?" I ask instead.

A sad, knowing look crosses his face before he pecks my head and leaves.

"Everything okay?" James asks when I sit back down in his office. "Who was that?"

"Thomas, Nick's best friend."

163

No matter how much I pretend I don't notice the small things Thomas does outside our strictly sexual arrangement, I do notice. Something's changing between us. The more I think of it, the more I understand that although we agreed to sex only, we were never purely physical.

Not even the first time we ended up in bed.

And that scares me even more than the inability to see Adrian for the monster he became.

"When I left Adrian, I felt like I jumped out of a plane with nothing to break my fall," I whisper, glancing at James. "And Thomas... I think he's my parachute."

Nineteen

Asshole persona

THOMAS

Nick had a silent fit when he found out Nadia took my car for the day. I never lent him the BMW, no matter how much he pleaded. No one drives my car. *No one*, but I didn't think twice about handing the keys to Nadia.

Go figure.

It's already half past three, and Nadia's due back any minute. She rang half an hour ago, saying she was done with the meetings and only had one more thing to do before she'd pick me up.

"Just tell me one thing." Nick clips, readjusting his tie as if it's choking him. "*Why*? Why are you suddenly so fucking thoughtful? Don't get me wrong, I appreciate that you're helping her, but you're acting nothing like your usual self. I don't like it, Thomas."

I smirk. Does he hear himself? How is my thoughtfulness toward the light of his life a bad thing? "Would you rather have me treat her like I treat other women?"

"No, but—"

"I thought so. Don't be an ass, Nick. If you're looking for answers, ask the right questions."

A ringing silence coupled with Nick's eyes burning a hole in my face lasts longer than it should. Why did I say that? Why the fuck am I encouraging him? My palms grow cold as I wait for his reaction. How will I answer if he asks whether anything is happening between Nadia and me?

Way to dig your grave, Thomas.

I'm with her every evening. She limits the time we spend together to sex, but I steal a few minutes before, asking about her day and telling her about mine. I steal many more minutes after sex when she falls asleep. I sneak back into her bed to hold her close, toy with her hair or stroke her arm.

I'm falling headfirst.

So fucking fast it makes my head spin.

Nick folds his arms over his chest, lifting his chin higher— a silent challenge. "Fine. Why did you lend her your car?"

Phew. Good thing he pretends he doesn't have the slightest idea about Nadia and me, the same way Nadia pretends we're just physical. They're both, consciously or not, turning a blind eye, afraid to face the truth.

"Because you didn't," I say, closing my laptop. I won't get any work done while he's here. "She's struggling, Nick. Forcing her to cut therapy short so she can run errands is fucking low. I know what she's going through. I've been there, and I won't sit back when I can help."

It took me a year before I told Nick about Adam's death and the darkest times of my life when I drowned in self-loathing. The three months I spent in the Army after Adam died remain a blur to this day. I don't remember much, running on autopilot the whole time: eat, train, kill, sleep.

The three months after I came out were full of Claudia, whiskey and pills. If I wasn't helping her set up the baby room,

I was washing down sleeping pills with vodka, so the nightmares wouldn't wake me every few hours. A total of six months passed while I tried to cope by myself—six months while I searched for a single reason that'd justify me being alive.

I got a hold of myself after Maya was born. I promised Adam I'd take care of his girls, and I did my very fucking best. Maya is the reason why I reached out for help. She deserved better than the pathetic drunk I was.

Four months of weekly therapy sessions cured me to some extent: I'm no longer tormented by flashbacks and nightmares every day. The sense of emptiness and worthlessness swims inside me to this day, along with the notion that I don't deserve a meaningful life. Flashbacks of Adam's lifeless body in my lap still wake me up sometimes, but the pain has lessened over the years. It's still there but bearable.

During the past three weeks, my world has turned brighter. Colours seeped in, painting vibrancy into the black and white canvas. I no longer firmly believe I'm doomed. Now, I fucking hope I'm not.

"I know she's struggling," Nick says with a sigh.

He won't dare question my motives after what I said, even if he still has doubts about my intentions. I'm sure he does. He acts oblivious, but he's not stupid. He knows there's more to my sudden change of character.

"I tried talking to her, but she's not letting me in."

There are two groups of trauma survivors: those who find it therapeutic to talk through the issue with their close ones and those who keep their pain to themselves mostly out of fear.

Just like me, Nadia belongs to the second group. I didn't talk about Adam's death with my parents for months. Not just because I was downright scared, but also to protect them. If I told my mother I wished I were the one dead, she'd worry sick.

Nadia's the same. She's protecting Nick by keeping secrets.

"I know my brother. I can screen-write that conversation for you. I

know what he'd say and how my words would impact him."

Just like misery, secrets like company—lies. Lies get out of control sooner rather than later.

"I wanted to give her time, but it's been three weeks!" Nick says, taking his phone out. "If she won't tell me, maybe *he* will."

"You're calling Adrian?" I rest my elbows on the desk, my heart picking up rhythm. "Don't. You think she'll appreciate that you're spying on her? You need to trust her, Nick. She'll tell you what happened when she's ready. Don't push."

I want to know what happened too, but going behind Nadia's back is a stupid idea. Satisfying curiosity isn't worth losing her trust.

"I need to know." He rubs his face, inhaling deeply.

The torment twisting his features acts like a bucket of water over my head. Sometimes I forget just how much he loves Nadia. He'd give his arm if it meant she'd never be sad again.

"I can't believe she's back in therapy. I can't believe it's happening all over again. You've no idea what the months after our father died were like. She was a wreck. A shadow. A teary, vulnerable mess. She built a wall and hid behind it for so fucking long." He shakes his head. "Nothing, not even Dad's death, hurt me as much as watching my sister transition from a happy, innocent teenager to a tormented, struggling woman. I can't go through that again." He meets my gaze. "I can't watch her hurt and do nothing. It'll fucking kill me."

"She's not a lost cause. She's getting help. She's getting better. Can't you see that?"

"Better?" he scoffs. "I thought she was just upset, but then she got stuck in her own head last week, and I realised just how bad she is. She's a much better actress now. I can't fucking read her anymore." He taps the screen of his cell. "That's why I need to know what happened."

The in-call volume on his phone is at the loudest setting, every ringback tone reverberating in my silent office.

I'm fucking torn. Should I stay? Should I leave? Find out now or wait until Nadia tells me the story when she's ready?

Argh fuck.

I get up.

No way I'll risk the little trust she put in me so far.

Thoughtfulness sucks ass.

"Hey, man, it's Ty," I hear, stopping in my tracks halfway across the room, a mere foot away from the chair Nick occupies. "I guess you're after Adrian, huh?"

"Hey Ty, yeah," Nick mutters, frowning. "Is he there?"

"Nah, he ain't got his phone privileges yet. Another week before you can talk to him."

"Phone privileges? Where the hell is he?"

A moment of silence fills the air, broken by the rapid thumping of my heart. I feel like a five-year-old disobeying his parents. I should fucking leave. Whatever comes out of Ty's mouth next isn't meant for my ears, but my feet won't budge.

"Nadia didn't tell you, huh? Damn that girl. She's reckless."

"What does that mean? What happened? What did Adrian do?" Nick turns in his chair, aiming a puzzled look at me as if asking whether I'm making any sense of this.

I sure am not.

"If she chose not to tell you, I won't either, man. What I can tell you is this: Adrian's in rehab. You can try him next weekend. I'm taking his phone over there on Saturday. Is Nadia coming back here after the wedding?"

Questions multiply in my head and on Nick's face. His lips part, but no words come out. I almost hear his brain working hard to connect the dots, but the picture is an abstraction.

"Not that I know," he says. "Come on, Ty. Tell me what I'm dealing with. Why did they break up?"

Ty sighs, falling silent. I think he's debating whether to tell Nick what happened. "Nadia must have a reason why she didn't tell you what Adrian did. I just fucking hope it's not because

she wants to come back. The best thing you can do is keep her in London. I'll make sure Adrian doesn't follow her. God fucking knows they're both self-destructive."

He cuts the call, leaving us more confused than before. Instead of answers, we got more questions. Nick watches the dark screen with two wrinkles creasing his forehead. I regain the feeling in my feet when my phone chimes in my pocket. A text message waits on the screen.

Doll: I'm here.

"Nadia's here." I grab my jacket from the hanger by the door. "I'm not coming back to the office once I drop her off."

Nick stops chasing his thoughts, though he's still only partly present. "Yeah, okay. I'll see you tomorrow. Oh, and Thomas... don't tell her I spoke to Ty."

I nod once, gritting my teeth. Is withholding the truth classed as lying? I sure hope not.

Fucking idiot! You should've left the room when you had a chance.

Should've. Could've. Would've. Too late for that now.

Nadia's buckled up in the passenger seat when I take the wheel. She's tired, but a small smile touches her eyes when, ignoring possible onlookers, I lean over, weaving my hand in her hair and seal her lips with mine.

"Hey," I say, a rush of inordinate protectiveness radiating all over my body. "How was your day?"

Despite getting no answers or even hints from Ty, unease settled over me when he mentioned rehab.

Alcohol?

Drugs?

Either way, addicts have a way of ruining a person's life. Their addiction drags down everyone they care about, sucking out life and happiness, leaving a distressed shell behind.

"Busy as always. You've not checked the car for damage,"

she chuckles when we pull out of the car park.

I rest my hand on her thigh, stroking her smooth skin with my thumb. "As long as you're not damaged, I don't care about the state of the car."

"Aren't you sweet. You should work harder on the arrogant asshole persona I heard so much about because I feel cheated. You were supposed to be a self-absorbed douchebag, Thomas... you're everything but. What happened?"

We stop at the traffic lights. I take her hand, bring it to my lips, and kiss her knuckles. "You happened, baby."

A small smile is all she gives me, changing the subject to the band meeting. She's still fighting, but I'm not giving up. She'll cave at some point. She'll realise resisting what's growing between us is pointless.

A Merc is parked outside Nadia's flat, and the owner, namely Scorpio, leans against the hood with Jane. He motions to me when I get out to help Nadia with the bags my assistant collected this morning.

"Hey, sorry I'm late; Mel's outdone herself again," she tells Jane. "I've been running around like a headless chicken."

Jane pulls out a bottle of wine from behind her back. "I figured you might need a pick-me-up."

"I have a free house and a fridge full of beer." Scorpio elbows my side. "Join me, won't you?"

His tone and the unnatural eyebrow movement hint he's on a mission to find out what the deal is with Nadia and me. We've not had time to catch up since the housewarming party because I've spent most of my free time with Nadia. Looks like Scorpio added two and two together.

Clever boy.

"Yeah, sure. Hold on a minute, I'll take this upstairs, and we can go." I lift the bags higher, then follow the girls upstairs.

Nadia grabs two wine glasses and leaves Jane to fill them while she walks me out to the door. The last thing I expect is

a kiss. She rises on her toes, pressing those plump lips to mine for a short peck. I grip her waist, slipping my tongue deeper just for a second. She's not the one who steals kisses in this relationship, so I'm making the most of this. Nadia's cautious, refusing to act like we're anything other than sex buddies.

We are. We're so much more, even if she's asleep when the *more* happens.

"See you later?" she whispers, glancing over her shoulder to make sure Jane isn't eavesdropping.

I press my lips to her forehead. "Call me when you're done, baby doll."

Twenty

Action, reaction

NADIA

Every girl dreams about a best friend straight from the movies. The one you tell your deepest secrets. The one who'll always have your back. The one you laugh and cry with.

When you tell her you killed your husband, she grabs a shovel and pulls an alibi out of thin air. When she's getting married, it's a given you'll be the maid of honour.

You'll end up being the favourite auntie to her kids no matter how many sisters she has.

Yeah, every girl wants a best friend straight from the movies—so did I, except... I ended up pulling the short straw and landed Amelia. The horror movie version of a bestie. The one who was the sweetest person and the personification of a perfect friend right until her status changed from girlfriend to fiancée. The engagement ring must have magical powers. Mel's no longer my best friend. She's a crazy bitch.

I can't wait for the wedding to be over and done with.

Mel arrives at ten a.m. on Saturday morning, immediately

turning my living room into a makeup salon to try out different options for the big day, which, by the way, is still *four weeks* away.

I wouldn't mind if she'd be trying out her own makeup, but no. It's *bridesmaids'* makeup. Two makeup artists follow her in, and four bridesmaids arrive no more than twenty minutes later. For some reason, Mel thought I wouldn't mind seven women in my flat. I don't even own enough cups to make them all coffee, so I jog to the nearby cafe for takeaway lattes.

"Do you complicate things on purpose or just by accident?" I ask three hours and seven makeup options later.

"What suits one won't necessarily suit the other," Mel huffs. "Jane has blue eyes, so blues suit her, but not Alex because she has dark hair."

It makes little sense to me, but Mel's exasperation keeps my mouth shut. The makeup artists work hard, creating masterpieces every half hour, aiming for something delicate but visible, elegant but not too elegant, frivolous but not slutty... something that'll satisfy the future bride and suit four girls.

They probably had no idea what they signed up for when they agreed to work for Mel. She was never an easy-going person, but with the wedding ahead, she's ten times worse.

"I'll make your life a little easier," I whisper to one of the makeup artists when Amelia heads upstairs to use the toilet. "Forget greens, blues and pinks. Stick to grey, black and maybe champagne."

She nods, returning to the task at hand. Two hours and five more makeup options later, we have a winner—classic smoky eye paired with coral lipstick.

Well, I could've done that.

It's already past three in the afternoon before everyone except Mel leaves. The focused, annoyed look on her face tells me she stayed behind to make my afternoon miserable.

"Whatever it is you're not happy about—"

"How much longer will you be sleeping with Thomas?" she clips, crossing her arms. "I can't keep lying to Nick, Nadia. He doesn't fucking shut up about you two."

"Weren't you the one who said I *should* sleep with him again?" I hand her a cup of steaming coffee.

She should be glad that I love her, or she'd suffer second-degree burns.

"I thought you'd both be done by now! It doesn't look like just sex from where I'm standing. He gave you his car yesterday! Do you have any idea how much Nick whined about that? I'm sick and tired of listening to him say how much Thomas will regret it if he hurts you. God, you're *all* he talks about. If he's not angry about you spending time with Thomas, he's whining that you don't trust him because you still haven't told us why you dumped Adrian." She takes a big sip, hissing when she burns her tongue.

I cheer inside.

Karma's a bitch.

"Tell him." She huffs again. "If you can't tell him the truth, make something up. I don't care."

Expecting that she'd be pleased about my deal with Thomas or that I'm keeping secrets was wishful thinking, but I never would've expected her to sound so mocking. Bitter. *Condescending.*

That stings.

Hell, it fucking hurts. We stood by each other since day one in primary school. Always there whenever one needed the other. Looks like much has changed while I was gone.

"Do go on," I say, settling into the corner of the sofa. "I see you've got something to add. You think you know why I broke up with Adrian? Or why I didn't tell you?"

She raises her chin, looking down at me. "I think Adrian met someone else, cheated on you or just got bored. I think you're blowing this out of proportion because you're ashamed, and you want attention. Do you know why I think that? Because you slept with Thomas a few *hours* after you met him."

My mouth parts into a small *o*. I wonder if she really thinks

so or if she's trying to hurt me because she's jealous that Nick focuses on me, not her. More than once in the past, we got into stupid fights when Nick and I spent too much time together.

Amelia's territorial. Half the time, I understand her, but she should've shut up this time. Instead, I'm the one speechless, dumbstruck even. Anger runs through me, and all the reasons she's wrong flash before my eyes, the words piling up on the tip of my tongue. I swallow hard, inhaling a deep breath. This is neither the time nor the place to scream my mind.

It's not really what she thinks. She's just overwhelmed by the wedding plans, and Nick, unloading on her, tipped the scales. I can't even blame her for pointing out that I slept with Thomas the night we met, though she was never the judgemental type. Still, she's not wrong.

I grab my cigarettes, crossing the room. "You know where the door is."

Not waiting for more venom, I walk outside, angry tears dancing in my eyes. Amelia wouldn't be so hostile if she knew the truth... she'd cry with me, and that's why I can't tell her. I don't want her hurting for me. It won't change the past. It'll only ruin the happiness she's building with my brother. They deserve better than dealing with my messed-up life.

The door to my flat slams shut less than a minute later. It's been a while since we argued, a year at least, and even then, it was something silly. Today is the first time I feel like I don't belong here anymore. Maybe I'm too damaged, too different. Maybe I changed too much to fit in with my family.

Maybe I can only truly fit in with the man who turned my life upside down in the best and worst way.

Two cigarettes don't put a dent in my foul mood. Flashbacks start when I get back inside and look at the painting in the living room.

Soon enough, I rip the box of diazepam open, swallow two pills, and curl into a ball on the couch, the pathetic little me. Once again, I recall the good times instead of remembering the bad ones. I recall every time Adrian made me believe that I could conquer the world; every time he told me there was nothing more important in his life than me: every kiss, every whispered *I love you*. This isn't fair. He hurt me beyond forgiveness, but my mind refuses to let the truth sink in, protecting the monster, and drowning *me* instead...

"You've not locked the door again," Thomas says hours later, entering the living room.

The sun has already set, and it's getting dark outside. I peer up from my laptop to find him draping his jacket over the wing chair, a bottle of wine in hand. A familiar warmth wraps itself around me, chasing away the demons.

If he could hear my thoughts and knew how powerful the effect he has on me is, he'd never come near me again. I still can't understand how his presence can soothe my tormented mind, healing the scars and bruises. Temporarily—yes, but even those short moments are steps taken in the right direction.

"I never do."

He lectured me about safety yesterday. *"London's not a safe place, doll. Lock the door,"* he said. It went in one ear and out the other. You'd think I'd be obsessed with locking doors after the abuse I suffered, but it's not that simple.

After the first few times Adrian took his delusional anger out on me came a phase of locking myself in the bathroom or locking him out of the apartment. I quickly learned that Adrian's wrath grew proportionally to the time he waited for me to come out.

"Wine?" I eye the bottle he sets on the coffee table.

"I heard you and Mel had a fight." He casts a look of annoyance my way, spotting a box of diazepam beside a cup of peppermint tea. "Why didn't you call me?"

I bite the inside of my cheek, holding a smile on a tight leash. He's so... *unfair*. So thoughtful, sweet and fucking caring. "It's nothing. I'm fine."

He sits down, pulling me onto his lap the way he does every evening. His lips catch mine, and a forceful but calm kiss follows. I love how he holds me flush against him as if he knows the closer we are, the better I feel. He weaves his long fingers in my hair, his hot tongue skimming mine slowly as if kissing me is his favourite part of the day.

"Don't lie," he whispers, pressing his lips to my temple before he repositions me, my hands, and my legs, cradling me in his arms like a lost little girl. I rest my cheek on his shoulder, skimming my nose along his neck, inhaling the intoxicating smell of his body and cologne. "Mel was in tears when she came home. I was helping Nick set up the new barbeque. Mel said she was a right bitch to you... she's really upset."

And so is he. We only met three weeks ago, but we've spent enough time together already that I've learned to read his body language and the tone of his voice. Now, he's worried. The way he holds me wrapped in his arms and stroking my back, how he's pressing his lips to the crown of my head, the unnatural, lively unease in his voice—it all betrays him.

I lean back a little, enough to see the crinkle between his brows. It gives way when my eyes skip from his cinnamon eyes down to his lips. "Kiss me again, please."

No hesitation. No second thoughts.

Action, reaction.

His tongue teases my bottom lip before he deepens the kiss, tilting my head to the side and letting out all the air from his lungs. There's nowhere else I'd rather be. He spreads his fingers over my back, climbing higher until he cinches my nape and draws me closer, exploring my mouth in the most delicious way.

I peck the tip of his nose, nestling my face back in the crook of his neck. How the hell can I feel *this* safe? Nothing can touch me here. Nothing can hurt me. My demons are locked away, their presence untraceable.

"I know she's under a lot of pressure, and Nick's not helping freaking out about you and me and about Adrian. Mel had enough of being the third wheel, which I understand, but she said some things she can't take back."

"Why didn't you call me? I told you I'll be here whenever you need me."

"You're not my personal antidote. I'm doing well without the pills because you're around, but—"

He scoffs, halting my rant. He grips my wrist, pushing me away far enough to see my face. "If you say you shouldn't rely on me like that, I'll flip, Nadia. Be selfish. *Please* be selfish. Focus on yourself. Take what you need."

If only that was so easy. How can I be selfish when Thomas acts selflessly despite saying he's using me as much as I'm using him? He set me, my well-being, and my happiness on a pedestal. I want to do the same, return the favour somehow, even though I have no idea what ghosts hide in his closet.

"You never told me what happened to you," I say, clinging to him again. "Why did you end up a bitter-sweet asshole who favours meaningless sex with those perfect blondes?"

His muscles bunch under my fingertips, harder than reinforced steel. He stops stroking my back, and a tremor of panic fills my gut. I shouldn't have asked that. We agreed to no questions and no pushing. A cold shiver navigates down my spine, forcing my heart into a higher gear.

For the longest time, he's silent, probably reliving whatever happened, and I want to kick my own ass for asking. The cold sweat coating my hands spreads fast, making every inch of my skin feel clammy. I cup his face, trying to right my wrong as I stamp a soft kiss on his forehead.

We're way past the friends-with-benefits stage. I don't think we ever were just friends-with-benefits, but I wouldn't dare spew that truth aloud. Thomas deserves better than me, my baggage, and my diseased mind. It's best to keep pretending we're just physical.

"When you're ready to talk, I'll listen," I say and try to get up,

but he digs his fingers into my thighs, keeping me in place.

"So will I."

Something in his eyes, the kind of helplessness I know all too well, pushes me to play a dangerous game. "What's worse," I whisper, "pain or fear?"

He doesn't blink as if afraid to miss my reaction. "Pain."

"Fear," I counter, hinting too much. "It lasts longer."

"Fear is a reaction. It's the product of your own thoughts."

"Maybe, but the reason behind fear is real."

"Danger and pain are real, baby. Fear is just a great illusion. Everything you want waits on the other side of fear." He holds himself wound so tight, so tense, but his eyes don't veer away from mine when he asks, "Are you afraid of Adrian?"

I shake my head, lying with gestures. If I'd admit to fear, he'd draw his own conclusions. He already knows more than Nick and Mel combined. Nick doesn't even know I'm on meds. Thomas knows what I take, how much and how often. He even reminds me about vitamins every day. Nick's oblivious, but Thomas... he pays attention. He's perceptive, and I'm sure he'd figure out why I came back home early if I'd admit that I'm afraid of Adrian.

"Okay, so if he walked through the door right now and saw us together, what would your first reaction be?"

He's breaking the rules asking that question. He agreed not to push for answers. I swallow hard and choose the cowardly way out, shutting him off as I get up. I grab the wine, heading to the kitchen, but a pang of guilt hits me square in the gut before I exit the room. I stop in the doorway.

The answer rolls off my tongue before I think it through. "That depends whether or not he'd be sober."

Thomas's head whips, his attention narrowed to a pinpoint. I give him no time to reply, disappearing into the kitchen. I fill two wine glasses, my heart bruising my ribcage with irregular beats. He's closer to the truth than anyone else, and the trust I put in him surprises me most.

The burning need to let him in on the secret isn't something I expected. Speaking about what happened would start a chain of events I don't want to be a part of.

"Sober?" he asks when I come back.

He takes my hand, pulling me right back onto his lap. I straddle him, finding his lips, hungry for the safety that comes as a package deal with every kiss.

I nip his lower lip, leaning back to grab the wine. "Drugs. He's in rehab now." I cut the conversation short, sliding off Thomas's lap and opening the laptop.

He knows I won't tell him more tonight, so instead of pushing, he wraps his arm around my stomach, planting ghost-like kisses along the nape of my neck. "What are you doing?" He glances at the screen. "Bachelorette party planning?"

"Yes. I could actually use your help. Mel said Barcelona is your go-to weekend break. Do you happen to know any male strip clubs out there?"

Thomas sits up, his body stiff, jaw tight. I don't understand what got him so agitated in a matter of seconds, but it sure looks like a battle's raging inside his head. "Strip club?" He pushes the words through his clenched teeth as if they're something dangerous that shouldn't be let loose. "You think it's a good idea?"

"I don't really care, but Mel's counting on it. Besides, it's not like the bachelor party won't have strippers. It's only fair we watch men take their clothes off."

He gets up, pacing the living room and pumping his fists. "It's not safe, Nadia. They're all drunk and high, and..." He crouches down before me. "I'll be a thousand miles away, doll. I can't help you if something goes wrong. You need to stay safe, and a male strip club isn't a safe place."

My heart swells a little. There's nothing sexier than a man worrying about his girl.

You're not his.

True. It's hard to remember when he acts protective.

I take his hand, lacing our fingers. "No need to worry. I want a big, organised show. My friend went to one last year, and she says it's fun and safe. Maybe Mel will get lucky enough to join them on stage. Apparently, in every show, a few girls cover their manly parts with baby lotion, and then they splash it all over the room."

Thomas forces a sharp gush of air down his nose, his shoulders rolled back, a muscle on his jaw feathering furiously. "What if they want *you* to join them?" he growls, pacing the room again. "I told you I won't share you. You're with me, and—"

"No. I'm not!" I tear myself out of the seat. "I only sleep with you. It's just sex! You have no right to dictate what I can and can't do. You won't control me!"

"That's it," Adrian seethes, standing over me while I press my back into the wall, my lip bleeding. "You don't leave the apartment without me, understood?! Every fucking douche bag on campus wants to fuck you!"

Tears are absent. I only cried the first few times Adrian took out his paranoia on me. Then, I stop crying. I stopped fighting too. There's no point to it... he's stronger. He always wins.

I wipe the blood off my chin with my sleeve. "Okay."

He's not appeased. There's no pattern to his behaviour. Words and actions that calmed him down last time just as easily infuriate him the next time he comes home high. I can't prepare because I never know what will work or make him stop.

The one constant is the reason behind his anger—me, or the mere idea of any guy getting anywhere near me. His territoriality gets out of hand on drugs, and Adrian sinks deeper into the madness.

He grabs my wrist, yanks me to my feet, then pins me to the wall, closing five fingers around my throat. "I'm not fucking kidding! You don't leave unless I'm with you."

Warm hands cup my face; long fingers disappear in my hair. I blink a few times, coming out of the vivid memory.

Thomas stands before me. The pressure of his worried, cinnamon eyes burns my cheeks. "It's not *just* sex, but I am sorry. I don't want to boss you around. That's not what I'm trying to do; I'm just worried."

"I know." I rest my forehead against his chest. "And I know why you're still here despite me proving time and time again that I'm not all there." I pat my head. "But I'll pretend I don't."

"Whatever you need." He sits back down, taking the laptop with him. "I know a place that organises male strip shows."

We drink the wine, organise the bachelorette party, and then we just lay there, talking until I fall asleep with my head nestled in the crook of his neck. It's the first evening we spend together and don't have sex.

Twenty-one

Asking for Trouble

NADIA

"Mum called last night. She asked about you." Nick treats me to a wary glance from the driver's seat of his Range Rover.

We're on our way to C&G Records. After only four weeks, he finally found time to show me around the place and let me meet some of the stars he mentors with Thomas.

I'm excited and annoyed too because Thomas won't be there. He's on his way to the airport, flying out to Madrid in two hours for a few days. He's got a meeting scheduled with a woman selling her late husband's independent record label.

He did show up early in the morning to say goodbye and make me come twice under the shower, but since he left, my mood's been deteriorating. I got used to his presence over the past two weeks, and now I'm supposed to survive almost four days without his help? Not likely.

"Will she be at the wedding?" I ask. It's a stupid question, one I know the answer to, but I can hope...

Nick doesn't despise our mother, so one of the two hundred

and fifty gift bags I assembled with Jane must be for Karen.

Taking the passenger seat in my brother's car, I was prepared for a few uncomfortable topics—Thomas, Adrian, and even my argument with Mel, but not our mother.

I've not spoken to her in three years, and I sure won't change that any time soon. Or ever, to be honest. I've no respect for her, and I still can't believe Nick forgave her for what she did at my eighteenth birthday party.

"Of course she'll be at the wedding. Don't you think it's time to let it go?"

Not the first time we're having this conversation. Any mention of Karen always ends with us arguing, but not today. I've got enough going on without adding the slutty, cheating, poor-excuse-for-a-mother to the equation. She's just not worth it.

"Why did you forgive her? I mean, he was your friend... I'm fuming at the very thought of seeing her face."

"I didn't forgive her. After a while, I learned to live with it. She's still our mother, sis. Do you really want to pretend for the rest of your life that she doesn't exist?"

That's the plan. Nick's wedding is the first and last time I'll be forced to see her face since Dad's funeral. She sure as hell won't be invited to my wedding.

I sigh, looking out the window. "I keep seeing the look on Dad's face when he caught them."

Arthur Grimwald was amazing. He considered his family his biggest accomplishment and gave us his undivided attention whenever possible. Karen was his muse, the love of his life. His winning lottery ticket, as he always called her. He never failed to show her how much she meant to him. We were a perfect family—the kind you only see in movies.

Until the night of my eighteenth birthday.

Karen cheated on Dad with Jake—Nick's friend from school and my crush of a few years. Dad found them in the guest bedroom when it was time for the cake.

Needless to say, the party was ruined. Karen's stuff started flying out the windows a moment later, and within a month, they were divorced. Dad was devastated. He couldn't move on. The only reason he kept it together was Nick and me, but I knew that Karen had destroyed him. Less than a year later, he died of a heart attack.

My world splintered apart that day.

I blamed Karen, and my hatred grew tenfold. She's pure evil. Devil incarnated. Nothing can change what I think of her because nothing can bring back Dad.

"Just let her explain." Nick plays the role of a mediator as always. "You never gave her a chance."

"I'll think about it." I won't, but lying is the fastest way out of this conversation.

Nick cocks an eyebrow. He's right to disbelieve me. There's no point in listening to Karen's excuses because what she did was inexcusable. Nothing justifies cheating. *Nothing.*

We turn right off the main road, and Nick parks the car in the Managing Director's spot next to Thomas's BMW. I guess he took a taxi.

We walk inside through a set of glass doors that open onto a spacious lobby. A reception desk stands in the centre, occupied by a stunning blonde. She greets us with a dazzling smile on her thin, red lips, getting up as if to show off her tight-fitted, grey dress accentuating her extra-long legs and extra-large boobs. She's gorgeous. A blue-eyed, blonde model. Thomas's perfection. My imagination fires up, creating images of them together... I push those aside fast. Thomas wouldn't sleep with anyone else while we have our deal.

He's a decent guy.

Nick nods at her and then takes me down a long corridor before the receptionist can try and introduce herself.

We reach another reception area where two black desks stand outside two pairs of doors. Looks like Nick and Thomas have private assistants.

I don't have to ask to know who works for who. Nick chose a young guy who rises to his feet when we approach and flashes me a beaming smile.

With a notepad in hand, he asks, "Can I get you a coffee?"

"Sure." The cheeky side of my personality arrives out of nowhere. I've not felt playful in so long that I don't dare fight it. "Tall, extra shot, extra-hot, extra-whip, sugar-free vanilla latte."

His smile slips, but he forces it back on, scribbling in the notepad. "No problem, I'll just be..." He scratches the back of his head. "I'll be just a moment."

"Relax, Anthony," a voice I know so well says, making my insides flutter. Thomas stands in the doorway to his office. He's not in a suit today, probably because it wouldn't be too comfortable on the plane. "She's messing with you. Black coffee, one sugar for Nadia, and the usual for us."

"Sorry," I say to Anthony, turning to Thomas. "Didn't you say your flight leaves at eleven?" I ask and immediately bite my tongue when Nick's head snaps to me.

"When did you talk?"

"Last night," Thomas says, just as I say, *this morning.* "Yeah, that too. Nadia needed help with the bachelorette party."

"Oh...." is all Nick says, shaking his head as if dismissing the information. "Why aren't you at the airport? Don't tell me she sold the label to someone else."

"No, but she rang saying she can't meet me until dinner time. Marie rebooked my flight." He looks at his assistant, his features pinching. "Manners, Marie."

She tears her round ass from the chair, and I wish she'd stay seated. High heels, an hourglass figure, boobs twice the size of mine, and a skirt that covers strategic parts only.

I glance at myself, embarrassed by the plain, yellow skater dress I chose for the day. I look about fifteen.

"We might as well get started and come back for the coffee

in a bit," Nick says, backing out to the main corridor. "Right, so those are our recording studios. They're all occupied, but Aaron's happy to let you watch him work." He opens the door to studio number three, letting me in first.

Goosebumps cover every inch of my skin when I hear the voice I love. The guy behind the glass wall is my age, and though he lacks good looks, his voice compensates. The song ends, and he peers up with a smile as he jumps off the chair.

"Hi, I'm Aaron. You must be Boss's sister. Nadia, is it? It's great to meet you. I hear you like my music." He speaks faster than a machine gun. "I heard a lot about you, but Nick forgot to mention how pretty you are."

My cheeks warm up. I'm not used to being complimented. "Thank you. You've got an incredible voice."

"Oh, do you want to hear more? You can stay here for a while. I'll sing for you." His straightforwardness is adorable.

"We just started the tour, but I might take you up on that when we're done."

"Please do." He winks, locking himself back in the booth when we turn to leave.

We tour the building, but nothing is as exciting as hearing Aaron sing, and half an hour later, we enter Thomas's office to drink our lukewarm coffees.

"Your taxi is here, *sir*." Marie stands in the doorway, blue gaze fixed on her boss. She bats her eyelashes, licking her lips.

I'm nauseous again. Images of Thomas's hands on her body flash before my eyes like a nasty fin out of the water. *No. No, okay? He wouldn't.*

I turn to Thomas, breathing a sigh of relief. He doesn't pay Marie any attention, his gaze fixed on *me*.

"Come on, baby doll." He grabs his travel bag. "We'll have a smoke, and I'll get going."

"Don't call her that," Nick clips.

We let his attitude slide and walk out the room, through the long, bright corridors and outside, turning left toward the smoking area. Thomas lights up his Zippo, then rests his back against the wall, taking my hand.

"Stop it," I hiss, but a smile ruins the effect.

"Nick can't see us here from my office." He tugs harder, making me take a step forward and rest against him.

We're asking for trouble.

"He's not the only one here."

A cloud of smoke hides his handsome face for a second, and then he dips his head devouring my lips in an affectionate kiss. This must be my favourite kiss to date. We're in public. Anyone can see. Nick might follow us out, but I don't care, parting my lips, tasting the coffee on Thomas's tongue.

"Call me when you need me." He kisses my head. "And call me when you don't need me." From the back pocket of his trousers, he takes out the keys to his car. "I'll come get it on Thursday when I land."

"You just want an excuse to come over straight from the airport. No excuse is needed. Call me when you land."

He drops the cigarette in the ashtray, grabs his travel bag and kisses me again. "I will, baby."

Two minutes later, the taxi disappears among other traffic on the main road, and I make my way back inside. Nick's talking to his assistant in the reception area outside his office. Marie walks past me, heading toward the restroom, and both Anthony and Nick watch her, wincing.

"It must be some kind of a record," Anthony says.

"It sure is. Either that, or he realised there's a limited number of blondes in London and wants to keep this one longer."

"You might be onto something, Boss. He asked her to stay after hours, not even a week after she started working here."

I stop by Nick, my stomach like a wrung-out rag, my legs spongy. Their words confirm what I suspected since we entered the building—Thomas is sleeping with his assistant.

He said he wouldn't share me with anyone, and I assumed it worked both ways... apparently not.

"Did he?" Nick asks, shaking his head. "I wish he'd quit fucking them in the office."

"At least he waited until we both left this time." Anthony looks at me with another smile. "Can I get you another coffee?"

"Um, no." I clear my throat. "No, thank you. I'll get going. I have somewhere to be."

Nick drapes his arm around my shoulders, making me shudder. I can't focus on anything other than Thomas and Marie. His hands on her hips, her lips on his neck, his dark eyes watching her come beneath him.

"Are you okay? You're pale, sis. What's wrong?"

"Nothing. I'm fine, but I should go. James is waiting."

He's not, but I need to run before I burst into tears. I peck Nick's cheek to calm him down and rush away, my eyes watering more with every step closer to the door as if it represents the end of Thomas and me.

***

I never felt like an artist, but since my early days, I loved the smell of pastels on my hands, the vivid colours and images that spilt from my imagination, filling a blank canvas with a part of my soul. As a child, I filled notebooks with scribbles and got quite good at drawing before I turned ten. Dad bought me a set of acrylic paints, professional brushes, and canvases for my twelfth birthday. The moment my brush touched the canvas, I felt at home. Years later, painting is still the main thing helping me clear my thoughts.

Not today.

I've been painting for two hours, hoping to forget about Thomas and his perfect blondes. Unsuccessfully. The painting looks as if I bled out on it.

I throw the brush aside, punch the canvas, making a hole, and almost fly down the stairs to turn off my phone. Thomas has called every few minutes, but I'm not ready to talk. Regret morphed to anger, and now I'm just mad.

Mad at Thomas for messing with my feelings, mad at myself for having those feelings, and mad because I agreed to the stupid no-strings-attached deal in the first place.

Drama queen much?

Hell yes. Aren't we all?

Apart from Anthony's words, I've got no hard evidence to prove Thomas slept with Marie, but I still feel cheated. The worst part is that I only have myself to blame, and now I need to find the safest way out of the situation.

The phone rings again, but this time it's Mel.

"Hey," I answer, taken aback that she decided to end the silent treatment. She's not the kind to apologise first.

"Look at that! Your phone works," she mocks, unaware she's fuelling the fire burning bright inside my head. "May I ask why you're not answering Thomas's calls?" Irony coats words, sticky like honey and the countdown on the bomb I am ticks faster. "He just called, asking me to check on you. Trouble in paradise, is it? *Boo-fucking-hoo.* Get a grip."

I take a bottle of white wine from the cupboard. I couldn't be more pathetic if I tried. "I don't want to talk to him."

"And you can't tell him that? You're adults, damn it! Act like it." She sighs, and her attitude changes, her tone now patronising. "He's worried. He's *worried.* I've never heard him like this. He's going crazy because you missed his call! You won't convince me it's just sex. What's the problem? What did he do?"

I shrug, aware she can't see that. "Nothing. Nothing I should be upset about... I saw Marie today and then heard Nick and Anthony talking. Looks like Thomas is sleeping with her." A jab of anger jolts me back upright. "I'm so pissed off! He didn't promise me anything, Mel. We were just supposed to

enjoy good sex, so why do I feel so... *used?*"

"I told you he's not a monogamist, honey."

She has to get the *I told you so* out of her system, or else she'll get ill. At least she's trying not to sound condescending.

"I know. I remember." I fill my glass to the brim, then throw half at the back of my throat as if it's a shot. "I thought we were exclusive. I know I was." I fall back on the couch again, hugging a pillow. I stare at the Puppeteer piece on the wall. Once again, I wonder if I gave up on Adrian too soon.

"Ladies' night!" Mel exclaims. "You need a girls' night out. I can't tonight, but we'll go out tomorrow. You can drown the sorrows in tequila."

A small, pathetic laugh flies past my lips. A few shots won't help, but tequila won't do any harm. I'm not even sure if I'm more upset about losing Thomas or the peace he offered.

The latter is more probable.

But it's also such a goddamn lie.

Maybe it's not a bad idea to call it quits. He's a player, but he deserves more than someone like me. It's cruel keeping him close and expecting that he'll piece me together when half of the elements are missing.

Twenty-two

Thanks, but no thanks

NADIA

Nick parks the Range Rover outside Vertigo—Mel's favourite cocktail bar.

She jumps out, blowing him a kiss. "We'll get a taxi back."

"No, you won't. Call me when you're done. I'll pick you up. And take care, okay?"

We nod, closing the door, so he can head home and enjoy a few hours of peace. He deserves an evening without Mel more than anyone.

We enter the bar, greeted by an overdressed bouncer. Jazz music filters throughout the spacious room, creating a relaxed background noise for quiet conversations. Mel blends with the crowd in a fashionable emerald dress and too much jewellery. Nick's been spoiling her rotten over the past two years. She now owns enough bling-bling to rival a small jewellery shop.

I'm not blending in so well in a black, tailored, sweetheart neck jumpsuit and a single, delicate necklace. I like dresses, but sometimes I don't want to watch how I sit.

Brown leather sofas surround small tables and framed pictures of London at night hang on the walls covered in red wallpaper. A couple pool tables and dart boards stand at the back, a long bar to the left.

"A bottle of tequila, please." I pull a bank card out of my clutch bag.

The bartender looks us over, one eyebrow raised. I think he doubts we can polish a whole bottle by ourselves. Drinking isn't the problem. It's getting up afterwards that poses a challenge.

Mel takes the tray with shot glasses and tequila, leaving me to grab the salt and a bowl of lemon slices. We climb onto high chairs by the window, downing two shots one after another while Mel fills the silence, telling me Nick's opinion on the flowers and menu choices.

"I'm beyond confused, Mel," I interrupt her monologue about pink orchids, focusing on a small scratch on the table above a metal plaque with the number seven. "I won't tell you everything, but I'll paint part of the picture so you can understand me better and give me some advice. Okay?"

She drapes her red locks over one shoulder. "You know I'll listen whenever you want to talk."

I wish I could tell her everything, but I can't find a reason that'd justify breaking her heart a few weeks ahead of the wedding. She loves me. Knowing what Adrian did would affect her almost as much as my brother.

"There are many things that came together to tip the scales, forcing me to leave Adrian. They say the fault is always on both sides, but not in this case. We fell apart because of him." I massage my temples, chasing away the memories. "I wasn't okay when I left London, but Adrian helped me through the mourning. Now that I'm back, I'm worse than when I left, and it's all his fault." A bitter, sad chuckle slips past my lips. "I'm ashamed that I'm not doing better. I'm ashamed of the anxiety, the panic attacks and the fear that puts my life on hold. I'm taking steps in the right direction, though. James sorted through my meds. I no longer swallow pills like candy. It's a start."

Mel listens with growing concern in her green eyes. She chews on her bottom lip, fidgeting. "What meds?"

"Just diazepam and sleeping pills now." I point at the bottle, encouraging her to fill the shot glasses. She sure looks like she needs a few extra rounds to absorb the information. "I have panic attacks; I can't control my emotions; I hardly sleep... the list goes on, but I think you get what I mean."

"Why didn't you tell me before? I would've helped you sooner! I don't know how, but we'd've come up with something. You can't deal with this alone."

I swallow the disgusting liquor in sync with Mel, wincing as it burns a trail down my oesophagus, warming me up from the inside. "That's the problem. I'm *not* alone. I have Thomas. He's the only person I feel comfortable with, the only one whose touch I don't mind."

"You're bothered when someone touches you?"

Her reaction to that little piece of information proves that keeping the truth to myself is a good choice. I'm already uncomfortable seeing the worry in her eyes, and if she finds out that Adrian used me as his punching bag for months, she'll break down. And I'll break down with her.

She doesn't need that.

I don't need that. Not when I'm getting back on track.

"It's surreal, I know. When Thomas is with me, I'm not afraid. And if that's not enough, after those few weeks with him, I see a change even when he's not around."

Shame burns my cheeks. Admitting to helplessness isn't pleasant. There was a time in my life when I couldn't understand why people were depressed. I didn't understand how they couldn't talk themselves out of sadness or couldn't control their emotions. Dad's death and Adrian's abuse taught me a vital lesson—a mind can become a prison, and fear can destroy a

person from the inside out.

"It's too much to process so quickly," Mel says. "I don't know where to start! I'm so damn sorry you feel this way. I'm here for you, okay? I'll do whatever I can to help."

She can't just wave a wand to make the negative emotions go away. No one can. Not even Thomas. He only dials down the screams in my head. He's not a cure, though. Just a powerful form of therapy.

"I know. I'm sorry I'm only telling you now and that it's still not everything, but it's difficult."

Amelia grabs my hand, brushing the pad of her thumb over my knuckles, then jerks her hand back as if remembering what I said about being touched. "You told Nick he didn't, but I need to ask again. Did Adrian cheat on you? You can tell me, babe."

Another opportunity to take the easy way out goes to hell, but this time I say *no* not because I don't think better of it, but because I do.

Hiding behind lies will hurt them even more if the truth sees daylight. Many things can be said about Adrian, but not that he's a cheater. He loves me. He loves me more than anything, and he'd never touch another woman. I can't accuse him of something he didn't do.

"Okay, I had to know. As for Thomas..." She toys with her engagement ring. "He's different since he met you. He tries to keep up the careless image when he's with Nick, but he's not fooling anyone. Nick sees right through him, but he pretends he has no idea that there's something going on between you."

"It's just sex, Mel."

"Not to Thomas. We talked for an hour yesterday. It's the longest conversation I've had with him since *ever*. You got under his skin more than you think."

"Not enough if he can't give up the perfect blondes, and I won't be one of many."

Mel takes her phone out, showing me a text message.

Thomas: Remember to call me when you're done.

"Why does he want you to call?"

"Because he wants to know you got home safe. I can't believe I'm saying this, but I'm pretty sure Thomas is a monogamist now and has been since you came back from New York." A grin stretches her lips, making it hard not to smile too. "Call him. I know you want to. He called me five times today to check on you. He's worried and miserable."

So am I. Instead of telling him, we're over, I ignore his calls, afraid to push him away, afraid that I'll never let him go, and afraid that fear will win every time. It's not fair to him. Cheating is the one thing I won't forgive, but it's hard to talk about cheating when I have no proof.

And is it even cheating if we're just sex buddies?

"Did you tell him why I'm not answering his calls?"

Amelia turns pink. "I'm sorry... I snapped. No one can treat you like the third wheel!" She slams her fists on the table, then drops them to her lap. "I shouted at him a little."

Shouted a little in Mel's dictionary translates to *screamed her head off, swearing and threatening to castrate him.* There aren't many people worthy of Amelia's protectiveness, but those who are, get a bodyguard straight from hell. If she could, she'd tear apart everyone who says one foul word about people she loves.

"Come on, call him. Please. Do it for me," she whines, hands clasped together as if she's praying.

"Change of sides again?"

"For the last time now. I swear. I'll be rooting for you two like you rooted for Nick and me."

We drink another shot, and I rest my forehead on the cool table. If not for tequila, I'd spend a few more hours overanalysing, but José doesn't let me overthink.

"Get another bottle to go, call Nick and meet me outside."

She salutes, gathers her things, and walks away toward the

bar. Tequila whooshes in my head when I stand. I don't feel drunk, but my lack of coordination proves me wrong. I head outside, stopping around the corner and resting against the wall, a cigarette between my lips.

A phone call to Thomas while tequila courses through my veins, speaking for me might not be a good idea, but a decision once made shouldn't be questioned. I press the phone to my ear, exhaling smoke.

"Hey, sweetie, why are you here alone?" a tall blond guy in rimless glasses asks, appearing beside me out of freaking nowhere. "Pretty girls like you aren't safe here. You could get hurt. I'm Max. Are your friends around here somewhere?"

"Are you hitting on me?" Tequila says all fearless and arrogant. Stupid, too. His words don't hint he's into me. "Thanks, but no thanks."

"What are you talking about?" Thomas says in my ear.

Max gently cuffs my wrist. "You had too much to drink, didn't you? You shouldn't be alone."

I free my hand. Anxiety arrives acting better than smelling salts. "Don't touch me."

"Nadia, what's wrong? Who's there?" Thomas asks.

I turn on my heel, taking a few hasty steps away. As luck would have it, I step on a pebble, twist my ankle and fall face first on the pavement.

So very gracious.

The phone slips out of my grasp, bouncing off the kerb. The screen turns black.

"No need to do that." Max takes my arm, helping me up, then gathers my phone off the street and hands it back. "I'm genuinely just trying to look out for you. You're very pretty and a bit drunk. We both know this city is full of idiots." He crouches before me, pressing his fingers to my ankle. "Tell me if it hurts."

"It doesn't." I move my leg back, frowning at the intricate

web of cracks marking the screen of my phone. Great. Just great. I look back at Max. "Who are you?"

"As I said, I'm Max. And you are...?"

"Nadia!" Amelia screams, rounding the corner with a bottle of tequila in one hand and a phone pressed to her ear. "Oh my God," she pants, staring at the guy beside me. "*Oh my God!*"

She tucks the bottle in her bag, shoving her phone in there, eyes permanently glued to Max.

"Nadia," he echoes, testing the word. "It's French, isn't it?"

"You-You're..." Mel stutters, striding closer, her cheeks flushed pink. "You're Max Gawn!"

He smirks under his nose, gracing my exhilarated best friend with a cursory glance. "Yes, I am. Who are you?"

"I'm your biggest fan! Amelia Roberts, soon-to-be Grimwald."

I stifle a laugh. Mel sure is one of a kind. Looks like Max is famous, but I've no idea who he is. An actor? A singer? A news presenter? You'd think Mel would be used to famous people by now. She's surrounded by them daily.

"I've seen all your movies! You're *amazing!*" she continues, pulling out a notepad and a pen. "Can I please have an autograph?"

"Sure. You must be the first person in forever who hasn't asked for a picture."

She face-palms herself, muttering under her breath, "Picture, or it didn't happen. Can I have a picture too?"

Max signs a blank page in the notepad, then wraps his arm around swooning Mel, letting her take more selfies than necessary. She steps away, flushed and bothered.

Nick wouldn't approve.

"What a coincidence! I mean, I know you live here, but this is crazy!"

The sound of a large engine halts their conversation. A black Mercedes rounds the corner, and tyres squeal when it stops by the kerb, five feet from where we're standing. Scorpio shoots out from the driver's seat, leaving the door open and the engine

running. His eyes rove over my body as if looking for injuries.

"What are you doing here?" I ask.

"What do you think? I'm making sure Thomas doesn't fucking sprint back here. What the hell happened? He's losing his shit. Why aren't you picking up from him?" he asks Mel.

The pink shade of her cheeks disappears, leaving her skin ashen. "Oh God..." She looks at me wide-eyed. "He was on the phone thinking something happened to you when I saw Max."

All she said was *Oh my God* before she cut the call. I snatch her phone, dialling his number.

"Mel, what the hell is happening?" he fumes, a magnitude of powerful emotions ringing in his voice.

"It's me. I'm fine, and—"

"Baby," he breathes, letting out all the air from his lungs and waking up millions of butterflies in my belly. "What happened? Who was that guy? Did he hurt you?"

"No, I'm okay. He's an actor. He was looking out for me, but I misread his intentions." I send Max an apologetic smile. "Mel's a fan. She got a little carried away when she saw him."

"You scared the hell out of me. God, I'm glad you're okay. Is Scorpio there yet?"

I hand the phone to Scorpio, turning around when Max places his hand on my shoulder.

"I'll leave you now. You're in good hands."

"Thank you."

Mel swoons some more, lusting after him when he disappears out of view, and a moment later, Scorpio hands her the phone. She starts apologising before Thomas can say a word, and Scorpio opens the passenger side door.

"Get in. I'm taking you home."

Mel takes the back seat, muttering *okay*, and *I'm sorry* a few times before she hands the phone back to me.

"Amelia told me why you've been ignoring my calls," Thomas says, sounding calmer.

"This isn't a good time." I rest my head against the side window. "We'll talk when you get back."

"I won't let you wonder for two days if I'm being a selfish asshole. I'm not. It's just you, doll. I want you, and I'm yours."

I bite my cheek, glancing at Scorpio, who watches the road in great concentration. The bed creaks on the other side of the line, and I imagine Thomas in a snow-white t-shirt and sweatpants, sitting on a neat bed in his hotel room.

"I believe you, but now, I have to go."

Scorpio stops the car outside Nick's house ten minutes later and turns to me when Mel leaves, clutching the notepad to her chest. "You know, when he told me about you two the first time, I was ready to kick his ass because I wanted to protect you. Now, I think he's the one who needs protecting. He's a good guy, Nadia. Don't hurt him."

"I know he is. We have rules, as you may know, and Thomas knows better than to let me hurt him."

Scorpio scoffs, switching the gear to reverse. "I don't think he does."

Twenty-three

Lie better

THOMAS

The room's stuffy despite the open windows, which don't let the cool air in. That's because there's no cool air around. The clock shows twenty past one in the morning, but the temperature outside still oscillates around twenty degrees Celsius.

Welcome to España.

I sit in a comfortable armchair by the bed, the night lamp on, a glass of vodka in hand. The hotel bar closed at midnight, but the bellboy was rather keen to fetch me a drink. This isn't my first visit. He knows I tip well.

Instead of staring at the open window, sipping vodka, I should sleep. I've got another meeting scheduled for nine a.m., but the remnants of worry linger at the back of my mind, poking and prodding. I spent two days on high alert, calling Nadia on repeat. The moment my calls started hitting the answering machine, I figured out why she wasn't answering. A sense of unease, a dull ache like a headache, dropped over me when an unwanted thought entered my mind after the fifth time the machine answered for her—she's done with me.

If that wasn't enough to send my mind into overdrive, then Mel's seemingly terrified *Oh my God* a moment after I heard someone hitting on Nadia did the trick. I never went from calm to confused, annoyed and fucking scared faster.

Possible scenarios infested my mind, stripping me of the ability to think straight. Five minutes passed while I paced the room, waiting for Scorpio to arrive at the scene or Amelia to answer her phone.

The longest five minutes of my goddamn life.

Jesus, I'm losing it.

Losing it over a girl.

A girl who...

Sounds familiar? Good. You remember what happened last time I was losing it over this girl?

Yeah? Well... *replay.*

Unfortunately, the hotel room left a lot to be desired when it came to things that could be trashed. All I did was kick the armchair, pacing back and forth between the door and the window, a phone to my ear.

Not very dramatic.

Just as fast as the fear arrived, it died away when I heard my girl's voice. No whimpers, no sobs.

Yes, that's right. My *girl.*

Nadia can fight me all she wants, but I'll fight back just as hard until she waves the white flag and admits she wants more than we agreed. She's already taken small steps across the bridge leading straight to me.

My phone chimes on the nightstand.

Nadia looks at me from the illuminated screen. I took the picture like a true psycho pervert—on the sly, without her knowing. She's not smiling. She's not sad. She's *calm*—the most beautiful expression she can wear.

My doll: I promised to call when I wake up, but I don't have the

heart to wake you. I doubt you meant the middle of the night...

We talked for forty minutes when Scorpio dropped her off at Nick's. She fell asleep while I told her about the record label I toured earlier, trying to decide if it was worth the asking price. I didn't realise my work was so boring, but there you go.

The sad part? I don't mind. At least I know she fell asleep without pills.

The yet-another psycho pervert part? I listened to her steady breathing for ten minutes before I cut the call.

That girl has me wrapped around her finger. She's all I think about. The one person I want to spend time with non-stop. I've been gone two days, but I miss her like I've been gone for a month.

How did my life plan change so drastically during a few weeks? I turned from a rowdy, arrogant playboy without dreams into a rowdy, arrogant man with one goal—make Nadia mine.

It scares me. I can't make sense of my thoughts and choices half the time. The sudden territoriality and jealousy surprises me at every turn. I'm confused but determined because I like what Nadia does to me. For the first time in years, I'm looking into the future impatiently, not indifferently.

I dial her number, making myself comfortable on the bed. She answers before the first ringback tone ends.

"I didn't peg you for a light sleeper. Sorry."

"I'm not sleeping. You were supposed to call. If I were asleep, a text message wouldn't wake me."

"I didn't want to wake you." She lets out an exasperated puff. "Okay, I did. I had a bad dream."

"Do you want to tell me about it?"

"No. I just wanted to hear you. I miss you." She weighs the words, pausing for three heartbeats. "And I don't mean sex. I miss *you*."

"I miss you too, baby. So fucking much..." I say on a sigh. "I should've sent Nick here. I'll be back in two days."

"You sure know how to make a girl impatient." She chuckles, the sound making me fucking swell inside. "Can't you come back now? Pretty please?"

Say no more.

Eighteen hours later, I land at Heathrow after paying the lawyer twice the agreed sum so he'd get the paperwork finalised before noon. All in all, including a new plane ticket, I spent an extra seven grand getting back to Nadia ahead of schedule.

All because she said *please*.

She makes me no less crazy than Maya. The difference is that Claudia holds back my extravagant ideas wherever Maya's concerned. There's no one who'd talk sense into me where Nadia's involved, and I don't bother capping the crazy.

I get in the first taxi outside the terminal building, giving the driver Nadia's address. It's almost ten p.m. when I barge into her flat uninvited and unannounced.

Soft footsteps start in the living room, and Nadia rounds the corner coming to an abrupt stop when she sees me. "You came back."

"You asked." I shrug as if it's not a big deal.

Her face brightens, and just then, a chubby Cupid shoots his arrow right in my ass. The smile on her lips is the prettiest *thank you* I've ever seen.

She grabs my tie, pulling me down for a kiss. "You're crazy, you know? You didn't have to come back early."

I drop the suitcase, taking her face in my hands, enjoying the happy sparks dancing in her eyes. Nothing makes me more euphoric than knowing she's perfectly calm.

"No, I didn't, but I wanted to." I kiss her head. "I need a shower, fresh clothes, and you in my bed, coming on my lips. In that order. Grab whatever you need."

She frowns, stepping back. "What kind of a gentleman are you? Why should I take a taxi home in the middle of the night? Forget it. My shower works just fine, and you don't need clothes

in bed. Also, I—"

"You won't be taking a taxi. You're staying the night."

I don't expect her to agree. She clings to the no-strings-attached idea despite knowing we're way past being just physical, so she throws me way off when her lips part, but no words come, and then she nods.

I take it as a good sign at first, but once she goes upstairs, I realise she hopes her nightmares will scare me away...

Five minutes later, she comes back with a small travel bag and a cheeky smile. "I have something for you. Well, kind of." She winks, pretending to zip her lips.

There's no point in asking.

To be honest, when she enters my bedroom after a long, hot shower a little over an hour later, I'm fucking glad I didn't ask. Wet hair sticks to her neck and shoulders, glowing skin bathed in the orange, dimmed lights.

All I can do is sit, unable to word a coherent sentence. Unable to tear my eyes off her. I bite my knuckles, taking in her flawless body dressed in red lingerie with ribbons attached to her bra and panties, tied into a bow on her stomach.

She's imperfectly perfect inside out. Bruised, unstable... irresistible. I just know, watching the small smile on her lips, that I won't fall in love with her.

No. I'm already in love with her.

"The look on your face makes me want to run," she says, straddling me.

I brush my fingers down her spine, closing her lips with a kiss, ready to dive between her thighs. She stopped me every time I tried that before, but it ends tonight. I need to know how she tastes. I want her to come on my lips, and I'm not resting until that happens.

"Why?" I touch her hips, digging my fingers into her warm skin. "Why do you want to run, baby?"

"Because you're hoping for more... lie to me."

206

"You're delusional."

"Lie better. Please."

"I don't want more," I say, contradicting the words with a kiss. "I don't want you to be mine."

She rolls my t-shirt up and over my head, resting her tiny palms on my chest. "I don't want you to touch me."

Her hot lips ghost across my jawline. I catch her wrists, flipping her, so she's flat on the bed.

"Lie better," I echo, turning a fantasy into reality as I untie the red bow with my teeth.

"I don't want you to want more."

I unclasp her bra, closing my mouth on her breast, toying with candy-hard nipples. "Tell me what you did when I was gone," I whisper, pulling the red panties down her legs.

"I... *ooh*," her eyes fly open when I circle her clit with two fingers. "I-I... I can't talk when you're doing this."

"Try. Tell me what you did."

"I told you last night," she utters, fisting the sheets. "We talked on the phone, remember?"

"You told me what you did during the day. I want to know what you did at night." I graze her nipple with my teeth, then soothe the gentle sting with my tongue, intensifying the attack of my fingers, drawing tight circles over her clit. "Did you touch yourself thinking about me?"

Her cheeks heat and her eyes fly open. "That's non—"

"I did. I missed you so fucking much I couldn't wait." I kiss a line of open-mouthed kisses up her neck, then bite her ear as I push two fingers inside her. "Did you? Did you miss me?"

"Yes," she pants, weaving her fingers in my hair. She steers my face and seals my lips with a kiss. "Twice. I imagined that you were touching me. That I was at that hotel with you."

"Next time, you will be with me. Now, close your eyes."

She does, and I immediately dive between her thighs, hooking her legs over my back. I don't give her time to protest. No

time to push me away. I've waited too long already. It's been years since I last went down on a girl, but I've imagined my head between Nadia's thighs daily since I first pushed inside her.

I lick her bottom to top, flicking my tongue over her clit. Fucking finally. She squirms, throwing her head back, fingers fisting the bedsheets.

"Thomas—"

"Don't think, baby. *Feel.*"

She bucks against me, her spine arching away from the bed when I push two fingers in, stroking her G spot, and she floods my mouth, her arousal coating my tongue. She tastes so fucking good. Her pussy clenches around my fingers, her breaths coming closer together, short and strained the closer she gets.

I suck harder, increasing the tempo of my fingers, and not even a minute later, I look up, watching her thrash on the bed, her walls pulsing around my fingers as she comes, lips parted, pure, unrestrained pleasure painting her gorgeous face. I'll never grow tired of seeing her like this.

"There it is," I smile, dipping my head to lick her clean, my fingers easing the attack. She buckles with every sweep of my tongue, oversensitive and overstimulated. "From now on, you don't get to deny me this, Nadia."

"Mhm," she mumbles, eyes still closed, a ghost of a smile tilting her mouth. "That was nice."

"Nice?" I chuckle, shimmying out of my clothes. "You're hurting my ego, doll. Calling that *nice* is like calling my dick *little.* Chose a different word."

Her bright eyes pop open when I climb over her, parting her legs with my knee. She knots her fingers on my nape, yanking me down for a kiss. "It was mindblowing."

"Better," I say, sitting back on my calves.

My heart thuds against my ribs as I grip her ankles, resting them on my shoulders. A veil of dark hair is scattered around her face, her glossy eyes full of wonder. How can she be so gorgeous? So fucking perfect?

I push inside her slowly, watching her mouth fall open. High on the look on her face. High on how surreal this is. The pace of my thrusts differs from the previous times we had sex. I'm not rushing. The slow rhythm of our bodies moving together speaks the truths we can't say with words.

We can't because we're not ready for declarations and empty promises. The road to happiness is paved with small bridges we have to cross first.

That's okay. The wait, the work, the uncertainty—okay, because something changed. We went from desperately keeping our relationship purely sexual to accepting it's a lost fight.

We waved the white flag and let fate do its thing.

Nadia ghosts her small fingers up my thighs, arching off the bed to dig her fingers into my ribs, trying to pull me down.

"I won't let you down," I say, covering her body with mine, her legs falling onto the bed, knees bent.

I nuzzle my face in the crook of her neck, biting the soft flesh. I want to mark her, suck her skin until a hickey appears, but I don't. I just drive into her as if she's my fucking lifeline, pinning her to the mattress with the weight of my body, kissing the nape of her neck when she vibrates under me, coming with a staccato of soft moans on her lips.

She's not overly audible in bed, but I'd take those breathless gasps over any ecstatic screams. My own orgasm comes like a fucking earthquake, building in the base of my spine and erupting so suddenly I see black spots before my eyes. We're both still catching our breath when I roll onto the side, kissing her head when she flips onto her stomach. She looks at me from under long lashes as I cover her with the sheets.

"I'll be back in a beat," I say, kissing her again—shoulder this time. I can't fucking stop kissing her when she's this close.

I lock myself in the bathroom, splashing my face with cold water, chasing away the sleepiness creeping up on me. I'm

determined not to let myself sleep until Nadia nods off, but when I enter the bedroom again, she's already out. I snake my arm around her waist, pulling her warm, limp body closer.

That's a first.

I've never had a girl stay the night. I probably won't get much sleep considering her nightmares and general insomnia, but I'm so fucking glad she's here.

I'm prepared for a wake-up call at any given moment, but Nadia doesn't move all night. I'm the one waking up every hour on the hour. The alarm that blares at five-thirty doesn't wake her either. She's still asleep an hour later when I come back upstairs after working out in my home gym, and she sleeps still when, just after seven, I accidentally slam the wardrobe door. No one expects me in the office until tomorrow, so with a laptop and a coffee, I sit by the window in the bedroom catching up on work.

And Nadia's still asleep.

She wakes up three hours later, her hair a mess, as she glances around the room, stretching out like a pussycat. A soft smile curves her lips when her rested eyes stop on me.

"Good morning, sleepyhead."

"What time is it?" she asks.

"Half-past ten."

Her eyes grow wide, and she sits up, clearly alarmed. The bedsheets slip down her body revealing perfect breasts and hard nipples. I must've done something right in life to deserve this.

"I slept for ten hours straight," she mutters, covering my favourite view. "I didn't wake up once."

"No. You slept like a baby."

If it's the first time she has slept through the night in months, I can understand her surprise. There's no fear in her eyes, so I sit behind her, wrapping her in my arms and wait until she stops overthinking. She pulls away a moment later, taking the bedsheets with her as she climbs out of bed.

I catch her wrist. "Are you okay?"

"I'm always okay when I'm with you."

Somehow, that doesn't sound one bit convincing. She retreats to the bathroom, closing the door behind her, and my head hits the headrest hard. Something in her voice, a kind of dread, has me bracing for a breakup. *Again.*

And I don't think we're even officially dating yet.

The few weeks we've spent together are enough for me to know her way of thinking. Right now, instead of being happy that nightmares didn't bother her all night, she'll turn it around, making it look like a bad thing. Like it's wrong that she's calm around me.

Nadia's phone vibrates on the bedside table a moment after the shower starts running. Mel's calling, but before I make up my mind about whether I should answer, she calls my phone.

"Where's Nadia?" she huffs.

"Taking a shower. Should I pass a message?"

"Yes, tell her I'll pick her up in ten, and she better be ready. I have the dress fitting in half an hour."

"Can't you go alone today? She could use a day off."

"Does Nick know you're back early?"

I like Mel, but right now, I imagine my fingers clasped around her thin neck, squeezing the breath out of her. We talked a lot over the past few days when Nadia wasn't answering my calls. I was under the impression that Mel has my back. She was happy that I care about her best friend and even gave me advice.

"Whose side are you on?"

She huffs some more. "Yours. If I weren't, my fiancé would turn your balls into blown eggs by now. Be nice and don't mess with my schedule. Nadia was at my disposal today. I'll turn a blind eye this time, but try pulling that shit again, and I'll take all your toys!" Her stern tone is ruined when she chuckles.

She's like a firecracker—a loud bang and an impressive explosion that lasts a few seconds at best.

"Fine. You can pick her up from my house in two hours."

"I'll be at work by then. Just drop her off at the venue."

I use the time while Nadia's taking a shower to brew two coffees. When I return upstairs, she's already dressed in heels, slim black jeans and a white vest, brushing her hair out.

"Mel called—"

"I know. I called her back." She gathers her things, focused on the task. "Can you take me to James?"

No eye contact doesn't bode well for me, but I won't let her put a cross on us this easily. She's halfway through the bridge, and instead of pressing forward, she glanced down.

"Tell me what you're thinking." I hand her a coffee.

"I don't know what I'm thinking. I just... I don't know. You make me whole again. I'm taking advantage of you, and you're still here." Her attitude changes, the fake calmness exploding into mortified annoyance. She throws her hands in the air, pointing at me, eyes narrowed, bitch-face on display. "What is *wrong* with you?! Why aren't you running?!"

"You act like I didn't know what I was getting into," I say, leaning my weight against the doorframe. "Like you forced me to do something against my will. I volunteered."

"Yeah, because you wanted to fuck me."

I almost fucking laugh at the piss-poor attempt at riling me up. She's adorable when she's mad. "Because I wanted *you* for myself. And I still do. I accepted the rules you set out, and I'd still adhere to them if I thought you didn't give a shit about me, but you do. You want me. You want *more*," I say, taking a few steps toward her. "You're just afraid to admit it."

Silence falls upon us, ringing in my ears. Every passing second pushes me that much closer to madness. She sure knows how to build tension. It's like some freak horror movie when nothing happens, but you just know someone will jump out of nowhere and scare you senseless.

She exhales slowly, biting her lip, eyes full of uncertainty.

"I need to see James." She zips her travel bag and rises on her toes, kissing my lips. "There's so much I'm working through... I don't want you to get hurt."

"I'm not afraid of your past, baby. I'm afraid you'll let it ruin our present."

Twenty-four

Puppet

NADIA

The road to hell is paved with good intentions.

Funny. It seems the road to heaven is paved with selfish deeds. My relationship with Thomas hit a crossroads. He wants more despite knowing he's falling for damaged goods. I want more despite knowing Adrian still has a hold on me.

"You're always overthinking," James says, sipping his coffee. "You complicate simple things. I'm not allowed to tell you what you should do, Nadia, but you *know* what to do."

"I allow you," I say with a smile. "Let's pretend you're not my doctor. Just be a friend. Is it cruel that I want to be with Thomas when I'm still not out of the woods?" I kick my heels off, tucking my feet under my bum. "At first, I thought he was just an anaesthetic, but he's more. The longer I'm around him, the bigger my progress. I hugged Nick the other day and didn't mind his closeness."

"Well, *friend*. If you only want to be with him because he's helping you, then yes—it's cruel, but if you have feelings for him, the help he offers is just a bonus."

The longer I think about it, the more convinced I am that I've had feelings for Thomas since day one. Nothing but physical attraction at first, coupled with how normal he made me feel, but it quickly turned into more than that. Maybe it's partly why I fought him at first because, deep down, I knew friends-with-benefits wouldn't work for long.

I was protecting him from day one.

My phone rings and the ringtone alone makes my skin crawl. Soft, bluesy guitar riffs of "Stay Around a Little Longer" by Buddy Guy captivate my mind, soul, and all my senses. James's office becomes a blur, his voice distorted, a string of incomprehensible gibberish.

How on earth did he get my number? I changed it the day he was locked away in the rehab facility. No one has my new number save for Thomas, Amelia, Nick—

Nick.

Bile climbs up my throat. I can't catch a breath at the mere thought of my brother talking to Adrian and finding out the reason I fled New York. I slide my thumb across the screen, staring into the distance. All I see is Adrian's face; all I feel are his Eskimo kisses all over my face.

He breathes down the line introducing a wave of tingles down my spine. "Puppet," he whispers on a sigh. "Please don't hang up."

I can't move. I can't force words past my lips, my head like a giant screen divided into hundreds of squares, each playing a different memory.

He sniffles, inhaling deeply. "I miss you so much, Puppet. I miss you like crazy. I promise I'll do everything I can so you'll trust me again. I'm clean. I swear."

He sounds desperate... so sincere. I feel myself tremble, focused on the words, the tone of his voice and the unspoken *I'm sorry*, and *I love you* between the lines.

"Hey," I say, eyes closed. "How are you?"

His choked-back sob almost breaks my heart all over again. "I'm good. I'm better. Clean, sober. I'll be out in a couple of weeks. How are you, Puppet? Are you safe? Just tell me you're safe. I've been worried sick."

"I'm safe."

I hate hearing him hurt. He suffered so much, and now he has to live with everything he's done. He might be a fighter in the ring, but inside, my Adrian is an emotional soul. Now that he's sober and thinks clearly, the weight of the abuse he put me through is turning him inside out.

"Thank God. Can you visit me? Please, I want to see you."

A tear rolls down my cheek, falling onto my jeans to leave a wet mark. "No, I can't."

It doesn't sound like I mean it. I'm not sure I do. I just want him to keep talking in that soothing tone. There's no cell in my body that's not ruled by fear, but with every word he speaks, I'm relaxing more. Memories of the good times outweigh the bad things that crippled our relationship.

Adrian's a magician. He hurt me beyond measure, but the love and regret behind his every word crack the foundations of my defence walls as if I built them in a sinking city.

"Please, I need to apologise. I need to tell you how sorry I am, and how much I miss you, and how much I lo—"

"Don't say it," I squeal, scared half to death of how those three words will affect me. I hug my knees, rocking back and forth like a child terrified of the monster hiding under the bed.

"I love you, Puppet. I love you so much. I won't survive another day without you."

"Stop. Please, stop saying that," I plead, growing more hysterical by the second.

"I'll never stop. I'll always love you. I need you, I need to see you, and I need to kiss you. God, I miss your lips; I miss the way you taste. You're everything I need, Puppet."

I shut my eyes tighter, blocking the memories his words summon. The endless nights and days I spent in his arms, the soft kisses, the most endearing confessions, and the three words that make my heart skip a beat. Memories that make me want to board the next plane so he can tell me how much he loves me face to face.

"You called Nick, didn't you? What did you tell him?"

"Nothing, Puppet. I swear. Why didn't *you* tell him? You shouldn't protect me, baby. He should know what I did, and he should hate my fucking guts. I know I do."

"He shouldn't know. What good will it do? It'll only break him, and I won't do that to him. Neither will you. Promise me."

"I do. I promise, Puppet. Whatever you want. I leave rehab in two weeks. I can still make the wedding."

A firm grip on my shoulder jolts me out of the haze. James crouches before me, his eyebrows drawn together, face paler than normal. The hypnotic state Adrian trapped me in disperses, and I allow myself to hear James's voice.

"Should I call Nick?"

I shake my head *no*.

"Who is that?" Adrian asks, his tone defeated.

"I'm glad you're better, but I don't want you to come."

I press the red button, cutting the call. My hands shake just like my entire body, jolted by silent tears. How could he isolate me like that? Why does my own subconscious still see him as the victim?

The bluesy melody fills the silence again, but this time I don't answer, and when he stops calling, I block his number and delete it from my contacts just in case.

We can't stay in touch if I want to heal.

"He manipulates you," James says, the doctor-patient front long gone. "Don't fall for it, Nadia. He'll be an addict for the rest of his life. Don't let him trick you into taking him back. You'll live in fear forever."

He's right, but Adrian's call isn't the worst that happened today. Nick gave him my number...

"I need all the pills you took from me."

"No way. I gave you what—"

"Please. I need to show Nick why he should never hope I'll get back with Adrian. I can't tell him the truth, but I can show him the state Adrian left me in."

Twenty-five

Crazy rooster

THOMAS

Scorpio rubs his hands together. "I'm taking all your money tonight, boys."

Yeah, right. We've been playing poker at Nick's house every Wednesday for over a year now, and Scorpio won maybe ten games total.

"In your dreams. It's my lucky night." Ethan picks up his cards, his smile slipping.

I throw my chips on the pile. "I bet a hundred."

Nick grumbles, tossing his cards aside. "I fold."

Poker nights were his idea, but he rarely wins. The saying goes *lucky at cards, unlucky at love*, but Nick revised it into *unlucky at cards, lucky at love*, blaming his bad luck on Amelia.

Ethan calls my bet, and so does Scorpio. I discard two cards, dealing more to the three of us. I win the first two rounds, and that's my luck for the night. Ethan picks up pace, and two hours later, he has most of our money.

Nick plays it safe. After losing three hundred, he fills the role of our croupier. "Are you calling or what?" He nudges me.

"Yeah." I toss the chips into a pile. "I call."

There's no way I'll win with a pair of queens, but who cares?

I've not heard from Nadia since I dropped her off at James's office, and I'm starting to lose it, so I don't give a shit about money right now.

"Watch and learn." Ethan beams, revealing four kings.

Lucky bastard.

The front door opens, hitting the wall in the hallway with a loud clap. Nick and I exchange surprised looks as high heels click on the tiled floor, reverberating through the house.

I know it's Nadia even before she enters the kitchen, her face determined, shoulders square. She's holding herself wound up tight, but her eyes betray she's shaken up.

"Hey, sis. What's wrong?"

She stops by Nick and tilts her purse upside down, tipping the contents on the table.

"Do you know what this is?" she snaps, her eyes rimmed pink from crying.

Nick looks between her and me as if I can shed some light on what the hell is going on. I fucking wish I could. Seeing her close to tears feels like a punch to my throat. Too many emotions dance across Nick's face to guess which one takes the stage.

"Pills..." he drawls, taken aback by her attitude.

He grabs the first orange bottle, reading the label. And only then does anxiety take the lead. He tosses the bottle aside and grabs another, then another, his complexion blanching. "Why do you have so many?"

"I needed them," she clips, but her voice is a far cry from anger. She's breaking down. "Guess who called me today."

I slide out with my chair, ready to grab her and hide her in my arms. I don't need her to spell out who called.

"How could you give him my number!" Nadia cries, tears trailing down her cheeks. "I asked you not to call him!"

Nick's shoulders sag. He rubs his face, glaring at the meds littering the table. "He called this morning. We talked just for a few minutes—"

"What did you talk about? He sure didn't tell you why we split up. You wouldn't sit like that if you knew. Did he at least say where he is right now?"

Nick shakes his head, looking at me for help. Fucking coward. He knows exactly where Adrian is, but he acts stupid. He tries to get up, but Nadia pushes him back down and snatches my drink, downing half in one go.

"He's in rehab," she says. "He's been there for two months now, getting clean after his friend got him hooked on PCP."

Nick stands, taking Nadia's hand to pull her into his arms. I'd do the same, but her reaction would be different.

She breaks free, stepping away. "Don't ever tell him how to contact me, Nick. Don't ever think I'll take him back. You wouldn't want that for me if you knew—"

"But I don't know!"

I expected him to snap. Nadia's been back for weeks, but she still hasn't told him why she's no longer with Adrian. I get up too, but Nadia sends me a warning glare before I take one step toward her. Instead of pulling her closer, I refill the glass she already finished and lean against the wall.

"Tell me!" Nick booms, slamming his hands on the table. "What did he do? You left him because he was using?"

A nervous, whimpering chuckle slips past her lips. "I left because he deserved it. Because I didn't deserve what he did and how he behaved. And you... you should be on my side."

"I *am* on your side. I just thought you could work things out." He glares at the pills again. "I'm sorry. I won't give him your number again, and I'll find you a new psychiatrist."

"I don't need a new one. I'm doing well with James."

Nick squeezes the bridge of his nose, barely controlling his temper. "Apparently not. Look at those pills! It's fucking

ridiculous you're taking so many!"

"I'm not. Those were prescribed by my psychiatrist in New York. James sorted through them and only left me with diazepam for now."

Nick sighs, not having any of it. "You're not making progress, Nadia. You need someone better. The way you are, the way you have been since Dad died, isn't normal. You—"

"I'm not normal," she cuts in, hurt dripping from her tone.

"That's not what I meant."

"That's what you think!"

"What am I supposed to think?! You don't tell me anything! and neither does Adrian!"

He pumps his fists, cracking his neck as if to rid the tension bubbling inside him as his face twists into a tormented scowl. It's both genuine and fake. He cares about her, and it kills him that she's struggling, but right now, he's jumping at the opportunity to take advantage of Nadia's vulnerability.

"You can't rely on pills forever," he continues in a defeated tone. "I'll find you a new psychiatrist. You must get better, sis. I need you to get better. I can't stand seeing you like this."

I only see the profile of Nadia's face, but that's enough. My stomach somersaults back because she's fucking afraid of him; afraid to oppose him; afraid of his screams, orders and disappointment. Her hands shake more than her chin while Nick presses forward, sensing a good moment to strike harder.

"You need help, Nadia. You can't do this alone. James isn't the right doctor for you, and since you don't trust me enough to say what happened, I have to find someone you'll trust." He pulls a stray, beaten-dog face.

Blood boils in my veins. He's manipulating her—the tone of his voice, his attitude and every word are aimed at exposing her weaknesses. He's forcing her to cooperate against better judgement. I just hope he's doing it unconsciously.

I still feel sick because Nadia's too weak to defend herself.

"Stop brainwashing her," I say.

I can't watch as he reduces her to an obedient mess.

"Stay out of this," Nick snaps. "You don't know the first thing about it."

Nadia looks at me through tears, helpless and broken. She's not verbally asking for help, but the plea in her eyes is enough.

"I know more than you think. She doesn't need you guilt-tripping her." I turn to Nadia. "You're doing much better now than you did a month ago."

She bites her bottom lip, eyes darting between Nick and me before she lets out a shaky breath. "That's because you calm me down. You help more than anything, but you're not a cure. You're just a band-aid."

"That's a lie," Mel says, standing in the doorway. "You told me you're better even when Thomas isn't around."

Nadia's cheeks flush a faint shade of pink. "It's not fair, Thomas. You deserve better than this."

"Better than you? There is no one better. I *don't* deserve you, baby, but unless you tell me to leave, I won't move."

"I told you to stay away from her," Nick heaves, his voice spiked with the sort of calmness that precedes fury.

"I'm glad he didn't listen." Nadia takes my hand, lacing our fingers. "I'm sorry," she utters, pumping her delicate fingers around mine. "This isn't how this was supposed to happen. I didn't mean to put you on the spot."

I snake one hand around her middle. "The end result remains the same no matter how he found out about us."

Scorpio grins in his chair, and Mel smiles from her spot in the doorway. Ethan looks as if he tried a lemon for the first time, and Nick... Nick changes colours like a kaleidoscope—white, green, red, and purple.

"I told you to stay away from her!"

The overprotective brother, instead of being overprotective and worried about the rapidly deteriorating condition of his

sister, is simply furious. His eyes jump between Nadia and me as if he can't comprehend what's happening.

He probably can't.

Too bad he can't prioritise either—calming Nadia before hitting Thomas.

Nadia steps forward when Nick charges at me. The look on his face betrays he's ready to throw one of his weak punches, so I yank Nadia back, hiding her behind me just as Nick's fist connects with my face.

"You *fucked* her?! You fucked my sister?!"

Scorpio grabs Nick by the shoulders. He means well but only makes things worse. Nick thrashes about, fighting to break free, murder on his mind. He sucker-punches Scorpio under the ribs and jumps at me like a crazy rooster. He pins me to the wall, gripping a fistful of my shirt.

"Let him go!" The girls cry in sync.

"Don't," I tell him. "Go on, Nick. Hit me."

He has to unwind, and to be honest, I deserve a black eye. I went behind his back... that's low even by my standards. I suppress my reflexes despite self-preservation instinct pushing me into action. Truth be told, I thought he'd back off, but it looks like I underestimated his rage. He throws his hand back, then forth, landing a neat blast on my jaw.

And I must admit that pissed-off Nick punches like a boxer.

He lets me go, turning back to Nadia. Tears stain her cheeks, but she's yanking his shirt, trying to pull him away from me. Her courage fizzles out when Nick steps forward, his fists clenched, steam coming out of his nose.

She stops fighting.

She stops crying.

She freezes, staring at her brother, choking back tears.

"You let him fuck you?!" Nick roars, clutching her upper arm and towering above her. "You're—"

I don't let him finish. Whatever shit he wants to say, he'll only trample Nadia's self-esteem further. I grip Nick's shirt, yanking him back. He lets go of Nadia, landing with his back on the table. Chips and drinks fly off. Glasses shatter on the floor, but Nick scrambles to his feet, swinging at me again. This time I don't suppress my reflexes. I dodge, then nail his face.

"You touch her again, and I'll break your fucking hands," I snap, then turn around, cupping Nadia's face. "You okay?"

"Get me out of here. Please."

I do. The last thing we hear before I close the door is Scorpio convincing Nick not to chase us.

Twenty-six

Jealous

NADIA

"Good morning," Thomas whispers, kissing the soft spot behind my ear.

I peek a little. He's dressed, his hair damp from a recent shower. I cringe at the sudden onset of a headache. No wonder. I cried myself to sleep, and I didn't utter a word since we left Nick's house. "Hey. What time is it?"

"Almost ten. I called James to tell him you won't make your morning appointment. He said he's got the afternoon free if you want to see him later." He kisses my forehead, moving away when I pull myself up. "How are you feeling?"

"I've got a headache. Why aren't you at the office?"

"I'm not going in today. Nick needs time to cool off, and it'll be better if he doesn't see my face this early." He hands me a cup of coffee, then opens the drawer on the bedside table, taking out paracetamol. "You should eat something."

"I'll throw up if I eat." I fall back, tugging his hand, until he takes the hint and lays beside me, hiding me in his arms. "I'm sorry about him. I knew he wouldn't be happy about us, but I can't believe he hit you."

"I can't believe it hurt," he smirks. Don't apologise. When he sees what you mean to me, he'll apologise himself."

"Have you thought this through?" I tilt my head, kissing his chin. "Are you one hundred percent sure I'm what you want? Because I'm yours if you want me, Thomas. It's pointless to delude myself that we're just physical when we're so much more, but you should really think about this because what you've seen so far is just the tip of the iceberg, and I want you to—"

"And breathe. I've never been so sure of anything in my life. You were mine the moment I laid my eyes on you at the airport. You just didn't know it then."

"Now I do." I nuzzle my face in his neck with a soft sigh, the emotional turmoil from last night gone. "Don't cheat on me."

He laughs. Then laughs harder when I smack his head.

"My reputation doesn't speak in my favour, but cheating is the last thing I'd do." He rests on his elbow, brushing my hair away from my face. "You'll need to be patient with me, baby. I'll make mistakes while I learn how to take care of you."

That one sentence is enough to melt me. I scoot closer to him, drawing tiny circles along his jaw. "If you're not going to the office, we can stay in bed all day."

"We do have a party tonight. I'm sure you wouldn't want to miss hearing Aaron live again, and I don't have a choice."

The headache intensifies when I realise we'll bump into my brother, but one kiss pressed to my head pushes the worry aside.

Nick can't hate Thomas forever. He just needs time to process the information. After all, they're best friends and business partners. I have a feeling his anger is in part triggered by fear. Nick cares about Thomas a lot, and he's afraid to lose a friend if our relationship doesn't last.

"I think it might be a good idea to hire two bodyguards next week when you're in Barcelona for the bachelorette party,"

Thomas says, gently stroking my back.

"You're joking, right?" I sit up, looking down at him. I don't think he's kidding. "No way!" As if I'd let him hire two vultures who'll report back our every move. "You can't. Promise you won't."

"If anything happens, we'll be a thousand miles away."

I put my finger against his lips. "We'll be fine. Do you see me sneaking spies to your party?"

He laughs, yanking me back to the previous position. "Spies? You plan on doing something I won't be happy about?"

"No, but I can't speak for the other girls. I won't let you control me. I lived through that once. I'm not doing it again."

"This isn't about control or knowing your every move. I just need to know you're safe."

"I will be safe. I'll stay out of trouble. I won't mix, and I'll text you throughout the night that we're fine."

"And if anyone bothers you, get the bouncers involved."

I kiss him, but a simple peck isn't enough. He teases my bottom lip, sinking deeper into my mouth, igniting my senses.

"Compromise," he whispers, his hand travelling down my stomach. "That'll take some getting used to."

***

If there's anything I learned about Thomas during the last few weeks of mindblowing sex, it's how much he loves when my neck and back are on display. He caresses the line of my spine, worshipping it with kisses every time, so I picked a simple, elegant, backless dress for Aaron's party. We'll be surrounded by a crowd of perfectly proportioned blondes, and I need Thomas to think about the bedroom when he looks at me only.

I stand in the hallway, clasping a gold necklace, when Thomas enters my flat. A fitted, three-piece charcoal suit hugs the tall, muscular perfection that is his body.

He stops two steps in, dark eyes roving my body. "Remember what you said about me having to work on my asshole persona? You'd change your mind real quick if you could hear the thoughts that'll scream in my head later when every guy at that fucking party eyes you up."

"We can stay here. I have Netflix and wine."

A sad smile crosses his face. "I need to be there, but don't worry. Nick won't make a scene with the paparazzi around."

I wouldn't bet my money on that.

Half an hour later, we arrive at Grande, a club around the corner from C&G Records. Almost two hundred guests crowd the space, and waiters walk around the room with champagne. I snatch a glass, expecting a power display on Nick's part as soon as he spots Thomas. He's a Grimwald, after all, and we rarely back down.

"They're by the bar," Thomas says, holding me to his side. "Come on."

"You want to go there? He hit you last night. I doubt he'll shake your hand today. Give him more time."

"Avoiding him won't help. He should see us *together*, baby doll. He needs to know I care about you."

"Do you now?" I aim for casual teasing, but it comes out nervous and pathetic.

He curls his finger under my chin, tilts my head and closes my lips with an affectionate kiss in the middle of the crowded room. "Like you can't imagine."

My heart picks up the pace with every step closer to my unpredictable brother. I like thinking that I know him well, but this time I can't guess his reaction

He's chatting with Aaron, seemingly relaxed, but his shoulders tense the moment he spots us, and an ugly scowl replaces his amusement. He glares at Thomas for a moment, then turns his head, pulling Mel into the crowd.

"Told you he wouldn't make a scene," Thomas says, disappointment clear in his voice.

All day he's been acting like Nick's disapproval doesn't bother him, but he can't fool me.

I squeeze his hand. "He'll come around. I promise."

"Nadia!" Aaron cheers, pulling me into a tight hug. "Nice to see you again. I hoped you'd come by the studio one day."

"I'm sorry. I've been busy."

"Well, the offer still stands if you're ever around."

"I'll bring her over on Monday," Thomas says, draping one arm over my shoulder, probably marking his territory. "You're recording all day, right?"

"Right," Aaron confirms, shaking his head as if shooing away unwanted thoughts. "I'll be waiting for you."

Nick re-emerges from the crowd, eyes narrowed on me. "Nadia, a word. *Now.*"

Mel stops behind him, panting, wide-eyed and apologetic, and Thomas chooses *that* moment to kiss my temple.

"Go," he whispers. "I'll wait here."

Nick takes me outside through the emergency exit, and I use the opportunity to light a cigarette.

"Don't be mad at Thomas, Nick. Well, at least not just at him. We're both guilty."

He scoffs, snatching the packet from my hand. "You're my sister, Nadia, and he's my best friend. He had no fucking right to touch you. I told you he's a player. He treats women like trash. You're better than that!"

Better than a one-night stand with a guy I just met? Maybe, but this isn't just one night and was never meant to be, no matter what I told myself.

"He cares about me," I say, resting against the building. "I'm not like the blondes, Nick. And I care about him too."

"He's not good for you, sis. I don't want you to get hurt. He might care now, but that won't last. It's *not* enough." He coughs when he inhales the smoke.

"It's a start. He makes me happy. He makes the huge hole

in my heart heal. I know I'm asking a lot, but try to accept this, okay? He's acting tough, but he's upset you're not talking to him." I butt the cigarette in the ashtray, kissing Nick's cheek. "Don't worry, I won't come crying to you if this doesn't last."

"I know you won't. You'll get my wife drunk instead."

With that, he turns around, marching inside the building. I stay behind, lighting another cigarette. Nick won't forgive Thomas right away, but the fact he talked to me means he *wants* to forgive him. He just needs time.

Twenty-seven

Permission

THOMAS

Thirty-two toddlers run around a function room I rented for Maya's birthday. A large, pink bouncy castle fills sixty percent of floor space, and whatever's left is occupied by sugar-rushed kids. Parents are squashed by the walls or tending to their spawns' every whim while I stand by the door with Richard like cheap security detail, stopping the wild bunch from escaping.

"One hour down, one to go," he shouts despite standing four feet away. "I'll get a drink. You want something?"

Giggles, screams and squeals fill the air. I can't hear my thoughts as I point to the water bottle in my hand. "I'm good."

"Maya's enjoying herself." Claudia takes Richard's place, grinning. "And you look like you're having fun too."

"Don't I just. I'll be glad if my head doesn't explode by the time we're done here. How can they make so much noise?"

I pull out my phone, checking for messages from Nadia, who rose bright and early to go shopping with Amelia, on a hunt for her perfect wedding dress.

A few messages wait on the screen, and I smile, flicking through the pictures of *my* girl in different dresses. A dark green one catches my eye—fitted at the top, loose at the bottom. I send her the picture back, and I get a reply within thirty seconds.

My doll: That's the one I bought. We're at Nick's. He still has a lot to say about us.

Me: Call me if you need me.

"You're smiling," Claudia says, her eyebrow raised. "You're smiling at your phone. Is it a *girl?*" she squeals, clapping her hands. "You're seeing someone?!"

"Kind of. It's complicated."

She comes closer, fidgeting as if she's on a sugar high too. "Why didn't you say anything? Who is she? Why isn't she here? I want to meet her! Why is it complicated? Come on!" She elbows my ribs. "Tell me something! Tell me everything!"

Then let me get a word in.

Why are women so prone to stacking the question marks until they run out of breath and ideas? One question at a time, please. Men aren't great at multitasking. Thinking about the answers to five different questions is multitasking-level hard.

"It's Nick's sister, Nadia. You'll meet her soon."

Claudia frowns, not appeased, and opens her mouth to ask thirty-two supporting questions, but my phone starts buzzing in my pocket. My muscles turn to stone at the thought of hearing Nadia's teary voice if Nick's being an asshole again.

There'll be fucking hell to pay if he made her cry.

Instead of *My doll*, *Amelia* flashes on the screen. It does nothing to relax me. If anything, I tense even more. She only ever calls when Nick and I hit the club after they argue.

"What's wrong?" I ask.

"Can you come over? Like, right now? I don't know what

to do. I think Nadia's having a panic attack. She's crying and shaking and won't let anyone near her. I don't know how to calm her down. Nick's scared, so he's screaming, and she's—"

"I'm coming," I cut her off, jogging up to Maya to kiss the crown of her head. "I need to go, sunshine, but I'll pick you up one day, and we'll feed the ducks at Uncle Nick's, okay?"

She's so excited about the bouncy castle she doesn't pay me any attention. I kiss Claudia's cheek before I push the double door open, hurrying down the corridor, keys in hand.

"What happened?" I ask Mel, who patiently waits on the line. "Did Nick say something to her?"

"No." Mel's voice fills my BMW. "Ty called. He's Adrian's friend. They talked for less than a minute, and she just broke down. What am I supposed to do? Call an ambulance?"

"No. I'll be there in ten. Tell Nick to stop screaming."

I slam my foot on the gas, rational thinking gone out the window. Seven minutes later, I jump out of the car outside Nick's house after breaking every traffic regulation. Mel waits outside, looking worried and a little scared.

"Where is she?" I ask, the gravel crunching under my feet. "Is she better? What the fuck did Ty tell her?"

Mel's bottom lip quivers. "Nick just hung up with him. Adrian... God, Nick called him yesterday and told him not to bother Nadia. He told him she's moving on, and he..." She pauses, inhaling a shaky breath. "He overdosed on sleeping pills. He almost died."

The guy gives *desperate men do desperate things* a new meaning.

"They're in the kitchen," Mel adds. "Nick gave her some of the Xanax she left here, but she's not having it. He wants to take her to the emergency room."

I hear him as soon as Mel opens the front door.

"Calm down!" he snaps. "Please, Nadia. He's fine! I spoke to Ty. Adrian is okay. I promise he's *okay*!" Worry shines through his voice, his tone bordering on desperate pleas. I understand his reaction, but he's making things worse. "I don't know how to help you, sis. Tell me what you need!" He stands with his back to me in the kitchen, oblivious to my presence.

Something fucking snaps inside me when I see Nadia sitting on the tiles, her back pressed flush against the patio door. Pale and trembling, she's staring into the distance with unseeing, pink-rimmed eyes, her alabaster skin a disturbing contrast to dark, messy hair and blood-red, bitten lips. She clutches her side with one hand, close to her heart, the left one holding her right arm the way I taught her.

This girl.

This broken, frail, timid kitten in tears...

She'll be the fucking death of me.

My heart thuds against my ribs. My first, *immediate* reaction is to lift her off the floor and manhandle her hands and legs until she's safely tucked against my body, unable to move. Unable to keep tearing her hair out.

Nick steps forward as if he wants to take Nadia's hand or embrace her, but she presses herself further into the unrelenting glass door and covers her face with both hands.

"Don't touch me," she utters, her voice breaking every few syllables, and my heart sinks every time. "I told you... I told you not to call him! He's so fragile. God, it's all my fault."

"It's not your fault. If you want, I'll book you the next flight to New York so you can see him, but *please* stop crying! Just calm down. Take the pills!"

She curls into a ball, a cornered, frightened animal panic etched into her beautiful features. She knots her fingers on her head, tear-stained face hidden behind her arms.

"What the fuck are you doing?" I snap, a ball of rage mixed with concern settling behind my ribs. "You think screaming will calm her down? You're just scaring her more."

Nadia's eyes snap to meet mine. Her spine straightens, and her brown eyes speak louder than words. She's waiting for me

to take her pain away.

"What the hell are you doing here?!" Nick yells, spinning around, a vein on his neck pulsing furiously. "Get the fuck out of my house!"

"Not without her."

"You think she'll go with you? Look at her! She's breaking down! You think it's the first panic attack I've seen? She needs to take this." He shoves an orange prescription bottle into my hand. "Or we're going to the fucking hospital."

I glance at the label. No way I'll ever force Nadia to take Xanax. James considered diazepam a better fit, and that's all she's getting if she wants pills. I leave the bottle on the countertop, ignoring Nick's mocking sneer when I take a few steps toward my girl. She scrambles to her feet, her tears coming on stronger. One after another, they trail down her cheeks and drop from her chin, dotting the white blouse she wears. Powerful shudders shake her small, delicate frame.

The dam bursts before my eyes.

She no longer fights the pain ripping her wide open. She welcomes it. Lets it consume her because she knows the negative emotions will subside once she's in my arms. She knows I'll take care of everything that bothers her. She knows I'll anchor her back in place.

I stop two steps away, leaving her in control. She needs to be the one who makes this choice. Either she lets go of the helplessness or drowns in it. She stands there, quaking under the powerful, silent, choke-back sobs, dark, mindless eyes not veering away from mine as she sinks her teeth in her bottom lip.

"Come here," I say, holding my hand out.

She doesn't hesitate. Doesn't skip a fucking beat. It's as if all she waited for was permission, a confirmation that I'll ground her regardless of who's watching. And I will. Always. The intense need to calm her, to help her see a way out of the maddening helplessness she's trapped in, rips me wide open. I can't fucking breathe around the intensity of my own feelings. I cradle her frail frame, lock her in my arms and tuck her head under my chin. She rests her forehead on my chest, then fists my shirt, inhaling uneven, shallow breaths as she slowly regains control of her own mind.

Jesus fucking Christ.

Seconds. That's all it takes. *Seconds* of my arms circled around her. *Seconds* of my lips pressed against her hair. *Seconds* of our closeness, and she's no longer violently shaking. No longer wetting my t-shirt with streams of tears. She feeds off whatever strength she finds inside me and uses it to pull away from the vile thoughts feasting on her mind.

"Do you want diazepam?"

"No," she whispers, her warm breath fanning my chest. She fists my t-shirt harder. "Don't let go of me."

"I won't." I slide my hands lower, cupping the undersides of her thighs, and lift her up. She wraps her arms and legs around me, face nuzzled in the crook of my neck, fingers entangled in my hair. She's so cold to the touch it absolutely guts me. "Mel, can you get her a cup of peppermint tea?"

Amelia jolts into action from her spot in the doorway. "Yes, sure. Just a sec." She hurries in, putting the kettle on.

Nick's eyes are on me as I walk out of the room. She holds onto me like a frightened, defenceless child when I sit in the armchair, manoeuvring her legs and arms until she's right where I want her, curved against me, snapping into place like she belongs there. She does. No one could ever fit me so fucking right.

"How did you—" Nick starts.

"Shut up for *five* minutes."

He folds his arms over his chest, throwing himself against the back of the couch, and swallows hard, watching the most important woman in our lives curled in my arms. The sound of the water boiling grows louder at a snail's pace while my fingers ghost up and down Nadia's spine. Her pulse slows down, her

heart no longer ramming against her ribs, and before the kettle clicks, she sits up, wiping the dampness off her cheeks.

"Thank you." She presses a cool, wet kiss to my cheekbone. The worst might be over, but she's nowhere near as calm as I'd like to see her. I can almost hear the screams in her head.

"Don't thank me for doing my job." I take her hand, grazing my lips over her knuckles. "I'm proud of you, doll. A month ago, you would've swallowed five pills and washed them down with tequila."

Mel brings the tea over, concern highlighting her freckled face. She's always the one who easily finds the positive side of things, but in the face of Nadia's issues, Mel's powerless, and so is Nick. I expected something else entirely. I thought they'd know what to do. After all, they've seen this before. They witnessed Nadia's meltdowns, panic attacks and cries, but they're fucking clueless, making every mistake in the book.

"How are you feeling?" Mel sits beside Nick, wary eyes on Nadia. "You need something else? Wine maybe?"

"No. Tea's fine." She looks at Nick. "You're right. It's not my fault Adrian overdosed, but I do feel guilty. I left him when he needed me most." She takes my hand, lacing our fingers as if unconsciously looking for support. "The psychiatrist at the rehab facility told me to leave. He said Adrian's a lost cause... I believed him. I watched Adrian hit bottom over and over. When I thought he couldn't sink lower, he proved me wrong."

Nick moves his gaze from my hand wrapped around Nadia's back to her face. "Will you ever tell me what he did?"

She gouges her nails into my hand, shaking her head. "Is his addiction dragging us both down not enough? That was the root of every problem we had. The cause of every fight. He used for months, and you know I'm not the strongest person."

"You shouldn't protect him."

Nick knows there's more to the story. We all do but pushing her for answers doesn't do her any good. I can't blame him for trying, though. The scenarios whooshing in my head turn more sinister by the day. Nick must have similar ideas.

"It's not him I'm protecting."

Nick rubs the back of his neck, pushing a harsh breath past his lips. "I'm sorry that I shouted at you. I just... I hate seeing you like this, sis. I wish I knew how to help you."

Nadia relaxes against me a little more, loosening the tight, almost painful grip she has on my hand. "You can't help me, Nick. No one can."

A muscle on his jaw feathers, eyes narrowing into slits as he motions his chin at me. "*He* can."

"Thomas numbs the pain and fear, but the bruises remain. He can't heal me. He can only dial down the hurt." She runs her thumb along my knuckles and tilts her head enough, so her lips brush against my temple. She leaves a kiss there. Nothing more than a quick peck, but that fucking peck is *everything*. A silent admission of feelings. A powerful, visual manifestation of that *more* she fought against so long. "Don't be mad at him, Nick. If you want to place blame, blame me. I'm the one using him here."

She untangles herself from the make-shift cage of my arms and sets the half-empty cup on the coffee table. "I need a cigarette, and you two..." She points between Nick and me, "...need to talk." She turns back to me and kisses my lips. Another peck. Quick. Featherlight... the most important kiss we've shared to date. "Come on, Mel. Keep me company."

I let go of her hand, my eyes walking her out of the room. I don't want her out of my sight. The moment they step out of the room, I brace for a fair dose of venom courtesy of my best friend. My hands ball into tight fists when Nick rises to his feet.

He hit me once, and once is enough. My muscles tense painfully as the atmosphere grows heavier, but it relaxes when Nick takes two crystal glasses out of the liquor cabinet and fills them with too-many fingers of his best whiskey.

"I was six when Nadia was born," he says, handing me a glass. "My father always said nothing matters more than family and that one day it'd just be Nadia and me. He said I should take care of her the best I can." He scoffs, shaking his head. "I hated that annoying little girl for *years*."

My eyes snap to him. Nick never told me why he loves Nadia so much—more than any other brother I ever encountered—but I assumed he'd been over-the-top protective of his sister since the day she was born.

Apparently not.

"She was so fucking annoying," he breathes, his tone loaded with indecipherable emotion. It could be anger, but it could also be shame or regret. "She kept breaking my toys and asked more questions than there were answers. She wanted to cuddle all the time. She giggled for no reason, clinging to me as if I were her security blanket. I couldn't stand her. God be my witness, I absolutely *hated* her. All I ever wanted was for her to leave me the hell alone." He rests his elbows on his knees, head dipped low, eyes on the carpet, a trail of crimson heating his cheeks. "Dad kept saying I should be patient. That I should play with her and love her because she's family and wouldn't stay so adorable for long, but I never once thought about her as adorable. She was a fucking *nuisance*. Whenever I was home, I slammed the door to my room in her face and locked the door so she couldn't come in."

He straightens up, eyes still avoiding mine as he downs half of his whiskey. "When I was eleven, Nadia caught the flu," he continues, shaking his head, clearly ashamed now. "I was *glad* she wasn't well because she didn't bother me for once." His voice grows smaller, but he inhales deeply, getting a hold of himself. "Two days later, she ended up at the hospital with pneumonia. It was bad. She was hooked to IVs, couldn't eat or drink, and every time she coughed, she turned blue."

He pauses, staring at the opposite wall as if reliving that

day, and I can tell by his face he hates himself for treating Nadia like a burden when she was little. I don't dare speak. I've been friends with Nick long enough to know that if I interrupt him while he's on a roll, in the middle of a rant, he'll need a lot of coaxing to finish the story.

"She was too weak to speak for two days," he huffs, rubbing his face before his gaze finally locks with mine. "She slept most of the time. She was so fucking pale, her lips almost blue... I sat by her bed, read her stories, and prayed she'd start asking those stupid fucking questions again. The lesson my father had tried to teach me since she was born finally sunk in. Family comes first, and Nadia's the most important part of my family."

That explains why he loves her more than any normal brother loves his sister. Nick crashed with reality when he saw Nadia in the hospital bed. Even if he pushed those thoughts aside, even if he didn't acknowledge them, he was a kid himself, and at some point, he must've feared he'd lose her.

There's no better wake-up call than that.

"I won't take her away from you, Nick."

"I know," he huffs. "I'm sorry I hit you. And I'm sorry about how I handled the situation. I pretended not to realise, but deep down, I knew something was happening between you and her. You're a completely different guy when she's around, Thomas." His head hits the backrest. "We both know how you treated women before, so don't blame me for freaking out. She's my *sister*. The last thing I want is to see her hurt."

"It's the last thing I want, too. Your reaction didn't surprise me. I knew you wouldn't approve right off the bat. I knew you'd hate my fucking guts. You need time to see that I love her."

His eyes snap to mine again, a deep eleven between his brows before they meet his hairline. "What did you say?"

"I love her," I enunciate, each word ringing loud and clear.

I didn't plan the confession. Fuck. Not even Nadia knows, but telling Nick was spontaneous... and it feels so right to say

it aloud. I'm lost in that girl, buried in her mindset, beauty, personality, and strength. She's stronger than Nick and I combined. Stronger than she should be.

Nick exhales again, calmer this time as if relieved. His expression morphs to poorly concealed satisfaction, one corner of his mouth curling up and lifting an enormous weight off my shoulders. We've been friends for two years, and if not for my lifestyle, I'd like to think Nick wouldn't mind me dating his sister. Hell, he probably would've set us up in the first place, but me fucking and firing the blondes doesn't put me high on the list of men worthy of Nadia.

He thinks I want to get in her pants, but I don't, so—

Okay, fine.

But as that's not all I want, he can't object.

"If you love her, why the big secret? Amelia said you were sneaking around since the day Nadia came back."

"You don't want the details," I say, uncomfortable in my seat. This is probably not a conversation any man should have with his girlfriend's brother. "Let's say she had me at arm's length this whole time."

I'd never admit I slept with the light of his world a few hours after we met. There's no rational way to explain how, since the first time Nadia looked at me, I had no fucking idea where was up and where was down. That I wanted her for myself from day one. Nick wouldn't understand that *something* drew us to each other, that we felt better when we were close. He'd think I exploited Nadia's weaknesses.

"I don't want any details," he says with a bitter look. "Definitely *not*. Just tell me why you didn't say anything. You should've come to me first, Thomas."

My mind fucking blanks. There's no way around this other than making up a lame excuse, but I've lied enough already. Nick deserves the truth. A mellowed version, at least.

"We weren't dating until a few days ago. I told you she kept me at a distance. She only caved when I came back early from Madrid. Before that, we were—"

"Sleeping around?" he clips, his nostrils flaring.

"Kind of. I know how it sounds, but don't twist it to your preference. I calm her down somehow. I don't know *how* so don't ask, but she feels safe with me. She uses that to work through her issues." Now I'm the one rubbing my face, treading lightly around the difficult topic. "She didn't want much, Nick, but after a while, she realised I wouldn't give up. As unbelievable as it sounds, she was the one who dictated the rules."

He doesn't look like he believes me but doesn't look ready to tear me apart either, and that's half the battle won.

"I know I'm the last guy you want around her—"

"It's not that," he says in a defeated tone. "I just had it in my head that Adrian's the one. I can't shake the idea, you know? Maybe because he was her first serious boyfriend, or maybe because they worked so fucking well together."

Kick me, why don't you?

He finishes his drink, crossing the room for another refill. "Shit, I *can't* believe you love her."

Neither can I. It feels great to admit it and even better to feel it, but Nadia has to work through her past and issues before she'll hear me say those words. She still cares about Adrian too much. Sometimes, I think if it weren't for me, she'd pack her bags and fly over there to hold his hand.

"You've been telling me to settle down since we met," I say.

He smirks, nodding along. "If I knew you'd pick my sister, I wouldn't have let her leave two years ago."

That's more than I ever hoped for. It's approval. A blessing I didn't expect. Trust I thought I broke.

Nick's smarter than most. He knows my asshole persona was just a front. He saw how I acted around Nadia and looked at her, and he sure knows she isn't just any girl.

She's *the* girl.

Twenty-eight

Lesser evil

NADIA

Adrian's lifeless body wakes me up three nights in a row. Thomas stays at my flat, but his proximity doesn't stop the nightmares.

Or maybe it does.

Maybe I wouldn't sleep at all if he wasn't with me.

Kelly, Adrian's mother, called the morning after my meltdown. She cried, pleaded, and then begged me to take Adrian back. I understand why she changed her mind, but I can't help feeling betrayed.

The doctor flashes a light in my eyes. "Can you see okay? No double or blurred vision?"

"No," I slur, closing my eyes. "Just dizziness and nausea. It hurts like no headache I've ever had."

He presses his thumb to my wrist, checking my pulse. "I'll give you painkillers for the ribs. They should help with the headache, although they might not work for the concussion. Depends on how bad it is." He hands me four pills and a disposable cup filled with water. "There's a prescription waiting for you in the pharmacy downstairs."

I've been a regular visitor at the hospital for the last five months. So much so that the doctors know me by name. They believed the stories about my clumsiness the first few times, but since I arrived with a black eye and a split lip that required two stitches, they've been convincing me to press charges. After that, Adrian learned to watch where he hits me so I won't walk around campus with visible bruises.

Instead of closing his fingers around my neck, he grips my arms, shoving me against the walls. Instead of hitting my face, he throws me to the ground, and I hurt my knees.

The physical pain is nothing compared to the fear he evokes by looking at me with dilated pupils.

The fear of pain is worse than the pain itself.

"You need anything else?" the doctor asks, his hand on the handle.

I drop my gaze, tears dancing in my eyes. My heart thuds against my broken ribs, each breath more painful than the last. I shudder, grabbing onto my side and doubling over, my mouth parted in a silent scream.

"Can I," I whisper, too afraid that nothing but a high-pitched sob will come out if I speak up. "Can I stay here for a while?"

"Let me call the police, Nadia."

I shake my head, regretting it when nausea intensifies.

"Please," the doctor says again. "How much more can you take?"

"No. He needs help, not the police. He needs a doctor, but he's not ready yet," I mutter, wiping away the first tear. "You're right. I can't take any more. I can't watch him destroy everything he ever cared for."

Adrian's boxing career is no longer an option; his grades are slipping, and he's one incident away from being kicked out of school. All his friends turned their backs on him. Ty lasted the longest—three months before he packed his bags and moved back home to New Jersey after pleading, threatening, and bargaining with me proved fruitless.

He tried everything to make me leave Adrian.

I couldn't, though. I was ashamed, scared and weak. I had no strength to save Adrian, let alone myself, but I hoped for better days. I hoped that one day he'd realise how much he lost, and it'd push him to seek help.

I'm done hoping.

Something broke inside me today. Whatever it was, it hit me hard, and every ounce of rage Adrian took out on me, every bruise, cut and tear resurfaced. I can't *take any more...*

That evening, I called Ty, asking him to meet me in Washington, where Adrian's mother, Kelly, lived, oblivious to her son's addiction. She cried for hours when I told her what Adrian had done to me. Within two days, she organised the rehab, paid off a few doctors to have Adrian admitted against his will, and made me swear I'd go home and never come back.

Now, she wants me to come back.

"I won't come," I told her, breaking through her pleading. "Please don't ask me to go through this again. Ty said Adrian's better. He said the anti-depressants are working."

"Yes, but—"

"He needs to get better for himself, Kelly, or he'll relapse a few months down the line. I'll stay in touch with Ty and call Adrian when he can take phone calls again." I cut the call and switched the cell phone off just in case she tried again.

My resolution not to visit Adrian hangs by a thread. I reached for my suitcase ten times over the past three days, but Thomas's voice echoing in my head stopped me every time.

"I've got you. I won't let go."

He said that when he witnessed my first meltdown after the housewarming party and he sounded like salvation.

***

Thomas stops by his bedroom door later in the evening. He snakes his hand around my stomach, pulling my back firmly against his broad chest and pushing the door open.

The bed is set with snow-white sheets and half a dozen matching pillows. Two bouquets of red roses stand on the night

246

tables, petals littering the floor. The whole room is bathed in a soft hue of dozens of candles. Romantic music seeps through the speaker on the windowsill. Two glasses and a bottle of champagne sit next to the third, largest bouquet on the ottoman.

It's perfect.

Breath-taking.

And I hate it.

Thomas kisses my neck, his lips cold against my skin. He's not his usual self. Not impatient or adoring. He's anxious, reserved, and hesitant. I can tell by the way he touches me and the stone-hard tension in his muscles that he's not adapting to the scenery he created.

"What is all this?" I ask.

He distracts me, ghosting his lips over the line of my jaw. "I thought we could do it right this time." He slides the straps of my blouse down my shoulders.

"*Right?*" I take a step forward, spinning on my heel to face him. "What was wrong with the other times?"

He straightens his back, holding himself up so tense it makes my back teeth hurt. "You don't like it?"

"No, I don't like it," I snap. "I hate it! This isn't you."

"But..." He trails off, seemingly lost in thought for a split second, the gold flecks in his cinnamon eyes dimmed. "Girls fall in love with impertinent bad boys and then spend their life trying to change them into stay-at-home romantics."

"And you decided to cut one step ahead of me? Well, whoever told you *that* doesn't know me, baby. I don't need flowers or candles." I cup his face, stroking the underside of his watchful, uncertain eyes. "If I wanted a romantic guy, I wouldn't be with you. I don't want you to pretend to be someone you're not."

"I knew this was a bad idea when I set to work."

"Next time, trust your gut. I like that when we have sex, you act as if you can't get enough of me. As if you're there to take what's yours."

"I am," he confirms. "And you are *mine*, doll."

I enter the room, take off my blouse, and toss it aside. Thomas is one step behind me, but I don't let him touch me this time. As soon as his fingers close around my upper arm, I wag my finger and push him onto the bed.

Careful, self-conscious of every move, I hook my thumbs over the elastic of my skirt and send it sighing to the floor as it fans around my short legs. My blouse follows, flying halfway across the room.

Thomas inhales slowly, his eyes roving my body dressed in black lingerie with a tight corset and matching stockings.

"No touching," I murmur, slapping his hands away as I straddle him, both knees digging into the mattress. I kiss his jaw, fiddling with the buttons on his shirt. I pop open one at a time.

Slowly.

Meticulously.

A song I know well plays from the portable speaker, "Heartbeat" by Haux. Thomas pumps his fists, itching to touch me. I slide the shirt down his muscular arms, ghosting my lips along the column of his neck.

"Take what's yours," I whisper when I reach his ear.

One second I'm straddling him, and the next, I lay on the white sheets, surrounded by rose petals, with Thomas's lips kissing the inside of my thigh. I weave my fingers through his hair, and my mouth falls open when he slides my panties down, latching onto my clit not missing a beat. The first time he did that, it took me a while to come. I was so self-conscious, thinking about what I looked like, what I tasted like, whether he was enjoying it and how exposed I was, but a lot has changed since then. I'm at ease. I know he enjoys this as much, if not more, than I do. I know he thinks I taste sweet, heady and musky like cotton candy you'd eat in the spring rain.

Thomas goes down on me any chance he gets, sometimes without it leading to sex like this morning when I woke up to find him under the duvet, between my legs, his tongue lapping and laving, bringing me to the brink within a few minutes. And when I came, he kissed my forehead, covered me back with the sheets and left for work, his impressive erection straining against the fabric of his black slacks.

"Oh... *oooohh*," I pant, unable to form a more coherent word when his fingers join the action.

"Good?" he demands, curling his finger inside me. "Tell me you love this, baby."

"Mhmmm."

He growls, the sound vibrating around my clit, fast-forwarding the oncoming orgasm. "You're so fucking wet, doll..." he sucks the sensitive bundle of nerves between his lips, thrusting his fingers deeper. "You better not be holdi—"

"Sh-sh-shut! Oh... oh. Shut it!"

He smiles against me, and within the next three seconds, my back arches away from the mattress, my moans lost, inaudible as my body vibrates under a powerful orgasm, and all my nerve endings fire up. Pure ecstatic anarchy seizes my thoughts.

"There it is. Fuck," he whispers. I feel him hovering just above me, the heat of his burning gaze on my cheeks. "You're so fucking beautiful when you come, baby." Hot lips press against my forehead when my back melts into the mattress. "We're not done here," he smiles against my skin. "No cheating. Look at me."

I await a restless, brutal thrust as he positions himself above me, parting my legs with one knee, but he slides in slowly, inch by inch. A muffled, satisfied growl builds in his chest, making me shudder. I love when he does that—a primal, animalistic, *raw* manifestation of how much he craves me. I wrap my arms around him as his moves become rhythmic, my moans drowning out the music.

"I'll never let you go," he says, and without warning, he pulls me up, resting his back against the headboard. "Take what will

always be yours."

I rise on my knees, taking him in, my fingers on his jaw, my mouth on his forehead. Eyes closed, I ride him, breathless and feverish, basking in the luxury of his unrestrained affection.

My moves grow faster, and my moans louder as the minutes pass, but I don't slow down until Thomas grips my hips, keeping me in place as he pumps his hips up and down fast, bruising my lips with forceful kisses. The pace alone is enough for the muscles in my abdomen to contract, but his urgent touch intensifies my orgasm. His body tenses, jaw shuts tight, eyes on mine as we reach that addictive high in sync.

Black spots dance before my eyes when after, once we can catch our breath and Thomas moves to my side, I bury my face in his neck, tucking my hair away behind my ears. "I'm afraid I can't move. My legs feel like jelly."

He smiles against my cheek. "Don't even think about sleeping. I'm starving." He grabs his phone to order a takeaway.

An hour later, showered and fed, we lay on the couch watching a movie—the they-killed-him-but-he-got-away kind. Unlike Thomas, who follows the action, I'm far more entertained by drawing little circles along his chiselled jaw. He kisses my hand every time it gets close enough to his lips and smiles when I nest my head under his chin, toying with his fingers next. I adore the little scar he has in the crook between his thumb and index finger—an inch-long perfect, pale line.

"How did you get it?" I ask.

"You know that game where you stab a blade in between your fingers as fast as you can? I got overconfident."

I chuckle. No surprises there. He's overconfident in all aspects of life. Arrogant. Bossy. Dominant. "You put a knife through your hand? Why did you play that game?" I don't want to think how much it hurt.

"It was the first night in the Army. We all did stupid things that night."

"Army?" I raise on my elbows to get a better look at him. "You were in the Army?"

A small wrinkle creases his forehead. "Of course."

It's the twenty-first century. No one's forced to serve, and I don't know a single guy who volunteered. Yet here I am, in the arms of a soldier.

"That explains a lot." I kiss his chin. "Arrogance, your huge ego, how you look down on everyone..."

Thomas flips me over, pulling me under him and ties my hands in one of his, pinning them above my head against the sofa's armrest. "You're the most annoying little creature I've ever met," he hisses, biting back a smile. "I can't be all flaws, or you wouldn't be mine, doll."

"Handsome. Protective. Passionate."

His lips curve, eyes sparkling. "Continue."

"You're big-headed as it is. No need to add to it."

"Stubborn," he pecks my nose. "Impatient. Delicate."

"Are those my flaws or qualities?"

"Both." He kisses my lips, moving back to the previous position. He focuses on the TV, and my fingers draw more shapes on his body.

Twenty-nine

Forever and always

NADIA

I sit on the suitcase, wrestling with the zipper. It's almost noon already. I don't have much time left. In less than two hours, the girls and I will walk through passport control and take first-class seats on a flight to Barcelona.

The guys' schedule isn't as tight, and Thomas is in no hurry, still occupying the bathroom. We're supposed to meet everyone at Nick's house at noon, but it's already twenty to, so I'm pretty sure we'll be fashionably late.

I growl, open the bag for the nth time and check the contents in case I missed something unnecessary all the other times that I looked for things I could leave behind, but all that's left is needed: gift bags, party gadgets and two changes of clothes.

Thomas descends the stairs wearing black jeans and a white t-shirt with huge, colourful stag antlers printed on his chest and *I DO CREW* in black ink underneath.

"Classy." I wink, folding my arms over my chest.

"Don't mention it. Thankfully, it's just until we land. We

change back to suits for the party."

"Yes, of course. God forbid you'd loosen up once in a while."

He cocks an eyebrow, then turns around, letting me read the list of dares printed on the back.

"Kiss *five* pretty girls?!" I exclaim, sauntering closer. "Kiss five *ugly* girls?"

"File your complaint with Scorpio. It was his idea, but don't worry. I never kissed an ugly girl and won't start now."

"Is that supposed to appease me?"

He grabs me by my waist. "Jealousy suits you, baby." He kisses me, sliding his hands to my hips and lifting me up so he can pin me against the wall. "That's one pretty girl," he mutters and kisses again. "Two."

"I'm just one girl."

"Are you saying I should kiss four other girls tonight?"

I smack his head, kissing him again. "Three."

"I've got *you*. I wouldn't kiss another girl even if you'd approve." He sets me back down, then grabs my suitcase, squeezing the top and zips it up as if it's freaking empty. "*A* for all you need, remember?"

Even in the obnoxious t-shirt, he looks like he just left a photoshoot for Armani. Dark, damp hair kisses his forehead here and there; long eyelashes make his cinnamon eyes pop, and he smells like amber, musk, and sex. That last one courtesy of yours truly. He could kiss fifty girls if he wanted to and wouldn't have to work for it.

"Look all you want, but no touching." I wheel the suitcase out to the hallway, the pink, strappy stilettos on my feet clicking happily against the marble floor. "I mean the strippers and the hookers," I add, seeing his bewildered expression.

"You think I'd risk losing you over a cheap whore?"

"They're not that cheap."

"I know. I'm paying for them." He takes both suitcases, taking them out to the car. "No kissing. No touching. And

you..." He closes the boot, then opens the passenger door while I lock the house. "Stay safe, okay? No mixing. If you have any problems, get the security, and let me know when you're back at the hotel. Now, get in. We're late."

Yes, we are.

When we arrive at Nick's, a white limo sits outside, and the girls are already in, sticking their heads out the windows and holding onto champagne flutes.

"What took you so long?!" Mel yells, waving me over.

Nick, Scorpio, Ethan, and three other guys wait for their limo, smoking and talking, but the audience doesn't stop Thomas from weaving his hand through my hair and devouring my lips, slipping his tongue past my teeth as if it's our first kiss.

"Have fun, baby doll. Just not too much fun." He opens the back door, letting me in.

Alex looks ready to tear my hair out when I sit next to Amelia. Her cheeks flush red when Thomas, who's already halfway toward the guys, turns around and sticks his head through the open window. "Almost forgot." He hands me a small envelope, pressing a soft kiss to my forehead. "Miss me."

The driver sets the car in motion when he steps away. I open the envelope, taking out six VIP passes to the hotel spa.

"Looks like we're getting massaged back into shape tomorrow," Jane says to Mel, peeking over my shoulder. "Are we even sure this was Thomas? I mean, he's like a brand-new person around you, Nadia."

"This was supposed to be an evening without boy-talk," Alex snaps, her baby blues drilling holes in my retinas.

"True, but have you seen the list of dares on their t-shirts?!" Camila, Amelia's friend from university clips. Her husband, Jake, is a part of the *I DO CREW*.

Jane bursts out laughing. "Oh please, as if they have the balls to go ahead with that."

Another bottle of prosecco waits at the first-class lounge,

but I refuse to drink just yet. There's still plenty of time for that, and since I'm the maid of honour, it's my responsibility to ensure the party goes as planned.

Besides, I want tequila.

Two hours later, we land in sunny Barcelona. Another limo takes us to the hotel where I rented a villa going off Thomas's recommendation. Once we're up on the tenth floor, I take my phone out, shooting Thomas a text.

Me: So far, so good. We're at the hotel, leaving in an hour. Thank you for the gift.

Thomas: You're welcome, doll. We're on our way to the hotel.

Holding a small package in hand, I knock on the bathroom door where Amelia's getting dressed. "I can't believe that after all those years of treating you like my sister, you'll finally be a true part of the family." I rest against the wall beside the mirror. "You make him so happy, Mel—" I pause because I spoke two sentences, and she's already emotional, her eyes brimming with tears. I have more to say, but ruining her makeup isn't my intention. I cut the speech short and sweet. "I love you, Mel, and this..." I hand her the gift. "This is to remind you of all the crazy times we shared together."

"Thank you," she hugs me, her eyes wet. "I love you too."

She opens the small box, taking out a silver bracelet with two dozen charms. Each one provokes a memory. There's the Eiffel Tower because we celebrated her eighteenth birthday in Paris; a giraffe to remind her of the time one spat on her when we visited a drive-through safari park; a wellington because we snuck into a festival when we were fifteen and danced the night away in the mud.

There's also a hen to remind her of whatever will happen later. I know it'll be a great night. Not because I planned it but

because we always have fun together no matter what we do.

"Forever and always," she says, clasping the bracelet.

"Forever and always. Now hurry up. We've got dinner reservations in half an hour."

I close the door behind me, quickly slip into a cocktail dress I chose for tonight and walk out to the balcony where no one will disturb me. I've been holding off calling Adrian for the past two days since Ty texted, letting me know the suicide watch is over and Adrian's doing better. I won't fly over there, but I want to check how he's doing.

I want him to explain *why* he overdosed.

I light up a cigarette, pressing the phone to my ear. I knew the moment we landed in Barcelona, the moment Thomas would be far away enough, I'd cave and call Adrian...

No amount of mental pep talk could prepare me for this conversation or the effect his voice has on me. How he isolates me even from the other side of the Atlantic.

"Puppet."

Relief washes over me, travelling straight to my heart, visiting every capital city of my soul along the way. The faint beeping of hospital machines resonates in the background. I can almost smell the distinctive smell of antiseptic and gauze, making me sick as I imagine Adrian, the strong man I once loved, defenceless in a hospital bed.

"Don't ever scare me like that again," I say. My voice breaks halfway through the sentence, and I whisper the rest.

"Don't cry, Puppet. I'm okay. I swear. God, you don't know how glad I am to hear you."

I bite my fist, closing my eyes. I take a deep breath through my nose and exhale through my mouth the way Thomas taught me. "Why did you do it?"

"Because I lost you." He heaves a heavy, defeated breath. "Nick called. He said you're moving on. He s-said you met someone, Puppet. He said you're happy... I tried to accept that you can't forgive me for what I've done, but I can't imagine my life without you, Nadia. What's the point of this if I don't get a chance to earn your forgiveness?"

"Don't say that."

All the bruises, cuts and screams, the fear, panic and tears, everything loses its significance in the face of Adrian's suicidal thoughts. It's not his fault he hurt me. It wasn't the same Adrian who's now on the other side of the line. It was the other guy, the one who's no longer here because Adrian's clean.

"I know apologies... won't change the past, but... I need you to... believe that I am *sorry*, Puppet." He's close to tears, pausing more often, his words barely a whisper. "It wasn't un-until rehab that I saw what... what I've done to you. Every day I'm buried alive under the guilt... I broke. I couldn't take it anymore when Nick said this is it—that you're done with me."

I believe his remorse. I believe that his guilt drives him insane every day. If he could turn back time and never touch PCP, he'd do it no matter the consequences.

"I don't need apologies," I say, whispering the words because I can't make my vocal cords work properly. "Just don't give up, okay? You're almost out of the woods, baby. You're stronger than you think."

"I love you, Puppet. So much. More than anything. I know you may never trust me again, and you may never be mine again, but right now, I just need you here. I need a chance to earn your forgiveness. Nothing makes sense without you. I won't fucking make it. I love you more than you can handle."

Those few words summon hundreds of memories. He helped me through the darkness, piecing together my broken heart, mind, and soul. He watched over me like a guardian angel—always there when I needed and wanted him and when I didn't want him, too.

Sometimes I screamed and cursed so he'd go away. So he'd let me fall apart in peace because I had no strength to fight.

He never left.

He stayed and fought in my name while I licked my wounds. Now, he needs me to rise to the challenge, but it's like jumping from the frying pan into the fire.

Thirty

Weed and dicks

THOMAS

When I booked the hotel in Amsterdam, I settled for the one that visually appealed to me the most. Distance to the strip club was irrelevant since a limo was at our disposal all night.

I stayed in dozens of luxurious hotels all over Europe, but once we enter Sofitel the Grand, it immediately becomes my favourite. A spacious, welcoming hall features a massive rect angular reception counter made of white marble with a larger-than-life chandelier hanging above. It must be ten feet wide and four feet long at least.

Three bellboys take care of our luggage while I check in, leaving my credit card details. Here's hoping no one gets drunk enough to Tarzan the shit out of the chandelier.

"Leave your things, and we'll meet downstairs in twenty minutes," I say when we're in the elevator, and I hand everyone a key to their respective rooms.

The window in mine overlooks the canal, and the room itself is almost as well equipped as my house. Above a double

bed hangs a long mirror, a desk stands by the opposite wall, and the bathroom features a walk-in shower large enough to fit three people.

Too bad Nadia's not here with me. I can already picture her beautiful tits pressed against the cool glass as I drive into her from behind.

I hang my suit in the wardrobe, ready for tomorrow. Unfortunately, I've been outvoted during the flight, so we're *not* swapping the stag-do t-shirts for smart shirts.

A soft knock on my door comes three minutes later.

"What the fuck am I supposed to do for twenty minutes?" Scorpio booms, barging into my room. "Oh, you've got one too." He points at a portrait of an old man. "What's with that? There's a hideous woman staring at the bed from her frame in my room."

"Kiss her. She'll be one of your five tonight."

A pillow bounces off my head, landing on the floor. I turn around, my eyebrows raised. "Are you high already?"

"No, but I better be by the end of the night. Jane's letting me do whatever I want if I keep my dick in my pants."

She probably threatened to castrate him if he doesn't. Still, giving Scorpio a free pass is not her brightest moment.

"How very fucking stupid of her. She should've at least warned me since I'll be the one carrying you back to the hotel and making sure you've got a bucket by your bed."

Scorpio joins me in the bathroom. "You gonna stay sober?" He grabs a bottle of my cologne, sprays it into the air, and then steps forward.

"You're supposed to spray it over your neck, not the floor."

"Bullshit. *This* is how you do this. You should educate yourself, mate." He puts the cap back on, tossing the bottle for me to catch. "So? Did Nadia say you can't have fun?"

"She didn't, but that doesn't mean I'll get trashed. Don't forget that I'm hosting this party. Who'll tell you where to go next if I'm unconscious?" I put a wallet, phone, and room key into my pockets, stopping by the door. "Are you coming?"

He rubs his hands together. "Where are we going first?"

"Downstairs. It's dinner time."

The smile dies on his lips, but he follows me down the hall to the elevator. Nick and the rest of the party are already waiting at the restaurant, studying the menus. A waiter comes a few minutes later to fill our flutes with Cristal and take our orders. We try keeping the noise down, but a bachelor party of eight excited guys is bound to get loud.

"Before we get shitfaced, I'd like to propose a toast." I rise from my seat. "Here's to Nick and his beautiful bride. May you never regret the journey you're about to embark on."

"This is it, isn't it?" he asks, clanking his glass to mine. "This time next week, I'll be a married man."

"You're getting cold feet?"

"No. No fucking way. I've been waiting for this to happen for years. I couldn't be happier."

"That's because you don't know what you're getting yourself into," Josh laughs. He's the marketing director at C&G, married, and a father of two. "I'm kidding. Nothing changes other than the ring on your finger. It actually gets even better."

"We'll all get there at some point," Scorpio says. "I'm next."

My phone vibrates a moment later. I take it out under the table, smiling at the text from Nadia.

My doll: Time to see naked firemen.

Me: No touching. You've got a soldier at home.

A smiley face arrives two seconds later.

"Wasn't this supposed to be a no-phones, no-girlfriends evening?" Ethan clips, gunning me with a murderous glare.

He's been pissed off with me lately. The fact I'm dating

the girl he's been crushing on for years might be the reason.

"Who said anything about no girlfriends? I only asked you to leave your phones behind so we wouldn't all text them every few minutes. You didn't expect us to not keep in touch with them at all, did you?"

The food arrives before Ethan finds his tongue. We eat, talk and laugh for two hours before we take advantage of the limo waiting outside. I've heard a lot about Amsterdam over the years. Unlike most other cities, everything I heard is true.

Last year, I spent a weekend in Paris. I expected a beautiful, romantic city filled with history, little cafés, and the best baguettes. The postcard image is just that—a postcard. In reality, Paris is dirty, crowded, and full of terrible drivers. The traffic around the Arc de Triomphe scarred me for life, and the street salesmen drove me nuts. The only impressive thing is the Eiffel Tower.

Amsterdam, however, is everything I expected. I wouldn't call it the most beautiful place on earth, but it has a pleasantly strange feel to it. The little bridges over the canal, hundreds of bikes wherever you turn your head, and iconic architecture make Amsterdam my second favourite European destination. And I can't wait to check if the world-famous Red-Light District is as impressive as the rumours imply.

The chauffeur stops the car, opening the back door. "I have to warn you not to take any pictures while wandering around the Red-Light District."

"Why is that?" Scorpio asks, clutching his Nikon.

"Out of respect," Ethan says.

"Yes, but also to avoid having your camera flung in the canal by the girls' enforcers. Moreover, watch out for pickpockets. Streets are narrow and crowded." The chauffeur raises his hat, seeing us off.

The first thing that grabs my attention when we wander into the closest street isn't the almost naked girls behind glass windows but the smell of weed. I know it's legal here, but I didn't expect so many people to smoke. It's not just youngsters either. An elderly woman selling roses sits on a small chair with a joint in her mouth.

"How much do you think they charge for a quickie?" one of the guys asks when we turn into a narrow passage.

It's just wide enough for one man, and the brothels are on either side every two metres.

I feel a little claustrophobic surrounded by prostitutes.

"Fifty euros," Scorpio answers, glaring at Ethan when he bursts out laughing. "What? I googled it."

The conversation about pricing lasts for a good ten minutes, during which we navigate the never-ending labyrinth of streets. Most girls are young and quite pretty. Some look excited, others bored. Most don't engage, but a few press their boobs against the windows, luring men in. The legal age to work in a brothel is twenty-one, but few of those girls look old enough. Some should probably still be in school.

"Look at that!" Josh yells, running toward a shop window. "It's a condom shop!" He pushes the door open, and the guys follow in, pushing and shoving at each other.

Scorpio stays behind, keeping me company while I take three minutes to grab a smoke. "We need to find a coffee shop before we leave. I'm not going home until I try Dutch weed."

"We've passed a dozen, and there's another one." I point toward the opposite side of the street.

Scorpio beams, knocking on the condom shop window. "Hurry up!" he mouths, waving the guys over.

Nick and I are the only ones not interested in weed. We wait outside the coffee house while the others buy their joints.

"Is that a sex museum?!" Ethan asks, jogging down the street. "Come on! We're going in."

Who put him in charge?

"You ready for the party now?" I ask after forty minutes when we exit the building.

"Tell me I didn't just see all that!" Scorpio grips my shoulder, acting like the drama king he is. "Make me forget, Thomas! Where are the strippers? I want boobs!"

"You almost broke your leg running in there; don't complain now."

"How was I supposed to know that the museum of sex is two fucking floors of giant dicks?"

Nick catches up, elbowing Scorpio in the ribs. "You're jealous of the size? Don't worry, mate." He pats his shoulder. "The size doesn't matter as long as you know how to use it."

"Enough with the dick talk. I say we find the limo and get wasted!" one of the guys yells.

A sensible one at last.

We find the limo parked on the kerb by the canal. The chauffeur has some fucking skills to drive a nine-metre-long car through the narrow roads.

"Did you enjoy the walk?"

"I love Amsterdam!" Ethan yells, bursting into giggles like a sixteen-year-old cheerleader. He could never handle his liquor, and obviously, he's no better with weed. I put my hand on his head, forcing him inside the car.

The queue outside the strip club wraps around the corner, but thanks to VIP passes, we walk straight past the line of impatient men. Music booms from tall speakers, and the place is packed despite my wristwatch only showing ten-thirty. A waitress that could just as well be a stripper considering she only wears thongs shows us to our table.

Another waitress slash stripper arrives two minutes later with a tray full of liquor: whiskey, vodka, bourbon.

The guys help themselves to alcohol, eyeing naked ass writhing around the poles. Instead of joining the stare fest, I check on Nadia.

Me: Safe and sound?

I press send, leaving the phone on my lap, expecting a reply within seconds. It doesn't arrive. I wait ten, fifteen, then twenty minutes, convincing myself that they are okay. That *she* is okay and just didn't hear the phone.

Nick starts his second drink when the escorts I booked arrive—Candy and Cookie. Twins. Tall, slim, pretty, and slutty twins. We all cheer when they sit on either side of Nick, whispering in his ears. He's absolutely mortified for the first few minutes, the tips of his ears bright red. His face turns red, too, when Cookie sucks his earlobe, moving her hand up his thigh, dangerously close to his zipper. They know they can't grab his dick unless he asks for it, so she backs away slowly, teasing him.

A reply from Nadia comes when I'm about to call her.

My doll: Safe and sound, baby.

I breathe a sigh of relief. She's making me crazy. Fucking paranoid. And jealous... so fucking jealous. Ethan cringes seeing me with the phone, and that's enough to boil my blood.

I'm Pussy Whipped, nice to meet you.

As the evening progresses, Nick gets more creative with the tasks for his escorts. They're supposed to fulfil his every wish, no matter how unusual, but no way in hell they could've anticipated what they signed up for. They're prostitutes—high-class and expensive, but still hookers. They probably expected a night of blowjobs, handjobs, and sex.

What they got is far from their normal day at the office, I'm sure. First, Nick asked Cookie to give him a massage while Candy ordered more drinks and fetched another bucket of ice.

Innocent, right? Better than sucking Ethan's dick, if you ask me. Things go downhill from there. At some point, I feel sorry for them when they dance "Macarena" to earn Nick's forgiveness because they couldn't down six shots in a row, but

then I remember how much they're charging for the night, and I no longer feel any sympathy.

The guys compete all evening, trying to fulfil the dares of the t-shirts, and Ethan wins as he's the only one who somehow organised a bar-wide conga, losing his voice while teaching everyone Chelsea's chant "Ten men went to mow".

He passes out around three in the morning, and not even a bucket of ice tipped over his head wakes him up, so Josh and I shove his sorry ass into the back of the limo, leaving him there to sleep it off. He doesn't stay alone long, though.

We join forty minutes later when half of the party can no longer stand without assistance. The groom, who should've passed out in a pool of his own vomit, is holding up surprisingly well, though.

Once we get back to the hotel, he's thrilled we can keep drinking. He's even more thrilled when I open the door to the Legendary suite I rented for the afterparty. The guys cheer, greeted by half a dozen half-naked hookers.

Nick delegates Cookie to make the drinks while Candy's three floors down, singing Ethan a lullaby.

It doesn't take long before the guys take advantage of the hookers. Even Josh pulls one over to the bathroom when he thinks we're not paying attention.

"Do you want one?" a guy whose name I failed to memorise asks me, motioning his chin at the two girls left in the room.

"No, mate. Knock yourself out."

Scorpio plops down beside me, his eyes heavy. "Have you heard from Nadia? Are the girls okay?"

"Yeah, I'd like to know how my wife-to-be is," Nick mumbles.

Two unread texts from Alex wait on my phone. My eyebrows draw together in confusion when I slide my thumb across the screen. The first message is a video clip showing Nadia and Amelia dancing on a raised platform at the club. Mel jumps off, and for a moment, her head floats in the crowd toward Nadia.

She grabs her ankle, and my pulse fucking soars when I watch my girl take a dive.

"Fuck!" I jump to my feet.

"What's wrong?" Nick asks, pulling himself from an almost horizontal position on the sofa.

I open the second message, scrutinising a picture of a random guy, his hands *touching* Nadia's back. Another guy sits at the table, watching them with a grin, which I immediately want to wipe off his face with brass knuckles. The glass in my hand goes airborne as blood in my veins turns hot and sticky.

"Thomas!" Nick booms. "What's wrong?"

"I don't know," I seethe, my chest heaving. "Nadia fell off a platform at the club. Alex sent me a video followed by a picture of some dickhead with his hands all over her."

I dial Nadia's number, pressing the phone to my ear.

No answer.

Of course.

I try again with the same result, and my frustration peaks at an all-time high. I try her a few more times, sending a few messages in between. Nick and Scorpio watch me clueless, not understanding why I act like I'm off my trolley.

The head of security at the hotel the girls are staying at is the next person I call. Three years of Spanish lessons pay off when I scream my head off over the phone, ordering the security to check the girls' villa.

Then, I call Jane. She's the most likely to answer.

"Thomas? Is everything alright?" she slurs.

Alright? No, it's not fucking alright, alright?

"What's going on? Who's that son-of-a-bitch in the picture? Where the fuck is Nadia, and why isn't she answering my calls?"

Springs creak on her side of the line as if she sat up on the bed. "Calm down. Nadia's here somewhere. She's okay. I think she's putting Mel to sleep."

"Let me talk to her."

"Okay, just—"

Her voice trails off. I almost send my phone to follow the glass, but I hold it together, redialling Jane's number. I squeeze the stress out of my neck with a free hand.

"Sorry," she mutters. "I dropped the phone. Let me find Nadia for you." I hear the door open, then a few rickety steps before another door opens.

"Hey, baby," Nadia says, her voice tired but calm.

Instead of that calming *me* down, it pisses me off more. She sounds sober enough not to act so fucking reckless.

"Where's your phone? You promised you'd keep it on you!"

"We just got back. I'm a little preoccupied—"

"I know! What the hell, Nadia? Who were those two assholes, and why was one of them touching you?!"

"How do you...?" She trails off, exhaling an annoyed burst of air down the line. "Let me guess... Alex told you."

"That doesn't answer my questions!"

"You're unbelievable!" she snaps, getting defensive. "You know she's obsessed with you! They were with Martha and Jess. Bill is a med student; he was checking if my bones were intact after I fell off the platform. You think I wanted him to touch me? You should know better than that by now. Mel said either he checks my bones, or we're going to the hospital!"

A commotion erupts in the background. A few male voices yell in Spanish, doors bang, and the girls scream.

"What the hell?!" Nadia cries. "You sent security up here?!"

"They're looking for those two jackasses. Are they there?"

"Yes! They came back with Martha and Jess. You thought they were here for me?! Are you insane? I thought you trusted me!"

I rub my face, letting out a long, calming breath. I collapse on the sofa, anger turning to shame.

She's right.

I flipped off before I found out what had happened. "You promised to take care of yourself," I say, controlling how my

268

voice sounds. "Yet here I am, watching you fall off a platform and some fuckhead touching you." *Suicidal fuckhead I may add.* "This is not what you promised."

"We were dancing. I had fun like you told me to."

When have I told her to endanger herself? Or befriend male strangers and let them touch her?

The door opens behind me. Ethan stumbles inside, followed by Candy, who does her best trying to keep him steady. "Thomas! This is the best party ever! I bloody love you, mate!"

I sigh, ignoring The drunk Jerk and focusing on Nadia. "Please take care of yourself, doll."

"Done," she barks, cutting the call.

Awesome. Now she's pissed off. She has every right to be, though. The green-eyed monster in my head turns off my rational thinking. All I have for my defence is that I never felt like this about anyone.

Nadia's *everything.*

The reason why my entire life has been turned on its head in the best way. The reason why I get up in the morning feeling happy. I can't lose that. I can't lose *her.*

Nick elbows me in the ribs. "And? What's going on?"

"They're fine. Nadia hurt her ribs, but she's okay. The security is kicking out the guys who came back to the hotel with Martha and Jess."

I tap out a text to Nadia.

Me: I overreacted. I'm sorry. It drives me insane thinking about someone touching you. Seeing it was beyond me. Don't stay mad long.

My doll: Stop acting like a lunatic and start trusting me!

"Am I acting like a lunatic?" I ask Nick.

"When it comes to Nadia? You almost took Scorpio's head off clean with that glass you threw just now, so yeah. You're

fucking cray-cray."

"I don't think you're cray-cray, Thomas," Ethan mumbles. "If you didn't steal Nadia from me, I'd be the same." He sits up, pulling his brows together. "I could still win her over her, you know? She'd love me."

"You'll die trying." Scorpio smacks him with a pillow.

What the fuck is it about the pillows?

Me: I trust you. I just don't trust anyone around you.

I don't know about you, but I'm off to bed," Nick says, pulling himself up. "It was a great night."

As if to confirm, one of the hookers moans in the adjacent bedroom.

Thirty-one

You should be dead

NADIA

The plane lands at Heathrow late on Sunday. Nick, Thomas and the rest of the party are due in an hour. I consider waiting at the airport, but Mel's green complexion changes my mind.

She dozed off during the flight, but nausea woke her up three times, and she threw up the colourful drinks she poured down her throat last night.

By the time I lay her on the couch in the living room, Thomas texts me to say they landed. A peculiar unease settles over me because I had no time to think about what Adrian told me or decide my next move.

It didn't help the case when he emailed me a one-way ticket to New York minutes after our conversation.

I've got a week to decide which road to take: stay or leave. I want to help him through the pain and suffering. He deserves the chance, but I can no longer imagine not having Thomas by my side. If not for him, I'd still consider myself a victim, a weak, bruised girl, not a fighter or survivor.

I'm choosing between bad and worse here. I can stay, risking Adrian will try to take his life again, or I can leave, wasting a chance at true happiness. A chance at healing my broken mind and living a normal life.

Immersed in my thoughts, I jump when the front door bursts open.

"Honey, I'm home!" Nick yells, chuckling.

I get to my feet, and the anxiety that arrived with Adrian's voice disperses in an instant. Thomas's presence pushes my worries aside. It's only been a little over twenty-four hours, but I missed him like crazy. That's not normal or healthy, but neither am I.

Dark circles surrounding his eyes betray he's not had much sleep. He drops his travel bag in time to catch me and lifts me into his arms. "What's wrong, baby?" he asks quietly, holding me close, his voice spiked with concern.

I inhale his scent, letting it overwhelm my senses. The choice between bad and worse is easier when he holds me close, his lips pressed against my temple.

He's the one I deserve.

The trouble is... he deserves so much more than me.

"Nothing," I say, nuzzling my face in his neck, the smell of his cologne better than peppermint tea. "I missed you."

"Jesus, it's been one fucking day!" Nick huffs aiming at irritation, but the playfulness in his tone ruins the effect. "Where's my lovely bride-to-be?"

"Asleep in the living room." I stand back on my feet. "I won't wake her if I were you. She's not well."

He ignores me, disappearing into the living room.

Thomas ghosts his fingers along my ribs. "Does it hurt?"

"It could be worse," I smile, dismissing the minor ache with a wave of my hand. I've lived through worse. Thomas isn't amused, though. "Don't tell me you didn't laugh when I waved my arms around like an eagle!"

"Laughed?" Nick comes back, eyeing Thomas, one eyebrow

raised. "He smashed a glass of whiskey against the wall."
Thomas sends him a warning glare before focusing back
on me. "All of this..." He sizes me up, "...is mine now. I'd
appreciate it if you took better care of it." He stamps a kiss on
my forehead, and we follow Nick into the kitchen. "Take a day
off tomorrow. I'll take care of the paperwork."

"You could use a day off, too," Nick says, pulling a bottle
of water out of the fridge.

The main door opens, and we all exchange confused glances
before a voice I loathe with a passion reverberates through the
house, sending cold chills down my spine.

"Hello! I'm here!" Karen enters the kitchen wearing white
cigarette pants and a red silk blouse. Suitcase in hand, she
beams, and every cell in my body screams in agony.

*"It's Dad," Nick says, tears in his eyes. He pushes the plate of fish
and chips aside. Silence rings in my ears as Nick swallows hard. "He had
a heart attack."*

My mind blanks.

*The fork slips out of my hand, taking an extraordinarily long time
to hit the plate.*

Time slows.

My heart stops working.

*Nick's words echo in my mind, travelling through my subconscious,
poisoning every thought. Cold hands grip my throat, and I can't breathe.
I can't utter a single word, staring at Nick's fake composure and the forced
strength he emanates.*

*He grits his teeth, wiping his eyes before a single tear rolls down his
pale skin. "He's gone, baby girl."*

For months I was convinced my only reaction was silence.
I thought I cried for hours in Nick's arms. I thought I dreamt
the screams, but the reality was much more sinister.

The sheer madness coursing through me, the pain ripping

my chest wide open... I pushed it out of my mind, not wanting to remember the darkness filling my heart and soul, but months later, Amelia confessed she was never more scared than when she walked through the door, finding Nick's flat trashed and my hands covered in cuts from breaking every glass and plate in the kitchen. Nick sat on the floor with my head on his lap when he told her Dad had died.

I was numb by that point, clutching a teddy bear Daddy bought me the day I was born, and Nick held me until dawn, singing a lullaby Dad sang when I was a little girl.

"Hey, Mum," Nick says, his words like a bucket of water in my face. "I thought you were coming over on Thursday."

The darkness resurfaces. Pain threatens to morph into rage and unleash itself on the woman before me. I squeeze Thomas's hand, willing him to work his magic, to turn into Xanax, diazepam, and any other sedative out there.

"I thought I'd surprise you and maybe help a little," Karen says, her voice seeping through the cracks in my composure.

"Let's go," I tell Thomas the second Karen walks into the kitchen, leaving the doorway unobstructed.

"Stay," Nick says, looking between Karen and me. "Come on, we'll have a coffee. Catch up?"

I shake my head, holding Thomas's hand for dear life.

One step at a time. Left leg, right leg, left leg, right leg. Leave. Go. Don't turn back. Don't listen. Don't engage.

"Leave it, Mum. She won't talk to you," Nick says when we're halfway down the hall.

I focus on my senses: the way my heels click against the tiled floor, the warmth of Thomas's hand, the creak of the doors opening, the crunching of the gravel, the smell of water and grass in the cool evening air.

Thomas lets go of my hand, taking his car keys out, and the lock clicks. I stare at the orange letters printed across his t-shirt, unable to make out the words.

"Hey," he says, his long fingers curling under my chin.

He opens his mouth to say more, to ask a question or maybe repeat something I didn't hear, but instead, he closes my lips with his, the kiss firm, soothing, and demanding. The door to the house bursts open behind my back. I inch away from Thomas, the effect of his lips gone, replaced with a feeling of impending doom.

"Nadia, wait," Karen says, rushing down the driveway. "Will you please just talk to me?" She grabs my arm.

The touch of her hand brings to life a side of me I considered buried. I was wrong... it's still there, just asleep. Karen woke the Cerberus, and the gates to hell stand open.

"Don't touch me," I snap, facing her. "Don't look at me. Don't speak to me."

Her eyes glisten with fresh tears, but that doesn't work on me. If anything, her sadness gives me a sick sense of satisfaction. Short-lived, but satisfaction, nonetheless.

"Nadia... sweetie, please, at least let me explain."

I scoff, crossing my arms over my chest. "Spare me. Nothing you can say will change what I think about you."

"He blackmailed me!" she cries when I flinch toward the car. "He knew things about Arthur and—"

Dad's name sliding off her tongue diminished any inhibitions I hoped to have. "Don't ever mention his name again, you unfaithful bitch!"

"Nadia, calm down," Nick says, appearing behind Karen.

The pure lava coursing through my veins, the hot, white frenzy in my mind is unstoppable. I'm too far gone to see reason, reconsider, or understand she's not worth my time.

"Please, let me explain." She steps closer, and for each one of her steps forward, I take one back. "I loved your father."

"You killed him!" I scream at the top of my lungs. "He's dead because of you!"

"I wish I could take it back. I do. Please, I need you to

understand, sweetie. Let me tell you my side of the story. You never let me explain."

Dad's face flashes before my eyes, and I cross the line between anger and pure, unrestrained hysteria. "You should be dead," I whisper, shaking all over. "*You* should be dead, and Dad should be here!"

"Nadia, stop." Nick jumps between us, grabs my arm and shoves me back at Thomas. "Go home and calm down."

Thomas wraps his arms around my middle, but I step away, anger quivering inside me like a loose wire.

"You were the one who wanted us to talk! What did you expect?" I glare at Karen, who stands there, sobbing. "I'll never forgive you. And after the wedding is over, you won't see me again. You're dead to me. I *wish* you were dead."

I turn on my heel, bumping straight into Thomas's arms. He hugs me tight, weaving his hands through my hair. He's trying to calm me down, but I don't want to numb the pain this time. "Take me to Dad." I say, getting in the car.

No one dares to stop me.

When Thomas backs out of the driveway, I pull a notepad and pen from the glove compartment, unbuckle my seatbelt, and climb to the back so I can write a letter to Dad.

"We're here," Thomas says twenty minutes later. He cuts the engine, turning in his seat. "You want me to come with you?"

"No. I want to be alone. Go home. I'll get a taxi back."

He did nothing wrong and shouldn't suffer, but my mind is like a nest of snakes. My thoughts don't stay in one place for longer than a second lately. I need a time-out. I need to get my priorities in order.

I open the door, expecting Thomas to drive away, but he steps outside, pinching a cigarette between his lips. "Take as long as you need. I'll wait. Maybe you'll change your mind about being alone when you're done talking to your dad."

I rise on my toes, kissing his lips, unsure what to say. It's getting dark, but I don't mind the cemetery at night. The bench in front of Dad's grave is one of the few places I feel truly safe.

Daddy,

I hate her so much it hurts. You used to say hate causes a lot of problems but fixes none. It's true. My hatred solves nothing. It doesn't ease the pain, just hurts Nick. It doesn't bring you back, just takes away the one parent I have left.

I tried to forgive her, but I can't. I'd forgive Adrian over her every time... at least I know he hurt me because he was using. Karen has no excuses. She made a conscious decision. Maybe if you were still here, if her actions didn't take you away from me, I'd find it in me to forgive her.

But you're not here. You're dead, and so I'm lonely.

It's funny how I came home to start over, and just when I thought I found a way to do so, my past came back, laughing in my face.

There's no escaping him, Daddy. I think he'll forever be a part of me no matter how far I run or where I hide. I owe him so much...

The time has come to pay my debt.

Why is life so complicated? Why can't it be simple? Why can't there only be wrong or right, black or white? Why aren't you here to help me choose? What am I supposed to do? Which door should I take? I wish you'd tell me which one of them is right.

But you're not, and I'm stuck.

I know it should be easy. Adrian turned my life—our lives—into a nightmare, and Thomas is leading me out of the darkness. He makes me happy, Daddy. He makes the bad memories fade. He makes me forget the pain, and when he's around, the huge hole in my heart is almost healed.

I still miss you, but now that I have him, it's easier to find peace. He's the one I want. He should be the one I choose, but it's not that easy. Nothing ever is, right? Isn't that what you always said?

I don't want to get hurt again. I don't know how much more I can take before I won't get up again. I'm scared of making the wrong choice. I'm scared of losing Thomas if I leave, and I'm scared Adrian will do

something reckless if I stay.
There's no wrong or right choice here.
It's a choice between what's best for me and what's best for them...

I love you so much, Daddy.

Thirty-two

You're next

THOMAS

Nadia's distant all week. She chases her thoughts most of the time we spend together, which isn't much. Amelia took the week off and dragged Nadia to every meeting, appointment, and dress fitting with her.

I tried talking to her, asking about her parents and Karen, but she dismissed every question. After a few tries, I gave up because the armoured wall started growing between us when Karen arrived.

I can't shake the feeling that Karen's only partially responsible for Nadia's daydreaming. I know she worries about Adrian. I've heard her on the phone with Ty a few times, and it fucking killed me every time, but I kept quiet. She's got a past just as I do. The difference is my past stays where it belongs. Hers doesn't.

The week drags as if it's dragging last week's dead body behind it. The anticipation ahead of the wedding hits an all-time high, and even I get a little nervous by Friday. The good thing is that Nadia's worries are pushed aside by excitement.

By Saturday morning, she's back to her normal self.

"Why aren't you here? I need you! Get down here right now!" Amelia screams down the phone so loud I hear every word despite standing in the doorway of my living room.

It's just past eight a.m., and the hairdresser is finishing Nadia's hair. I'm still in my gym trousers, sweaty from my morning workout. I half hoped for a morning workout session with Nadia's naked body writhing beneath me, but she was up before the alarm, and I had to settle for the gym.

"I'll be there in half an hour, Mel. Is the hairdresser there?" This time I don't hear the reply. "Good. Sit down. Let her work." She cuts the call after that, glancing over her shoulder. "Why aren't you ready? Mel's freaking out. We need to leave soon." She shoos me away, and the small chance I thought I had for sex is gone.

Twenty minutes later, we're on our way to Nick's house, and once we arrive, we're swallowed by the chaos.

No, really, it's fucking disgraceful.

Nick jumps out on us when we enter the house. "Do something!" he yells over the noise of seventeen people talking at once. "Everyone's everywhere! No one knows what to do! I don't know what to do! Mel's throwing up every ten minutes; her mum is crying, and—"

"Whoa. Calm down." I pat his back. "Calm down."

He's not wrong, though. People are shouting and running around like a flock of sheep without a dog to herd them into a pen. Scorpio's on the phone, screaming. Mel's foster parents, Jack and Grace, are in the living room, arguing. Karen's rushing down the stairs with Nick's suit jacket, and the bridesmaids giggle in the corner.

I take Nadia's hand when Karen approaches, half expecting another round of screaming, but Nadia holds her head up high, almost choking as she swallows her pride. She's only doing this for Nick and Mel's sake, but I'm still fucking proud of her considering how much hatred she harbours toward the woman.

"Enough!" Nadia yells, standing her ground in the middle of the hallway. "Everyone, shut up!" They all turn to her, surprised. "Here's how it's going to go: Grace, go upstairs and check on Mel. Groomsmen go into the living room and bridesmaids into the kitchen. Jack, you're in charge of the groomsmen—make sure they look decent. Karen..." She pauses and swallows hard, grinding her teeth. "Take over the bridesmaids." She rolls her eyes when no one moves. "Do you need an invitation?! Go!"

They do. As directed, groomsmen veer left, bridesmaids right. Karen eyes Nadia for a second, probably stunned she addressed her by her name, not by *bitch*, then spins around, getting to work as if fulfilling Nadia's order will earn her forgiveness.

"Make sure they don't get out of control again," Nadia tells me, looking over her shoulder. "I'm going upstairs."

The remark about Mel throwing up stops me from climbing the stairs to say *hi*. Instead, I get Nick a glass of champagne and blend in so no one can ask me what time it is, when the cars are arriving, or where their fucking bowtie is.

Nadia comes back five minutes later, once again taking control. Within thirty seconds, Ethan's on his way to the pharmacy for some over-the-counter anti-nausea medication, and everyone knows where their fucking bowtie is.

"I need you," she grabs my hand, dragging me out to the hallway. Long, manicured nails dig into my skin as she steps to my side. "Karen," she shouts, waiting for her mother to join us.

And I fall in love with her that much more. She trusts me to keep her in check and soothe her tormented mind.

I wrap my hand around her waist, leaning into her ear. "I've got you. And you've got *this*."

Karen emerges from the kitchen, pale and self-conscious.

"Grace is falling apart up there. It's not helping Mel. Take her place and calm Mel down. I need to get the dress ready."

"Of course," Karen says, her spine straight like a guitar string. She watches Nadia as if debating whether now is a good time for more apologies, but Nadia doesn't let her say a word.

She tugs my hand, rising on her feet and plants her lips on mine, apparently needing more than just my hand in hers to stay sane. The noise level drops as she devours my lips, paying no attention to the audience.

"You need me to do anything, baby doll?" I ask when she inches away.

"Yes. Take care of the groom. I'll handle the rest."

A calmness settles over the cottage once the groomsmen are made presentable by Jack, who had to tie everyone's fucking bowtie. Amelia stops throwing up, and the bridesmaids walk out to the back garden giggling some more.

Of course, nothing lasts forever. Chaos erupts again when we gather outside the church before and after the ceremony. Good thing Nadia knows how to handle an insubordinate crowd without offending anyone.

If it were me, I'd throw a few *fucks* and *idiots* at random people as a form of a reliable tactic designed to make them listen. Nadia settled for discipline. She's sexy as hell bossing everyone around, earning permission to order *me* in bed sometime.

The newlyweds are all hearts, kisses, and smiles when we arrive at the venue. Guests start the usual ritual of wishing them all the best, but since Nadia and I did that earlier, I take her over to the main table.

"Tell me this is *not* what all weddings are like," Scorpio says, leaning over the back of my chair. "It looks like torture. I'm starting to worry they'll never lose those idiotic grins."

Nadia punches his shoulder. "Stop being an ass. And to answer your question, yes, you'll have to do this one day, and if I were you, I'd make sure that day comes sooner than later."

"Why?" He pulls a chair out beside us. "Did Jane say something? She wants to get married? Have babies? When? Now?

What did she say?"

"Good job not freaking out," Nadia chuckles. "She only suggested all our hen parties should be in Barcelona, but you're what, twenty-eight? And you've been together for how long now? Unless something is holding you back, go for it. You're not getting any younger."

Scorpio glances at me, looking for help.

"I'm with her on this one."

"Of course you are," he scoffs, making a sound that's supposed to resemble the crack of a whip.

Nice one.

Disappointed I don't have his back, he forges his way through the crowd, looking for Jane. Nadia sips her wine, looking around, checking if anything requires her attention.

"Why don't you take care of the caterers, and I'll manage the band? We can entertain the guests together," I say.

She focuses on something on the other side of the room. "I'll be right back. Mel's having a hard time with her dress."

During the next four hours, we only have time for one dance. It'd be two, but Nick stole her from me, so I took Mel's hand instead.

An eye for an eye.

The first glass of double vodka on the rocks I ordered when we entered the venue still sits on the table. I had maybe two sips from it. The ice long melted, watering down the alcohol and deeming it undrinkable.

When midnight strikes, the bridesmaids almost end up in a group catfight over Amelia's bouquet. Alex grabs it, but she's immediately tackled to the ground by Jane, who tears the bouquet out of her hands. She stands up, smoothing out her dress, a big smile on her face.

I pat Scorpio's back. "Good luck, mate. You should get a ring on her before she scratches someone's eyes out."

Ethan scoffs, standing beside us. "Please don't. I hate

weddings. All these old people keep patting my back, saying, *you're next.* I don't even have a girlfriend!"

"Return the favour at the next funeral," I say.

The room starts emptying around one o'clock in the morning, and soon it's just the young ones still dancing, drinking and shouting.

"Can you check with the band if they can stay until we're done here?" Nick asks when I sit at the table with my second drink.

"They're booked until three, but we'll be here longer."

I set the glass aside, making my way across the room. Nadia grabs my hand, pulling me in for a dance before I reach the band. She's been dancing with every guy left in the room for the past half an hour, her cheeks flushed, but a big, *genuine* smile brightens her beautiful face. God, she's so fucking perfect.

I've no idea what she sees in me, I swear.

"Sit down, baby. You need a minute to catch your breath." I kiss her head. "I need to talk to the band."

"I'll get some air. Join me when you're done." She turns on her heel, walking outside.

The lead singer has no problem staying until everyone leaves. Nick pays him enough to cover the weekend, so they have no reason to be awkward. Besides, the guy has his heart set on a record deal... thanks to his unique, raspy voice, he actually has a shot at making that happen.

It's four in the morning when Nadia, cuddled in my arms at the main table, starts yawning. Eight of us are left in the room, but the band keeps playing. The singer sings a soft, acoustic version of "Cry Me A River" by Justin Timberlake.

"Should we call it a night?" I whisper in her ear, smiling when goose bumps cover her neck. "You must be exhausted."

"No less than you."

"Come on." I pat her hip. "Let's get you in bed."

We say goodnight and enter room thirty-one on the second floor minutes later. Nadia changes into a white nightdress, climbing onto the bed, where I lay, ready to pull her to my side and tuck her in.

She has different plans, though. Despite my exhaustion, the moment she straddles me, my batteries recharge, and desire takes the stage. I don't like the aura of insecurity surrounding her tonight. I don't like the sadness in her eyes that doesn't go away no matter where I kiss or touch her, and I don't particularly like the urgency of her touch, but when she opens her mouth to speak, she lulls me into a false sense of security.

"You're my heaven, Thomas."

Thirty-three

Jumped ship

NADIA

Inaudible sobs shudder my body when I close the door to room number thirty-one, taking care not to make a sound. I tiptoe across the long corridor, my footsteps muffled by the red carpet as I descend the stairs, a small suitcase in hand and a tote bag over my shoulder.

Once in the lobby, I set the suitcase on the floor, wheeling it toward the reception desk. An older gentleman sits behind it, reading a newspaper. The name on a gold plaque pinned to his navy jacket reads *Alistair*.

"Good morning. Trouble sleeping?" he asks, his eyebrow raised. "The groom hasn't yet made his way to bed, and you're already up."

"I have a plane to catch." I clear my throat, wiping my face. There's no hiding how upset I am, though. "Is my brother still in the venue?"

"No, he left with one of the groomsmen about an hour ago. I believe they craved junk food."

Mel spent a long time designing the perfect menu for the wedding, but Nick told me at least half a dozen times during the night that he was starving because the portions were tiny.

"Please don't tell him I left."

Alistair bows, taking my room key from the countertop. "As you wish. Should I order you a taxi?"

"No, thank you. One should be here in ten minutes."

"Well, then. Have a nice flight."

I wipe more tears, smiling as well as I can, then exit the building, my legs weak, stomach tied in knots and light a cigarette. Instead of calming down a little while the clouds of smoke fill my lungs, I'm freaking out more with each passing second.

Abandoning Thomas is the cruellest decision I've ever made. Abandoning Adrian can't compare. He deserved what he got. Thomas did nothing to drive me away, nothing to warrant the broken heart he's getting as a thank you for the help he offered. He gave me reason after reason to stay, but how can I stay if it means risking Adrian trying to take his life again?

Five minutes pass. I glance around, hoping to God that Thomas will stay asleep. Every sound has me jumping out of my skin. Every voice in the distance quickens my pulse. My hands grow cold and damp; my muscles tense, and every time I blink, Thomas's face flashes before my eyes, his cinnamon irises full of sadness.

It'd be better if I had the courage to face him and explain why I'm leaving to help the man who left me traumatised, but courage isn't my strongest suit. Like a coward, I wrote Thomas a letter and left it on the pillow.

"Nadia? What are you doing up?" Nick says behind me.

I spin around, my pulse like a blaring thunder. Nick's there with Scorpio, still in their tuxedos, but neither is wearing a bowtie. A couple of the buttons on their shirts are undone. Scorpio munches sad-looking chips from a polystyrene box, his eyes on me. My vocal cords stick together. A mild panic attack

lurks nearby when Nick scans my tear-stained face.

"Where are you going?" he asks, taking a few steps forward. "Are you..." He pauses, adding two and two together. "You're going back to New York?"

A whimper is my first answer. "I have to." I grip my suitcase in they decide to hold it hostage. "Adrian needs me... I owe him so much."

I look at my brother but aim the words at Scorpio. Between the two of them, he's the one who might try and stop me or run upstairs to wake Thomas. I half expect Nick to wish me a pleasant flight, but something entirely different leaves his lips.

"Where's Thomas? Does he know you're leaving? He doesn't, right? You didn't fucking tell him!"

Scorpio turns on his heel to enter the building.

I lunge forward, grabbing his arm. "Don't tell him. I left him a letter, but I can't—"

"You can't say to his face that Adrian's more important?" he scoffs, snatching his hand out of my grip. "Thomas loves you, Nadia, and you're about to fucking break him. Don't do it. Don't you fucking dare hurt him like that."

The taxi pulls onto the car park, stopping by the entrance. The driver gets out, and Scorpio bolts inside the building.

"I don't know what Adrian did," Nick says, looking torn, "but you told me time and time again that he doesn't deserve you. Don't go back there, sis."

"I'm not going back to him. I'm going back *for* him. Adrian's out of rehab. He's clean, but he needs me to stay clean... he needs me to stay *alive*. I won't be able to live with myself if he overdoses again. I can help him, Nick."

"Thomas won't wait for you, sis. If you leave, you'll lose him. He might act all tough, but it's just a front."

I wheel the suitcase toward the driver, who locks it in the boot and takes the wheel, ready to go.

"I know he won't. I also know he deserves so much more

than the mess I am. All I do is drag him down, Nick. He should be with someone who builds him up." I wrap my arms around his neck. "I'll call."

"Don't go," he pleads. "Please don't go. Scorpio's right. It'll ruin him, Nadia."

I can't believe the distance he walked since he found out about Thomas and me. From throwing his fist at his best friend to choosing him over Adrian—the one he hoped I'd marry.

"I don't want to go. I'd stay if I could but *have to* go. I won't forgive myself if Adrian tries again. Take care of Thomas, please. He'll need you."

I take the back seat of the taxi, ordering the driver to go. He pulls away from the kerb, and I turn around, stealing one more look at my brother standing where I left him, his hands clasped over his head, disbelief painted across his face.

Just then, Thomas runs out of the building.

Barefoot, in jeans and a grey t-shirt, his hair a mess. He's wide-awake despite being dragged out of bed an hour after he fell asleep.

"Don't stop," I tell the driver, choking back a sob, my vision blurred by tears.

Thomas runs across the car park at full speed, eyes on mine. I thought I'd lived through the worst, but looking at him now, I'm splintering apart, breaking in ways I've never been broken before. Thomas stops once we turn right onto the main road, and my heart jumps ship to stay where it belongs.

With *him*.

Other Books by I. A. Dice

Broken Rules (Broken #1)

Broken Promises (Broken #2)

The Sound of Salvation (Deliverance #1)

The Taste of Redemption (Deliverance #2)

Too Much (Hayes Brothers #1)

Too Wrong (Hayes Brothers #2)

Too Sweet (Hayes Brothers #3)

Too Strong (Hayes Brothers #4)

Too Hard (Hayes Brothers #5)

Thank you for reading! Thomas and Nadia's story continues in *The Taste of Redemption.*

Please take a few seconds to leave a rating or a review. It doesn't have to be long, few words is enough.

Please visit my website to sign-up for newsletter if you'd like to stay up-to-date with my releases www.iadice.com

Love x

I. A. Dice

Printed in Great Britain
by Amazon